Praise for Am

Longlisted – Branfor

'A **thoughtful and believable** fi
the nuances of cancel culture and the remorseless
nature of internet scrutiny.'
Guardian

'A deft and sobering novel about growing up with
the internet, **written with great skill.**'
Bookseller

'Fresh and believable.'
Observer

'An **incredibly thought provoking** and perceptive YA debut.
An essential read for both young adults and adults alike.'
CultureFly

'This **searingly memorable** story will be one of
the most talked about young adult novels. Pertinent
and likely prescient, *Influential* is **a must-read.**'
School Reading List

'Now this is how you write an **impactful** YA book.'
Five-star reader review

'I **LOVED** this book!'
Five-star reader review

'**I couldn't put this down** – such an important book!'
Five-star reader review

For all the women I love.

First published in the UK in 2025
by Faber & Faber Limited
The Bindery, 51 Hatton Garden
London, EC1N 8HN
faber.co.uk

Typeset by MRules
Printed and bound by CPI Group (UK) Ltd, Croydon, CRO 4YY

A CIP record for this book
is available from the British Library

ISBN 978–0–571–38591–1

Printed and bound in the UK on FSC® certified paper in line with our continuing
commitment to ethical business practices, sustainability and the environment.
For further information see faber.co.uk/environmental-policy

2 4 6 8 10 9 7 5 3 1

GIRL, ULTRA-PROCESSED

AMARA SAGE

faber

december thirty-first

It is six minutes to midnight, and nobody here's kissing me when the clock strikes.

(Questioning if I would want them to though.)

I'm surrounded by a bunch of legal adults who still call their mum *mummy*, which is unsurprising, considering this is a party in Poppy's halls. She's at the University of Bristol, staying in accommodation literally called Manor Hall.

'I don't believe anyone who says they prefer giving gifts rather than receiving them, do you?' I blink at her flatmate, Bella, who sits on the table, looking down at me. Her foot's on the edge of my chair, digging into my leg.

On the other side of the table Poppy's chatting to a boy. I watch his hand keep landing on her bare thigh, her sculpted quad muscle tensing each time.

Bella smiles at me expectantly, so I say, 'Same,' though neither of us is particularly invested in the conversation.

Bella's fine. Sure, she's a class-appropriating posh girl who boasts she's into grime because she has two of Stormzy's chart songs on her Spotify rotation, but she's nice enough. She's someone Poppy would've rolled her eyes at if she'd shown up at our humble parish school toting her Burberry backpack, but not now though. I notice her copying Bella's mannerisms all the time. She's reinventing. Mum called it something like keeping her gown friends separate from her town friends.

This party is the first time I've seen Poppy outside of work since November, and I don't think she's seen Freya since even earlier. August, September? Then again, neither have I. Which is sad, because at the end of sixth form the three of us were inseparable, and we assumed we still would be not even six months later.

'What do you study again?' Bella asks, picking at something stuck behind her acrylics.

'Social Anthropology. At UWE,' I add, before she can ask. She already knows I'm at the University of the West of England but will never miss out on an opportunity to tell me that it's *still* a good uni despite the rankings.

'Oh, yeah. You're such a good fit for there.'

I pull a tight smile, free-pouring vodka into the mug patterned with hand-painted poppies I bought Pop two birthdays ago.

She cheersed me with it when I told her I'd declined my offer at Manchester, even though it was my first choice. I knew I would the minute I submitted the application though, that I wouldn't have the courage to go. When I told Mum, she insisted I was sure of my decision, but I saw all the tension she swore was pre-results-day nerves relax once she knew I wouldn't be moving three hours away. They pretended they were, but no one was surprised, really. Not only was I never going to leave Bristol because I love my city, but Poppy was staying. And even though she's far from perfect, she's safe and she's been my person for the last ten years. No introductions, no icebreakers necessary.

Plus, the thought of spending months apart from my niece, my mini me, Rue, was not an option. Even the thought of moving to a new place in Bristol has me torn up because it'll put an end to our after-school hangs. His ex, Clara, works two jobs and doesn't have a good relationship with her own family, so between us, me, Mum, and Otis handle school pickups, and every weekend is a sleepover. There isn't space for Rue to have her own room at ours, and officially she sleeps on the pull-out in Otis's room, but sometimes I wake up to find she's crept in with me. There's no way I'd be able to spend whole terms without her.

I clear my throat. 'You're studying Business with Pop, right?'

Bella nods. 'Where's your other friend? The redhead. I like her. Pretty sure she hates me though. But she likes *all* my stuff, I love it, big fan energy.'

I hold my tongue firm to the roof of my mouth. The unironic conceitedness is crazy. 'You mean Freya?' I say slowly, pouring mixer into my mug. 'Her family come down from up north for her parents' annual party, she'll be here later, hopefully.'

'Cute. I think it's so adorable that Poppy still has her friends from primary school hanging about.'

I twist the lemonade lid tight. Something about the way she said that makes me think those are Poppy's words, regurgitated. Me and Freya, her little limpet friends. I keep my voice measured, not about to let Bella know she's getting under my skin. We definitely had this conversation the first time we met.

I correct her. 'Me and Poppy have been friends since then, yeah. Since we were eight actually—'

'A whole decade, *cute*. You guys should exchange Pandora bracelets or something.'

'—but we didn't meet Freya 'til year nine, when she switched to our school.' Bella uncharacteristically asks me why she moved and I just shrug. I'm not about to tell her Freya was, well, not exactly *bullied* at her old school, but she didn't have any friends. 'Her parents wanted her to go to the same school her cousin went to – this boy Jack, in our year.' I swallow, just saying his name making my heart race. For so long, I've avoided talking about him in case something gave it away we were together, that saying his name feels like swearing. Bella's nodding but looking into the crowd, losing interest. My eyes flick over to Poppy, fake laughing at something the boy's said. 'Anyway, I chose Art for GCSE, Poppy chose Drama, which is where she got close with Freya. They'd spend so much time rehearsing, we sort of became a three. Though we don't get to see each other as much anymore.'

Bella's not listening, distracted by someone asking for a bottle opener. 'I'll get it.' She jumps up, happy to oblige.

Now sitting alone, I get out my phone and find myself scrolling way back in my photos to when me, Poppy, and Freya first became friends. Selfies from those lunchtimes we'd spend in empty classrooms where I'd watch them run lines, script in hand so I could prompt them whenever they'd forget, channelling my inner Greta Gerwig. If they got through a whole scene without flubbing, it would always be Poppy who'd suggest celebrating with a slice of the canteen's tray bake. Dense sponge drizzled with white icing and hundreds and thousands. Always Poppy who would throw half of hers in the bin though, while me and Freya licked the rainbow sprinkles off our fingers.

I zoom in on Freya in a photo of the three of us, her golden retriever energy evident even in pictures, her chin doubled, caught mid-laugh. Looking at fourteen-year-old Freya – the way she was when I met her, the only other girl in our year built like me – calms some of the nerves I have about seeing her after so long. She'll still be the same Frey. Even though she's thin now and has a proper adult job at a bank, and a boyfriend to obsess over. I need to remember she probably still snorts when she laughs and has a pillow with Harry Styles's face on it.

But with no sign of her yet, and not even Bella to begrudgingly keep me company anymore, big regrets for coming here hit me. At first, I'd said no, but changed my mind when Mum announced she'd be away for SlimIt's New Year New You campaign, and Otis said Harrison had booked them a fancy dinner. A party at Manor Hall seemed like the better option than ringing in the New Year alone with Netflix and leftover Christmas chocolate. Plus, the makeup I got gifted this year was begging to be experimented with.

5

Getting ready earlier, my brush hovered over midnight blues and hazy purples, imagining the swathe of sky I could paint across my lids complete with gemstone stars. But in the end, I stuck with a blend of soft browns that don't stand out too much.

'Sorry, can I just get by?' A girl behind me presses up against my chair, trying to squeeze between me and a group of people dancing.

'Yeah, sorry. Sorry.' My chair was already tucked in as far as it could go, but I crush my body against the edge of the table.

My boobs topple the dregs of a beer can over and I take a deep breath, about to cringe to death as I mop it up.

Everyday embarrassments like this are why I stopped leaving the house, but I'm proud of myself for making the effort tonight. It's the first step to making sure this term isn't a repeat of the last one. Insecurity's had me hiding at home, ashamed of my size, attending lectures through a webcam. I needed tonight to remind me of everything I'm missing out on.

I glance at Poppy, running the pendant of her necklace along its chain as she listens intently to something the boy's saying.

I hate to say it, but I want what she's got: to be in a place of my own with a whole party's worth of new friends, to unselfconsciously wear a crop top. And to talk to a boy who isn't afraid to let people know he thinks I'm pretty.

Poppy's the vision board.

Across the littered table, the boy veers towards her, his eyes on her silicone E cups. 'So, how much does a pair of them set you back then?' he says.

Instinctively, I skirt over to them and take her hands, pulling her up. 'Come to the toilet with me.'

'Oh my God, *thank you*,' Poppy says out of the side of her mouth, flatly telling him that she has to talk to her friend. She squeezes my hand as she shoulders us towards the door, weaving us through the long kitchen crammed with people dancing and drinking. I take a breath to ask if she's OK, but she shoots me a look and changes the subject. 'I'm fine. Freya's not coming now, by the way. She just text saying her mum doesn't feel safe to drive on the one rosé she had two hours ago. Lol.' I hate it when she says lol out loud. 'And she's too skint to pay the Uber surge prices for New Year's.'

'Oh,' I say, kind of sad, kind of relieved.

I need to text Freya back. I'll do it tomorrow when I'm sober, and more often after that. She doesn't deserve to be ignored.

'I'm glad you're here though, babe, I've *missed* you, you never come out anymore—'

'Hey, where are you going?' Bella throws a cork at Poppy's shoulder as we pass. She shows us the time displayed on her phone screen. 'You're gonna miss midnight.'

'Oh, it's already? We need a photo, Saff. Our last pic of 2024. Will you take a picture of us?' Poppy thrusts her phone towards Bella.

Before she can answer, I say, 'I'll take a selfie.'

'But you won't see my outfit.'

'You will, look.' I angle my arm so the camera's almost got a bird's-eye view, though I'm massively in the forefront and it's

7

just my head and shoulders. You can still see Poppy in full length, standing behind me in her crop top and denim skirt. My camera flashes, and I turn to her triumphantly. 'See—'

'Now take one of me and Bella. Way further back though.' She waves me away and I nod, watching them as they suck in their already flat stomachs.

I stare at their cheeks pressed together, their arms around each other, and feel lonely. I've only made acquaintances at uni so far, people I can ask to copy lecture notes off, how to add printer credits. There isn't a closeness, a unique You-and-Me-ness like Poppy has with Bella. Because I haven't let anyone get close enough for that.

At uni everyone struts around campus so sure of who they're supposed to be, how to dress, what to say, what they want to do with their lives. And yet the person I am right now feels transitionary, not the me I want them to meet. Like, I'm still in my Very Hungry Caterpillar phase, yet to emerge from my cocoon, socially confident, snatched, with job prospects and colour-analysis-matched ASOS wings. Not like Poppy, a born butterfly, with her size eight wardrobe of 'light summer' outfits, 82 per cent grade average, and dreams to open her own gym.

I didn't think us going to separate unis would be such a big deal. But every night as I fall asleep under the ceiling I stuck glow-in-the-dark stars on when I was seven, I worry that it is.

When I accepted my place at UWE, I knew it meant staying home with Mum and Otis, staying still. I just didn't factor in that Poppy would keep going. And watching her live her best life all over Instagram from the comfort of my sofa has made home start to feel like a place I *should've* outgrown. But I don't go anywhere, do anything, because my bigger body feels like it doesn't belong out in the world.

It doesn't stop me wanting to live the experiences people move to melting pot cities like Bristol for though. Like doing my own food shop from the international markets on St Marks Road, or getting the number of a boy I meet amongst the crowded pub benches on King Street. Only I want to be doing all of that as the new me. Which starts tomorrow.

Poppy's clicking her fingers. 'Hello? Babe, what have you taken? Did you hear me, can you do one more?' She switches up her pose and I oblige. 'Thanks,' she says, taking back her phone.

Bella drags us over to where people are gathered to watch the fireworks being projected on to the back wall of the kitchen, and immediately, we split up.

I scan the faces of Poppy's friends, dappled with light from the projector. I say friends, but apart from Bella and a couple of people she's mentioned from the floor below, I'm guessing a lot of these relationships don't go much further than drunken introductions made during freshers. Strong male majority. She's always had this kind of magnetism with boys, even before her mum paid for her boob job for her eighteenth-birthday present. Her ability to get boys to fawn, to be nice to me to please her, was what protected me from getting bullied any worse than I did at school. It's probably the reason I still put up with her shit, because I guess I feel indebted to that.

And even if it makes me feel like I'm playing the part of an extra in my own life, billed simply as The Fat Friend, being a guest star on The Poppy Show is always a fun time. She's a loveable brat, unpredictable and hilarious. It's only recently that being in the shadow of her spotlight has been getting old.

'You OK?' Poppy calls to me over the top of some heads. 'How'd we get separated?'

'I don't know.'

'Hey, what's your New Year's resolution?' she asks.

'I don't think I have one,' I lie.

'I've just found mine,' Poppy says, pointing to a boy in the crowd, his afro in a bun.

Makes zero sense, but OK? Go off.

Everyone chants backwards from ten into the New Year along with the countdown lighting the back wall. Faces gazing, beaming at each other, basking in a togetherness I just don't quite feel a part of.

'... Six. Five. Four.' My eyes meet with a boy across the gathering. He stares at my mouth, lined and lipsticked with MAC's Velvet Teddy, my Cupid's bow a perfectly kissable capital *M*. My belly swoops with hot hope. Is this a boy who appreciates the artistry of makeup? Who likes the bounce of my 3B curls? For once will my face card not be declined? But then his eyes are travelling down my body. Lingering on my stomach. 'Three. Two. One.' His gaze rips away from me and he screams, 'Happy New Year!' into the face of the boy to his right, the rejection subtle but firm. *Not you.*

They go in for that diagonal hug boys do, clapping backs. I look for Poppy and see she's kissing the boy with his afro in a bun, resolution complete. The rest of us clasp arms, brush cheeks, come together with only a grazing intimacy.

'Happy New Year,' I say into the ear of some girl from the ground-floor who came to the party with her heated rollers still in.

'Yeah, happy New Year, Sophie.'

'It's Saffron,' I mumble, people around me beginning to sway, clanging out 'Auld Lang Syne'.

As I stare at the fireworks I acknowledge that my New Year's resolution is the same as it was last year, and every year before that as far back as I can remember making them. I want to lose weight, but it's about so much more than that too. I want to go on holidays, throw myself a birthday party, wear a bodycon dress.

I want to be thin. I want to be happy.

Poppy's still kissing the boy with the afro, a string of saliva spindling between their lips as they pause to giggle at each other. I glance down at my phone as it pings with a message.

Mum

HNY hon, this is going to be your year, I just know it!! Xx

This *is* going to be my year. I will be happy. I make a note on my phone of how I'm going to make that happen.

1. GO ON A DIET

january

Sunday afternoon squeezes through the slats of my blinds as I sit in bed. My attention flicks from my laptop to my phone. I scroll past not one but two more fitfluencers in a row promising me a hot girl summer as long as I pay for their subscription-only workout routines and meal plans, starting now *now* NOW.

imogen_shawcross Happy New YOU, tomorrow starts today

skyevaleriofit If you're tired of starting over, stop giving up

Oh, fuck *off*. I'm trying, alright?

Along with three thousand other people, I like a comment under Skye's post by a blue-ticked user named, bodiedbybliss.

bodiedbybliss You know what I'm tired of, girl? Every influencer and their mum's friend's auntie's dog out here acting like a qualified nutritionist 'cus they own an air fryer and a nutribullet.

I laugh, tapping into her profile. Her name's Bliss Adeyemi, a strikingly beautiful Black woman with glorious coily curls. Her bio says she's from Bristol too. I skim through her content. Her uploads are a fusion of beauty, body, and food, including makeup tutorials, mukbangs, plus-sized outfit try-ons, infographics about body neutrality, and a video series called, 'What I eat in a day as a Fat Girl who don't give a damn!!!'

My finger hovers over the follow button. She's instantly relatable, funny, and her makeup looks are fire, but I hesitate. I'm not sure this is the content I should be engaging with right now. I want my feed to be inspirational, full of people at my goal weight, posing with toned midriffs and offering up ten versatile ways to eat sauerkraut. No matter how insufferable they are.

Scrolling back up, I view Poppy's Story, frowning as I skip through *eight* slides of her reviewing a meal-replacement shake I recognise from the notably insufferable, Molly Mills's, page.

'Girlies, run, don't walk to FastOff's New Year sale. No word of a lie, this tastes exactly like triple chocolate brownie in a glass. I literally don't know how they make protein powder taste so good.'

Yeah, neither do I, but the results displayed all over their website make trying it tempting.

I peek out of the blinds. Not raining. I could go for a jog. (OK, a walk.) No, I should pack. If I trick the universe into thinking

I've already got somewhere to go, it might manifest an available room for me to rent.

I consult my refined Notes app list of New Year's resolutions.

1. GO ON A DIET
2. Find somewhere to live
3. Track meals in SlimIt app. Try not to go over 1,200 cals
4. NO SUGAR
5. Take self out on cinema date once a month
6. Do 30–60 minutes of cardio a day
7. Have beach body (weigh 10st) by summer
8. Find boyfriend to go to the beach with!!!

Ideally, I need number two ticked off *today*.

I contemplate the calories I'd burn dismantling my soulless IKEA furniture. Though I could get this room packed up in less than a day if I bribe Otis with the deep-fried plantain bites they serve at work. Or just food, any food. Otis has that enviable metabolism of tall, skinny boys who can eat whatever they want in any quantifiable amount and never look any different.

My stomach groans, gnawingly cavernous, having finally churned every ounce of energy out of the spaghetti he made for dinner last night. Ignoring its protests, I take a sip of tepid tea and click to view the next page of ads for rooms on sharespace.com.

Halfway through reading the description for a dental office

by day, studio apartment by night (!?), I notice my phone light up with a notification for a new match on Reveal. My hand grabs fast, a loneliness-induced spasm, and I unlock the screen to:

Nolan, 20
lazy sundays > pizza n beers > cult movie marathons in our underwear

Hey how are you lovely, he says.

I write back, Good thanks, you? Knee-deep into a lazy Sunday of my own tbh.

I bet this guy gets Revelation after Revelation on Sundays with a bio like that.

Reveal's matchmaking concept is purely personality based, with everyone's photos hidden until you've exchanged a certain amount of messages, so I pore over his Aura. It's this synthographic collage Reveal's AI technology generates out of your answers to their questions. Basically You in a virtual collage of emojis, quotes, colours, and personality traits. Swiping through them is supposed to leave you with a much deeper hook on a person than the typical dating app profile pics. (Beaming man holding dead fish. Mirror selfie. Windswept man dressed head to toe in North Face at the top of a big hill in Wales.)

Nolan and I engage in the back and forth of dating app niceties, our Revelation status progressing across the top of the chat as I try to keep my hopes in check.

I've got to 100 per cent with seven boys since I downloaded

Reveal a month ago but none of them have progressed to real-life dates. I'd heard of Reveal, seen the targeted ads, but I didn't think it was for me. First week of December, I downloaded it out of desperation. I was jealous of all the mistletoe kisses and matching pyjamas on social media. Freya and Tom, hands clutched in front of the Christmas tree in their Fair Isle onesies, paper crowns askew. Still, every single time I think I've found someone on here, once they see what I look like they disappear. The first three – OK, four, hurt me. But that was before Sydney. Now I feel un-ghostable, plasma-proof.

Sydney doesn't get unmatched.

After some time, I switch tabs on my browser, back to Facebook, to resume my room hunting. But I'm restless and swing my legs out of bed. Spurred on by the possibility of Nolan meeting the New Me me, I grit my teeth and step on the scales, record my start weight, then pick my ugliest, mismatched underwear for maximum 'Before' vibes. I take mirror pictures of myself from the front and side, shoulders slumped, breath blown out. On my phone, I hide them in a folder I name Saffron 2.0, and allow myself the briefest flash forward to six months from now when I'm finally happy. I see myself finally at my goal weight, so the obsession with reaching it is no longer hijacking my every waking thought. I've got the thinking space to concentrate on my course and the confidence to fully embrace student life. I see myself sipping guilt-free cocktails with new friends I've found the courage to make, not quietly calculating the empty calories of my drinks while Poppy's uni friends talk around me; no ducking out of group photos; no more shopping exclusively for baggy, shapeless clothing; and maybe, just maybe, a boy will tell me he likes me, and I'll believe him.

But six months is forever, so I google

how to lose a stone in two weeks

and come across something called the Military Diet. I take screenshots of the meal plan and feel a renewed sense of determination. This one girl in a forum from 2011 swears by it, says it's what doctors recommend to patients who need to lose weight before surgery.

But until it's worked, there's Nolan, and my unsubstantiated hope that he'll be different from the rest.

As I flop back down on the bed, my phone rings. It's Mum, FaceTiming. I answer, adjusting my head so my chin doesn't double.

'Hello— Oh my God.' Mum's head whips left then right as she crosses a road, giving me the whole panorama of yesterday's makeup still caked on to her deep brown skin. Oh, her poor pores. 'Where are you right now? Are you calling me mid-walk-of-shame?'

'I am walking, yes, home from a very good date. No shame.' She grins so wide, I see the glint of one of her gold teeth in the back.

'You know I know that.' I shuffle into a seated position, suddenly embarrassed at how starkly different our mornings are. Here I am, in bed on my phone after a full ten hours of sleep, while Mum's sneaking back to her car, hungover and wearing last night's clothes. She's meant to be living vicariously through me, not the other way round. 'What did you and Pete get up to then? *Before* you went back to his.'

'Oh no, not Pete, that's done with.' The traffic noise on Mum's end hushes as she turns on to a residential street. 'Last night was Eduardo, and we went salsa dancing.' She shimmies her shoulders, giddy.

'Oh. You didn't tell me about him.' Or maybe she did, maybe I mixed him up with Tamir – or no, Greg, who she did our Christmas shopping with only a month ago. Maybe she told me all about Eduardo and I'd already filed him under done and deleted. Despite popular belief, the dating pool for thirty-fives and up is seemingly depthless. Mum's always on to the next one. Too bad the next one is never the right one though. Or the last one. I want her to be happy, whether that means finding a man or realising she doesn't need one. So, I swallow my complicated mix of jealousy and concern, and give her my most heartening smile. 'Glad you had fun. Are you home tonight at least?'

I've not seen her since Wednesday, and I miss her. If she's not been on dates trying to fulfil the wish of all these men who must've put *find a wife* at the top of their New Year's goals, she's been at back-to-back work events. January is like diet culture Christmas, and SlimIt have had Mum touting their membership offers at every self-help seminar and gym reopening across the region.

'I am, hon.' The camera shakes as she gets into her car, leaning the phone against the windshield as she winds a loose braid round her bun. 'Duvet night?'

'Please. Much needed.'

It takes us our usual fifteen seconds of frantic goodbyes to get off the phone, and then I'm consulting my to-watch list for tonight's film. Duvet night's been a long time coming. Just me, Mum, the reclined sofa, her king-sized quilt, and something clichéd but characterful on TV. An *Eat, Pray, Love* or a *10 Things I Hate About You*.

Decided on *How Stella Got Her Groove Back*, I flip my phone face down to stop myself from waiting for Nolan's next message and refresh my room search, house share Bristol bills incl. I click into an ad for a five-bed house share in the centre and read its description.

Toby Booth Yoooooo fellow Bristolians and all you rahhhhh baccy types who've moved up here from Oxford and Kent because you got pied off by your chosen Russell Group . . . ATTENTION. We have a room available in a 5-bed terrace on Wilder Street that needs URGENT occupying. Spacious (well, the rats think it is) attic room with skylight, double bed, and built in wardrobe. £500 deposit and £675 a month including bills. (PS the rats was just a joke, pls reply.)

I check my online banking, even though I know I've got the deposit and enough for three months' rent up front if there's competition. The evidence of Dad's guilty conscience is still sitting there in my savings account. Last June I received £3,000 via BACS transfer on my eighteenth birthday. HBD x was the payment reference. It was the first contact I'd had off him since he emigrated in 2022. No card, no call. Just a one-off transaction converted from Australian dollars. HBD x.

All his life he's blistered lobster red in the heat, his pale skin not able to handle anything above twenty degrees. I hope he's got a perma-sunburn out there.

Putting my well-versed Tinder tone to good use – a breezy blend of self-assured yet slightly self-deprecating – I comment on Toby Booth's post.

Saffron Saldana Hey! I'm a friend of the rats, they told me to message about the room – we're cool with sharing. Will DM you x

Straight away I send Toby a follow-up message letting him know I'm *very* interested in the room, don't need to view it, and can pay a couple of months' rent up front. He insists I come view the house first – a condition of the landlord's – and I say,

Saffron Saldana OK, totally get that. When?

Toby Booth Sound. Friday?

Saffron Saldana Cool, Friday works

And he sends me the address as well as his number.

I save him to my contacts as Toby – Facebook Rat Boy and tuck away the blossoming, wishful feeling of a boy giving me his number.

*

Because it's January and the Caribbean café where Poppy and I work employs its staff on zero-hour contracts, both our shifts get cancelled, so we have the next day off. Though we both work front-of-house at Jemima's Jerk Café, we don't see as much of each other as you'd think. Most of our contact happens in fleeting moments behind the counter. In the hour where my afternoon shift overlaps with her evening shift, or vice versa, we bitch about rude customers and make bets on which tables will leave good tips. It's rare we're both off rota on the same day, so when Poppy asks me to meet her in town to look through the sales, I go, wondering how many steps I'll clock in traipsing round the shops.

The hangers squeal against the rail as Poppy parts the size tens from the size eights. 'Oh my God, did you see Freya's Story last night? Do you think they'll actually get married?'

I don't mean to, but I scoff. 'Would be a big, expensive waste of a ring and all those engagement pictures if they didn't intend on getting married, Pop. But no, I didn't see her Story.'

I swallow. Did that sound bitter? Back in September when Freya announced her engagement, I nearly dropped my phone into my cauliflower rice. (Mum was, unsuccessfully, trying to convince me it was better than basmati.) Tom had the content-savvy foresight to record the moment he got down on one knee silhouetted against the sunset, and it had just popped up on my timeline. I showed it to Mum and Otis across the table, jaw-dropped, then scrolled through the accompanying carousel of golden-hour shots of them on a beach in the south of France. I watched the likes and comments rack up in disbelief. The caption read when you know, you know 😌💍 to

21

address that, yes it was soon (after only three months!), and yes, they were young, but they were happy. I fled the table to FaceTime Freya, and she answered from the balcony of their hotel, hair in a towel, surrounded by cloudless blue sky. She'd propped the phone up against an ashtray on the table, her chin cupped in her hand. As I stared at her sharp cheekbones and the diamond-clustered ring on her finger, I remember thinking how much I wanted to be her in that moment, about to go out to dinner and not have to choose between a starter or a dessert, and gaze into the eyes of a boy who loved her so much he'd publicly declared he wanted to be with her forever. I also concluded I might be rotten inside because I kind of hated her for it.

'What about this?' I ask Poppy, holding up a denim corset top with a chunky gold zip, wishing something like this would look good in my size. Pop says the gold's a bit tacky, so I put it back.

'She posted a Boomerang of them cheersing with Bride and Groom to Be glasses.' Poppy considers this. 'I liked it but it's still weird though, right? Like who gets engaged at our age, let alone commits to planning a whole-ass ceremony about it? I fear she's a future trad-wife victim.'

'It's quick, yeah. But if it's what she wants . . .' I trail off, keen to move on from talking about Freya's perfect life.

'Just imagine if we're bridesmaids and Jack's part of the groomsmen.' My hand stops swiping through discount dresses. 'Like, I know he's *her* cousin, but surely Tom will have Jack as a . . . a pageboy or whatever for Freya's sake.' I eye Poppy over the rail. 'And don't act like you won't be glad to see him, it was *so* obvious you fancied him in school.'

'I—'

'It's OK, he's hot, we all did. And like, I know he was a dick ninety per cent of the time, but he was alright when we used to walk home with him, remember? It'll be like a school reunion, so cute.'

'Yeah. Cute.'

Or not, considering we haven't seen Freya in months, and Jack and I have had a whole relationship begin and end without Poppy or Freya knowing anything about it. So, yeah, you could say I fancied him. Quite a bit.

I don't know why Poppy's acting like we were some kind of tight foursome anyway. Like, let's be for real, Jack was a scarily different person in school to the one he was in the twenty-minute walk home from the bus stop we all shared. Even more so when we were alone in his room, just me and him. During school, he'd spend the day negging Poppy about her flat chest with the other boys, or else sniggering as Charlie yelled, *'Earthquake!'* after Freya and I in the hallway.

But away from boys like Billy Ferris and Charlie Webster, he was quieter, and away from everyone else, he could even be kind.

Later, over the changing room curtains in New Look, Poppy hears me groan.

'What?' she says.

'I hate everything. I swear, fat girl hell's gonna just be one big changing room. And these lights—'

'You are not fat. Stop saying that.' Her words jig with the

23

motion of shimmying her jeans back up. 'If I hear you say it one more time, I'll call you out on my Stories and you'll be cancelled.'

'As *if*,' I say under my breath.

Poppy's an ex-Olympic-adjacent swimmer with abs and fake boobs; her Instagram's followed by a league of fuckboys and simps of the amateur athlete genre. Boys in V-necks cut to their belly buttons that send her messages like, We should gym together, and I love a girl who prioritises her body. Do it, post your Story. There's no way her DMs would be filled with the passionate, politically correct outrage she's expecting, shouting in all caps that FAT IS NOT A DIRTY WORD.

'You're beautiful, babe.'

I roll my eyes, folding up a pair of too-tight mom jeans. The words fall flat with a kindness that feels performative. And aren't I allowed just a little self-deprecating comic relief every once in a while? Must we be so yass queen about ourselves *all* the time?

Handing back the six pairs of jeans that didn't fit, I tell Poppy something to that effect. 'I can call myself whatever I want.' I shrug, standing in the queue for the tills, fronting, but actually feeling quite shit on the inside. 'Anyway, I thought we took that word back. I'm *allowed* to call myself fat.'

Poppy tuts, exasperated. 'I just don't think it's very helpful to give voice to your inner critic all the time, I saw this TikTok about it.'

'Right.'

But I need my inner critic, I want to say, staring at the visible sculpted hipbones of a shop mannequin. As much as I try to align myself with the feel-good philosophy of plus-sized models and bo-po Instagrammers like that influencer, Bliss Adeyemi, I came across the other day, I am not unapologetically voluptuous, or curvy, or thicc. I'm fat, and that's all Nolan's going to think once we reach 100 per cent and I've Revealed myself to him.

Poppy snaps her fingers. Another Bella-ism. 'I said, where'd you want to go for lunch?'

'Sorry.' We walk out of the shop and into the throng of bodies and food smells. Wall-to-wall restaurants and retail. 'You pick, I'm not hungry,' I lie. 'I'll get lunch at home.'

The lunch at home: black coffee, a tin of tuna, and a slice of unbuttered toast.

By Tuesday, I'm at 97 per cent with Nolan.

I can tell you're a brunette, he sends. Wrong. I mean, naturally, yes, I am. But my curls are bleached blonde right now, my dark roots growing through. It was something I decided to do on a whim about a week before first term started and now kind of regret. I already feel like we have such a connection. I can't wait to see you. I bet you're beautiful.

I swallow. About to hit 100 per cent in the middle of a packed lecture hall, I tilt my phone towards me, shielding my screen, embarrassed about the person sitting beside me seeing Reveal's interface.

Saffron Me too. It's been nice talking to you anyway ☺ So . . . here goes

As that last message delivers, the app refreshes and an animated pop-up updates me with the notification, **Revelation Status: 100%**.

Around me, everyone's hand shoots up at something the guest lecturer's asked. I raise my hand too, my phone cradled by my pressed-together thighs. It's the first lecture back after Christmas and I'm not paying attention at all, anxious because I'm self-conscious, and thus distracting myself with Reveal.

This New Year New Me mantra I keep kidding myself with had me lulled into a false sense of security, thinking that I'd feel surer of myself already, confident enough to be here. That's why I made the effort to come in today. But honestly, I wish I'd kept it virtual. All I can think about is the extra couple of pounds I put on over Christmas and whether or not Nolan's going to end up ghosting me.

Which is frustrating because Modern Kinship and Belonging was the only module on the syllabus that really spoke to me.

My concentration was the same all last term, my mind blanking whole presentations, not retaining anything. If I've learnt one thing from my university experience so far, it's that my interest is not piqued by Social Anthropology. Sitting here, giving my screen more attention than the course I'm paying over nine grand for, I'm realising how stupid it was to base my whole degree on what my mum studied twenty years ago because I had no idea what else to do. Before Mum got the job with SlimIt, she used to be a social worker, and, like, *actually* help people. Mainly getting mothers with kids Rue's age into safe housing and organising outreach programmes to feed and clothe Bristol's homeless. And when the time came to apply to universities, faced with indecision and a list of barely B-average predicted grades, I decided helping people wouldn't be a bad career path to take.

Hand still in the air, I glance up at the lecturer in her late thirties, her face crowded by a pair of thick-framed glasses and a cable-knit turtleneck.

Surveying the raised hands, she says, 'Yeah, as I suspected. Now, keep it raised if swiping through a dating app has ever felt quite overwhelming to you.'

I glance along my row, arms lowering. My elbow bends, half up, half down. I think there are only women left with their hands up, girls my age, a mature student I recognise from my Research Ethics module last term. All of us signed up to the same apps, compressing entire personalities into five pictures and a 300-character bio, uploading ourselves to be categorised as a yes or no. Squished under the thumb of serial swipers, ghosters, and unsolicited dick pic senders.

'Thank you for being honest.' The lecturer nods, and I sigh, dropping my arm into my lap. She sweeps her hair back and secures it with a claw clip as she speaks. 'I personally found the whole thing so panic-inducing, I shut down at the notion of someone *super-liking* me. You have to pay to be able to send super-likes. I freaked, deleted everything.' Low, relating laughter shuffles through the class. 'Are you surprised then, that when society moved to a more digitised approach to dating, rendering love and emotion as algorithmic and datafied responses, we started seeing rising levels of anxiety and stress among our dating population? Of course we're all anxious.' As I listen, my phone slips off my lap. It clatters and a few people look over. The guest lecturer notices me, holding my stare as she fixes her stance behind the podium. 'Though initially culturally liberating, the problem we're seeing with prolonged dating app use is that because their algorithms give the illusion that our potential partners are infinite, it amplifies the pressure to make the right choice. To pick the right person.'

I scrabble for my phone, my body not fit to bend between the narrow, tiered seating. On the screen is what I suspect to be my last unrequited message to Nolan. Watching as it's marked as seen, I presume that for him, I will not be the right person.

A growl from my stomach eats into the near-silence of the auditorium. I lock my arms across my middle, letting my curls fall over my face as I stare at those two ticks, willing a speech bubble to pop up to tell me he's typing. But as my stomach growl grows, it feels like the whole auditorium can hear how hungry I am. Embarrassed, I grab my stuff and slip out from my end-row seat.

In the canteen, I'm surrounded by people who have found their people, grouped together laughing or working, and here I am, desperately checking my phone. The screen refreshes and I've been spat back into Reveal's swipeable catalogue of Auras. Nolan's already scrolled through my Revealed pictures and unmatched me before I had a chance to see what he looked like behind his faceless grey avatar. I watch a girl bite into an iced bun at the table opposite me, my throat aching with the urge to cry.

It's not that deep, I know – *he's* not that deep – but the rejection stings.

Overwhelmed, I go into a toilet cubicle and cry under the cover of the hand dryer.

After some minutes, I fish my phone out of my trouser pocket. There's a Facebook message from some girl named Veronica.

Veronica Farrington

> Hey. Toby says you're coming to see the room Friday – I live there, hi!! Gutted, I'll be in lectures all day, so I won't see you. Just wanted to make it clear that THERE ARE NO RATS, and if we pick you, please don't bring your own rats!!! 😇

I smile, drying my eyes on my sleeve, because one of my potential new housemates just reached out, but it's not enough to stop me from what I'm about to do. I reply with a *Ratatouille* GIF, then go to Reveal's settings, where I log off as Saffron Saldana.

log in
email sydney.darlinghurst@gmail.com
password fuckujackday

Two days later, and Sydney hasn't found Nolan yet. I'm on my phone, searching for him with hard, impatient swipes.

I lie in my unmade bed, next to a book I borrowed from the library, spine-up, abandoned halfway through the introduction.

There's no way I can concentrate on it now, when I'm still searching for Nolan.

Sydney swipes through boys like flicking through pages of a book with spit-licked fingers. She knows the exact part she's trying to get to, the end, the happily ever after. Not in the traditional sense and not for her, for me. Her purpose is strictly revenge, a five-minute fuck-you to the boys who reject the real me.

Once I set up her profile, I realised pretty fast just how therapeutic hot-girl ghosting was.

When I'm Sydney *my* body doesn't matter. I know when I'm Revealed, nobody's going to be unmatching me because I'm wearing hers. Which is technically my body all dressed in reality-bending filters. I asked ChatGPT to make me into a goddess-like beautiful Instagram model with a hot body and ChatGPT understood the assignment. AI *delivered*. Kilos have been erased off my body, my waist an impossibly balanced hourglass, my boobs dragged high up on my chest, not softly sitting atop my belly rolls like they are in reality. A rigid gap's been carved between my thighs, and my double chin's been sculpted away.

My gaze flicks to the mirrored wardrobe door. Even on my best days, I don't live up to what AI understood to be *the* beauty standard.

The only thing that comes close is my makeup. Today it's soft-glam and glowy, even as I sit here in trackies and a SpongeBob tee because I had seminars to virtually attend. After how being on campus went on Tuesday, I decided to play it safe. I'm much more at ease and willing to participate in classes when I can control how others are perceiving me. No bad lighting, no unflattering angles, just me, perfectly poised in my square webcam window.

On my phone, I thumb to Sydney's profile. When I stare really hard, I still catch glimpses of myself. It's scary, should probably be illegal, but it isn't, and neither is catfishing. I've watched enough of the TV show to know it isn't, and that most of the people pretending to be someone they're not aren't evil, sadistic, old-lady scammers, though some of them definitely are. Most of them – oh God, most of *us* – are unconfident or dealing with shame or trauma, and just after a little ego massage.

I skim through Reveal, making and ignoring more matches until I find him again.

Nolan, 20

lazy sundays > pizza n beers > cult movie marathons in our underwear

The afternoon drips closer to early evening as I type my way back into Nolan's affections as Sydney, weaving insider information into her flirting. Saffron knows his favourite band's The Smiths (in hindsight, a major red flag), so Sydney says she's obsessed with The Cure. Saffron remembers Nolan went to a *Rocky Horror* drive-in showing last month, so guess what Sydney did last week! Our artificial instant chemistry makes him reply faster.

I send the cry-laughing emoji alone in my room as the street falls dark outside my window at 4 p.m.

My pulse thrums in the base of my throat as our Revelation status hits 99 per cent. Nolan's obviously also free this afternoon and doing the exact same thing I am, not putting his phone down between texts. This is the fastest I've ever progressed a Revelation status, even while pretending to be Sydney, who I've character developed to be a cool girl, dripping with wit and composure and references that boys like. *Pulp Fiction* and football transfers.

Nolan tells me for the second time this week that he can't wait to see me as I let his excitement tip us over to 100.

Nolan Shiiiit. 99%. I'm nervous, why am I nervous? What have you done to me!

Nolan Come on come on. How many messages count as a single per cent??

Sydney That should do it

I let out a little involuntary shriek that spoils into a cackle as we hit 100 and Sydney's pictures are revealed.

Nolan Oh my god

I imagine Nolan's palms sweating, his heart tripping, his dick getting hard, and I sit here feeling despicably, delightfully sick with the knowledge that I did that and it was all a lie.

Nolan Whoa. You're literally the most beautiful girl I've ever seen

Downstairs, the front door slams, keys clattering into the bowl on the hall shelf.

'Alright!?' Otis shouts up the stairs. 'Anyone home?'

Usually, I like to sit awhile and actively ghost someone, watching their messages slowly sour with the same insecurity I felt when our roles were reversed – You there?? Come on babe, don't leave me hanging aha – until they've either been reduced to nothing but punctuation – ???????, !?! – or their innermost incel is revealed – Bitch u arrogant. I didn't like you anyway. Think you're better than me, do you? Slut.

But Otis being home feels like there's a witness to my mind games and immediately my stomach's squirming with guilt.

'Yeah, be down in a sec,' I call, lurching off the bed.

Pacing, I tap into Nolan's profile for closure, needing to put a face to the name that's been living rent-free in my head all week. But the interruption means there's no vengeful surge of adrenalin as I anticipate the big Ghost, awaiting the satisfaction of deleting myself from his phone right when he thinks I've let him in.

Nolan's pictures load and—

I gasp.

A sharp, sudden pitching of my stomach. My phone clatters on to my desk. A disorienting kind of confusion prickles at the nape of my neck. It can't be him, it *isn't* him. Why would anyone want to pretend to be him? And yet that has to be what's happening here, because talking to Nolan was like talking to a stranger, new and exciting and never-before.

Trembling, I stare down at the smiling face of my ex-boyfriend, Jack.

The next day I wake, anxious as hell, and rot in bed until late morning when the house is empty. I heard Otis leave for work hours ago, then Mum's hairdryer blaring, and the car starting a bit after that. It was raining when I snoozed my GO FOR A FUCKING RUN 🐻 alarm at seven, and by eight, the clouds were letting through licks of lilac and it was too light to go running.

I don't have to leave for the house viewing until twelve thirty anyway, so I have time to properly process last night's Reveal.

My stomach swirls with unease as I flick through Nolan's pictures again, because they've been ripped straight from Jack's social media accounts.

This whole thing is so unprecedented. I've been revenge-catfishing someone who just so happens to also be catfishing *me* as my ex. Like, however and whenever this all concludes, I'm going viral telling this story to TikTok, I don't care. Get me that Creator Fund coin. But right now, this person's motives are uncertain, and seeing Jack's face attached to a different name feels all kinds of uncanny. I need to disengage. I stare at the last message Nolan sent.

Nolan Aha, hope my pics haven't scared you off. Night x

Considering I've just found out you're digitally masking as my ex-boyfriend, Nolan, I am somewhat scared.

There's no denying Jack Day is attractive. He's over six foot with long-lashed, chocolate-cake-coloured eyes, and a tousle of dirty-blond waves. Trust me, he's someone whose pictures you'd steal if you wanted a lot of swipe rights. But then I remember that this is *Reveal*, where these photos are hidden behind a wall of conversation. So, what's the rationale? All I know for certain is that I'm being catfished. There's no doubt in my mind this isn't the real Jack using a fake name.

Back in school, Jack resented the fact he liked me. I wasn't a Poppy or any of the other girls from our year who could knot their polo shirts into crop tops. Girls he wouldn't have to get to swear not to tell anyone he was shagging.

At first, I thought Jack *did* like Poppy. He started walking home from the bus stop with us when Freya did, which he later told me his mum asked him to do because of all the trouble Freya had at her last school. He'd flirt with Poppy in that weird, pestering kind of way, like pushing her into puddles and pinging the back of her bra. We'd get to Freya's house first, then Poppy's in the cul-de-sac fifteen minutes further, so the last part of the journey was always just me and him. We started texting. About normal stuff at first, exams and plans for university, TV shows, and people we went to school with. He kept insisting that Charlie and Billy were *decent lads, really*. Then before I could get over the fact that Jack Day was texting me, he was asking if I'd ever had sex before and what bra size I was. And when he asked me not to tell anyone what we talked about, that's when I realised he was being serious, that this wasn't some elaborate joke or fucked-up dare.

One time, after enduring twenty minutes of Billy Ferris's new game of shouting, *'Hey Free Willy, I think you missed your stop,'* every time the bus passed a chip shop or a McDonald's, when Poppy left us, Jack asked me to keep walking. He wanted me to come back to his house to see his new car. His parents were out, the implication obvious. I said yes because no one had ever liked me before and I was willing to do anything to keep a hold of that.

'I think you're hot. Who cares what they say?' he'd said after kissing me in his parked Vauxhall Corsa. He'd emphasised the 'I' hard, as if he'd accepted that, objectively, I *was* a big, blubbery beached whale, but it was OK, so long as he got to stick his harpoon in me.

My phone goes off and the message preview makes me utterly convinced whoever I'm talking to on Reveal is *not* Jack.

Nolan What a morning, winter sun and frosty grass is my favourite kind of day. Hope you slept well

I close the app. As if I needed this on my mind today, when I'm already nervous about going to meet Toby – Facebook Rat Boy later. I wish Veronica could be there. Her account's set to private, so I'm only going off her messages, but she seems kind and I think we vibe. After responding to my *Ratatouille* GIF with, OK, that guy's allowed, I asked her if she liked living in the area, which led on to her sending me a list of recs for the best local coffee shops and markets around. I *so* hope the room checks out and I get to move in. Veronica's friendliness, and all the places she suggested nearby, have made me want this ten times more than I did before.

I screenshot the house listing and send it to Mum, then the girls' group chat with a line of fingers-crossed emojis. Poppy replies instantly.

Poppy
Love it. That blue carpet is uni accom chic at its finest

She sends back a picture of her feet standing on an identical square of wiry, scratchy carpet in shade Public Library Blue.

Poppy
Excuse the pasty feet

Freya
Ooh, you found somewhere! Sleepover at yours when you move in pls

I heart react Freya's message and reply, 1000% yes, to the group, then open up a separate message thread with just Poppy.

Saffron
What're you doing today? Wanna meet after the house viewing? I'll be in town anyway

I watch as my message gets seen, tapping my nails against the hard plastic of my phone case. It's not that I don't want to spend time with Freya, I do. But every time I see her these days, it's like talking to everything I want personified. I get bitter and petty, mad about nothing and everything, and I hate what it's doing to our friendship. I'm jealous, but it's different to how I'm jealous of Poppy. Poppy's always been leagues above me. But with Freya, I look on like a covetous sore loser. Her three-stone weight loss and subsequent relationship feel like they could've been happening for me if only I'd tried harder.

Poppy

Can't babe. Me and Bella are venturing to IKEA for a new wok and some cute cushions. Let's all try and meet up soon though. We haven't seen Freya in LONG

Saffron

True

I type Freya's username into Instagram and pore over her recent pictures. They're all of her and Tom. The latest, in the mirror at the gym, posing with personalised his 'n' hers water bottles. I click her haloed profile picture to watch her Story and see they're out for brunch. She looks amazing, her rust-red hair loose but off her face, a cream, fitted rollneck jumper clinging to her slim figure. She's an After where I'm still a Before, someone whose picture you'd stick on your fridge or post to your Story as

38

#thinspo. I *should* be inspired. Yet because she used to be like me, I instead feel ravaged with envy.

While I'm on my phone, Mum's reply comes in.

Mum

Room looks good, let me know how viewing goes! Very happy it'll only take me 15 mins to get to you in Stokes Croft, rather than 3 bloody hours up M5 when you were thinking of Manchester 🙏😂

Mum

Tina asks how's your diet going? Any loss yet? xx

A picture comes through of her and her friend Tina, sitting at Tina's kitchen island. They're in white robes, wearing those terrifying, Stormtrooper-esque red light therapy masks and holding glasses of green juice. Tina is Mum's for-life friend through and through, the way I thought things were headed with me and Poppy. They take each other everywhere, from plus-ones to weddings, to mammograms, so it tracks that Tina would know about my diet.

Saffron

What are you two up to?? And tell Tina I'm just staying the same. Don't know what I'm doing wrong

Mum

Tina's throwing me a pamper day ... found chats with six other women on Eduardo's phone, after we agreed to be exclusive, so my salsa days are over. Still, happy Friday. And hon, why don't you join SlimIt again? We've got a New Year New Me discount on atm. 30% off your first month when you sign up in Jan, and if you use that with my 30% waived members fee for staff, you'll be laughing!! xx

Saffron

No way! I only joined last time because I had Frey. The thought of doing it alone is BLEAK

Saffron

Also sorry about Eduardo, boy bye!!! Though maybe a bit soon to have been exclusive ... ? Good riddance anyway.

Mum

When I want dating advice from my 18 yr old daughter, I'll let you know!!! 😂 . Also, you won't be on your own! That's what SlimIt is all about. The community! Women supporting women xx

Saffron

Have a day off lol

I search fat burning hiit workout on YouTube and follow along barefoot in my bedroom, Freya on my mind. Then I shower and dress in baggy clothes.

I get off the bus in Stokes Croft and the knife-slice January wind cuts under my clothes. I shiver. My coat from last winter still just about fits me unless I need to do up the zip. So, with the wind constantly flapping it open, my jumper's soaked, and my teeth are chattering. I should just size up and get a coat that keeps me warm, but I can't. It's like, as long as I still have the smaller coat, the promise to myself that I'll fit into it again one day is kept.

I follow Maps to the address Toby sent me, hood up, with my head bent over my phone to stop the rain from dotting today's face. I went for playful minimalism, my base layer and lips natural and dewy, with a little dust of colour on the lids. I take a right off City Road, go all the way down Brunswick Street, until I'm on Wilder Street. As I huddle under the stoop outside number nine, I *pray* Veronica was telling the truth, that the rats really were just a joke and I'm not about to walk into an utter hellhole. I get out my phone, dancing with the delete key over putting a kiss at the end of my message to Toby.

Saffron

Outside 👍

In the end I settle on a thumbs up, deciding it looks unhinged the moment I hit send.

As I hear footsteps thumping down the stairs, it occurs to me that I don't know what Toby looks like. Too swept up in first my, then Sydney's talking stages with Nolan, I didn't even think to do a bit of light Facebook stalking. Still on edge from all the catfishing, I brace myself as the door swings open and—

'Oh.'

He's so fit.

'Oh?' Toby says.

'I said that out loud, didn't I?' I also said *that* out loud. 'Sorry, you're just not what I was expecting, I convinced myself you'd be weird.' As the words leave my mouth, my eyes gape at him in horror. What am I *saying*?

Toby strokes his chin stubble, cocking his head slightly as his mouth wrestles with an amused frown. 'OK?'

Awkward laughter raspberries from my lips. 'Oh my God. Now I'm spitting at you. Look, I'm having a *day*. Like a … a bumped into your ex kind of day.' (In cyberspace.) 'And just to clarify, I don't think you're weird.' We stare at each other for a few seconds of excruciating silence. '*I'm* being weird.'

He laughs, thank God he fucking laughs and it sounds fuzzy and warm, from deep in his chest. 'Good to know. That, you know, you don't find me weird.'

'I'm Saffron. Obviously,' I say, waving my phone at him.

'Toby. Obviously.'

We laugh and as it settles, a smile rests on his face that feels small but sincere. He steps back to let me in, his sliders shuffling against the laminate floor. Toby's dressed casual, in white Adidas socks, baggy joggers, and an oversized basketball jersey tucked in on one side. And he's also dictionary-definition beautiful. Close-cropped brown hair, broad shoulders, at least six two. If I were to match his skin tone to a generic foundation shade name, it'd be something like Light Sand, Warm Fawn, or Nude Honey. No, it's definitely honey I'm seeing, a warmth hinted at under his presumably White but maybe mixed skin. His eyes are honey brown too.

I squeeze past him into the narrow hallway – the handlebar of a bike jabs me in the ribs as I stumble over a pile of kicked-off shoes – and for a second, I press up against him.

'Sorry, I'm soaking,' I say, plucking at my sodden clothes.

'Hang on, let me get you something of mine.' Toby shuffles down the hall as I stand there dripping. He leans into a room off to the left, then comes back holding out a dry hoodie. It's red, and has UWE's basketball team logo on it. 'Keith washed it, and he never uses softener, so it'll be like a bit of cardboard, but here you go.'

'Keith?'

'Guy in the room opposite yours. If you take it, that is. Which I hope you do.' I know he probably means for rent reasons, but my hopelessly romantic heart swoons. 'We're kind of desperate,' he says then, slamming me back down to reality. 'Our old housemate peaced out over Christmas. Mass-texted everyone he knew from uni saying he was *in too deep* and his parents were paying for him to go to some rehab facility in Kent.'

43

'Too deep in what?' I ask, intrigued.

'He was in too deep in his head, that kid, but ...' As Toby offers up a bunch of pop psychology buzzwords to explain that you can in fact become addicted to weed, all I can think about is how hot he is and how comfy he seems within himself, how he speaks, how he moves, like he's got a lot of head space. '... And that's why I don't smoke anymore.' He runs a hand through his grown-out buzz cut.

'Not gonna lie, a lot of that went over my head, I'm sorry.'

'I know. You look cute when you're zoned out.' I— What? Toby smiles, and I toy with one back. The cramped hallway makes it impossible not to feel close to him. Our eyes meet and the tension of almost-touching is palpable, quickening my pulse. When he coughs and looks at the ground, I realise with fierce regret that I've responded with stone-cold silence to him calling me cute. 'Anyway, you want this? I won't be offended if not,' he says, shaking the hoodie.

'Thanks. It probably won't fit, but ...' I finish the sentence with a shrug.

'It'll fit. You can change upstairs,' Toby says. I don't know *what* is happening, but I know I did not just imagine his eyes taking a little round trip down-up my body, his lips pressing together in a smile. Is it really me he's doing that face at? 'You good?'

'Oh, I'm good.' Thrown, but good.

'Cool, let me show you around. Here's the kitchen ...'

I peer inside the door he ducked into a minute ago and see a recently refurbished kitchen with cleanish worktops and a dining table mountained with cardboard recycling.

'If I'm honest, it doesn't get much tidier than this. We've all got different schedules so as soon as one person cleans, the next person's in here cooking.'

'Got it. I don't really like eating in front of people anyway.' I speak the confession like a shrug, surprising myself with how Toby makes me feel so at ease and *here* in my body. Not dissociating, losing myself in a constant commentary of negative self-talk, which is what usually happens when I'm around boys. *Don't slouch your shoulders, it'll make your boobs look saggy. Breathe in, breathe in! Fold your arms across your belly. Press your tongue to the roof of your mouth. Breathe in!*

'Oh. That's cool,' he says, thinking nothing of it, because to most people that is such a nothing comment. When you're thin, people don't eye-track the trajectory of the doughnut going towards your mouth like you're about to swallow a sugar-glazed nail bomb. When you're fat, people watch you eat.

He shows me the living room, utility space, and downstairs toilet, and then we're heading upstairs, the butterflies in my middle flurrying.

'Cool cactuses,' I say, noting the row of spiky potted plants on the windowsill.

'Thanks. They're my babies. I have 'em dotted all over now. Mama cactus is in my room, she's an *Echinopsis calochlora* and they offshoot like crazy. There're already some in your room you can keep.'

'As long as you help me. I can't keep anything alive.'

He smiles over his shoulder. 'Sure. What do you study, by the way?'

'Social Anthropology. What about you?'

'Nutrition and Food Science.'

'Oh cool, food *science*? What's that?'

'Well, the basics of it is all about how what you eat impacts your cells and your organs, and we study the link between food and disease, food and growth. It's mad interesting.'

'It sounds interesting,' I say, really meaning it.

'Yeah. I've just started a module on the microbiome.'

I nod. 'My mum's always banging on at me to eat probiotic yoghurt.'

He laughs. 'Your mum knows. Did you know they call your gut your second brain?' On the landing, Toby looks back at me with his eyebrows raised, one hand on his stomach.

'I did not.'

He points. 'Bathroom. My room. Veronica's room, Nairong's room.' Veronica's door is patchworked with wristbands, train tickets, and stickers that say things like, *empowered women empower women*, and *pro-choice*. I smooth down the edge of one that's peeling off, even more excited to meet her than before. I'm peering through the open bathroom door when Toby says, 'They're gonna love you,' and our eyes lock. He thinks they're gonna love me? He looks away first, shy. 'You'll also love them, they're great. Keith is tolerable.' He laughs.

I face away from him, hiding my smile. I take in the sink

clutter – three electric toothbrushes, two manual – flicking the light on and off. 'Five toothbrushes? I thought there were only four of you?'

'Ah.' He leans past me and shoots one of the manual brushes into the small bin in the corner. 'She doesn't stay here anymore. My ex. Been meaning to do that for weeks.'

'Nice shot.' I want to ask what happened but get the sense his feelings are still raw from the swift precision of that throw, so I don't.

We go up a second flight of stairs before Toby stops in front of a paint-flaky door and lets us both inside. The room's bigger than the ad made it look, even with its snug sloped ceiling and dark carpet. Rain taps against the skylight as I blink at the empty space, mentally painting the room with a lick of me. Fairy lights strung from corner to corner where the ceiling dips, my *Kill Bill* and *Little Miss Sunshine* posters above the desk (3.5/5 and 4/5 respectively), waking up sunlit as morning drips down through the skylight, yawning through a smile as I feel him stir beside me, my thigh snaking over his—

'So, what do you think?'

'Huh?' I gulp a lungful of air before I speak. 'I love it. Genuinely. Though it would've had to be literally on fire for me not to take it at this point. I've been living at home during first term. Not ideal.'

'Say no more, say no more.'

I shiver again, my wet clothes clinging to me. 'Um, I'm gonna put this on, can you ... ?' I do a little air spin with my finger and

Toby faces the corner, hands in his pockets as I peel off my wet jumper. My heartbeat trips and my hands move clumsy. I wonder if he feels it too, the tension I'm feeling, knowing I'm standing half-naked behind him. I pull Toby's hoodie over my head, surprised that he was right, it fits, and tell him he can look now.

Toby drops on to the bed and I sit next to him, the broken mattress springs dipping in the middle and sinking us together. I can't believe I'm having *this* kind of moment with a boy. A skittish, fumbling moment that the early noughties romcoms I grew up on made me believe couldn't happen to me. Big girls don't get meet-cutes, grand gestures, or asked to prom. And yet, his hand grazes the thick crease of my thighbrow as he tries to shift from basically being in my lap, and we laugh awkwardly.

He *has* to feel it too, the tension thrumming between us.

'Mattress is not looking promising. I need to test it out,' I say as I lie back, leaning on my elbows to look up at the rain running in rivers against the skylight. 'Look at this rain, it's like art. How am I ever gonna get out of bed?'

'Don't,' he says, lying sideways next to me, his arm bent to prop up his head. 'We should just go to bed for a year.'

'Me and you?' I turn to face him, my heart jumping up my throat.

Toby laughs a light breath out of his nose. In answer, he fights with that tentative smile he has. 'I meant everybody, like the world should have a year-long siesta for everyone to figure their shit out. I like your hair.'

'Thank you.'

He sweeps the rain-frizzled strands off my face. His Adam's apple bobs. 'I like it like this.' I'm wearing my hair in a bun, dangly curls at my temples. 'And I like it when it's down, all big lion, like in your profile picture. My mum has hair like that.'

'Look at you, noticing me! Thanks.'

'I might've.' I swear he moves closer and my breathing shallows. 'Don't act like you didn't stalk me too.'

'I didn't actually, but I should've done. God knows who I could've been walking into a house viewing with. Lucky it was you though.'

'Lucky, yeah?' Eyes on mine, his chin tilts. A moment of *could I, does he want me to?* flits by. There's only the hush of the rain against the glass above us. I look at his lips, imagining myself leaning in, and my breath snags. But then the fantasy warps to an outer point of view, as if I'm seeing myself tagged in someone else's candid photo of me and Toby kissing. I see me, huge, hulking over him, my body swallowing his. 'I've lost you again,' Toby says. He's smiling, mistaking my shame for nervousness. 'Earth to Saffron, you good?'

I blink at him a few times. 'All good. I just have to go,' I say, picking up my wet jumper and stuffing myself inside my coat that feels even smaller than before.

I feel Toby watching me as I search for my phone, which must've fallen out of my pocket when I got changed, my brain practically humming with all the overthinking it's doing.

We were almost kissing (were we, or did I dream up that possibility from wanting to so badly?) but he's beautiful, and I look like *me*, so how can I not question whether his intentions were genuine, if there at all? OK, he was undeniably flirting, but I just can't believe someone like him could ever want to kiss me for any other reason than convenience. Quick fun. My obvious low self-esteem must give off a certified *Yes, I will sleep with you* signal, which Jack picked up on too.

But the way Toby's face creases with concern now also makes me question if I brought my guard up too fast. 'You're leaving?'

'It's, um— It's my niece's birthday tomorrow, I said I'd help my brother bake a cake.'

Toby sits up, his hands running back through his hair. 'OK?' He laughs awkwardly. 'Must be some cake.'

'Yeah, he's planned some eight-tier job, so it's gonna be an all-day thing. I should go, I've got unicorns to ice.' I laugh though it falls flat. 'Sorry. It was nice meeting you.' He stands, his brow furrowed, but I'm already bombing it down the stairs, not able to keep the tears in my eyes from spilling over. 'I'll take it, by the way,' I call behind me, slamming the door on the first place, the first person I've felt invited in by in the longest time.

I shelter from the rain under the bus stop, checking the times on my phone. The next bus home isn't for another fifty minutes. I stare out into the road as the rest of the scene I yelled cut on back in my new room plays in my head. As I see our imagined kiss unfolding, my big ol' self straddles Toby, and I cringe.

With quick thumbs, I google those FastOff shakes Poppy was hyping up on her Instagram stories and head towards the nearest pharmacy that stocks them.

'What's the deal with these milkshakes then?' A lady in her sixties with bubblegum-pink hair swivels the contactless card machine my way. 'All the young'uns been buying these up. Not a scrap on 'em, some of these girls, mind,' she says, nodding to a girl about my age serving someone else. 'Our Jamie reckons all it does is give you diarrhoea.'

I say I don't know and pay. Though I do know, everyone does, we're all just willing to shit ourselves skinny if FastOff promises to give us bodies like Imogen Shawcross, Molly Mills, and all the other influencers promoting it.

I sit upstairs as the bus rumbles home, reading mixed reviews under FastOff's latest paid influencer collab. A message preview from Toby appears at the top of my screen, and seeing his name reminds me of the way he looked at me. With sincerity and intrigue, and then confusion as I walked away.

But how could I not doubt his interest in me? Jack spent the last five months of sixth form shagging me in secret, and avoiding eye contact with me in English every day. He said we couldn't tell people we were together because then Billy, Charlie, and all the other dickheads he hung around with would only make fun of me more to piss him off.

'But you could stop them, tell them to shut up,' I'd said, our uniforms crumpled at the foot of his bed as we ate sweets he'd pocketed from the shop on the way home.

Jack had sucked the Haribo ring off my finger and shook his head. 'As if they'd listen to me after that.' He looked away, splitting the gelatine with his front teeth. I knew *after that* meant after admitting to being with the fattest girl in our year, but as he kissed me, it silenced all those blaring bad truths in my head, his lips dusted with sugar crystals from the sour cherries. 'Trust me, it'll be better if we don't tell anyone.'

And I let him convince me it was, until last summer was close to being over and he realised what a burden it would be to carry on stringing me along come September.

As I slouch against my seat, Toby's hoodie rides up, making me realise I ran out still wearing it. I hope he doesn't think I did that on purpose. I shuffle down into it, burying my face, sniffing what I imagine the inside of his room smells like – the faint spray of aftershave I caught on his neck; overripe citrus fruit; old, thread-bound smoke from a spliff.

I tap into our messages.

Toby

Hey, I know you said you wanted the room, but I just wanted to check you're sure before I delete the Facebook post. You didn't seem very . . . happy when you left. Hope you're good?

I sigh, cringing at my dramatic exit. Nothing actually happened. And still, I left him with a parting image of me babbling about sugared unicorns with tears in my eyes, before legging it out the door, stealing his hoodie.

Saffron

Ha, I'm OK!! Sorry for being weird – you were so nice. No way not to trauma dump when I say, I'm not used to that. I really do want the room. Which is why I stole your hoodie, so you have to see me again haha

Saffron

But seriously, I'd love to live at Wilder Street if you'll have me? And I meant what I said, it was really nice meeting you

Toby

It's yours! The hoodie too if you want it, ha. Technically your tenancy starts from February. I'd say move in now cus it's empty, but our landlord's a bit of a twat and he's always coming up with reasons to be round here. So as long as you've got somewhere to stay until then?

Toby

I honestly loved meeting you too

I reread that last message over and over.

Later, in my room, the house is quiet. No one's home.

Saffron

Where are you??

I message both Mum and Otis. Predictably, Otis replies instantly.

Otis
At Harrison's. Girl, I told you this earlier. U OK? I'm just leaving

I heart react the message, then take my makeup off in the bathroom, do my skincare, and when I come back there's a text from Mum too.

Mum
Hi hon . . . pamper day turned into cocktails downtown. Won't be home too late. All OK?? Xx

I sink into bed and pull out my phone, eyes straying to the pile of Christmas presents I'm yet to put away, to the box of truffles Poppy's mum bought me. I'm salivating as soon as I think about them, imagining my tongue holding one to the roof of my mouth as it melts.

But I claw on to my resolve not to eat refined sugar, distracting myself with my phone. Before I know it, I've typed in Toby's name and I'm scrolling through his profile. He doesn't post much, save the odd restaurant food photography or action shot of him on the basketball court, but he gets tagged in a lot of photos.

In a tagged picture from two weeks ago, I recognise the cluttered dining room table from earlier. I imagine a phone propped up opposite the four of them living there, squeals and shoves as the self-timer ticked down. A stainless steel pot's been placed on an old pizza box in the centre. On one side of the table are two girls who must be Veronica and Nairong. The closest in shot is East Asian and dripping in Y2K – khaki cargo trousers and a pink mesh baby tee. She looks cool, and I imagine I'll be nervous meeting her.

I stare a little longer at the second girl, who I assume is Veronica. Do I recognise her? She looks so familiar, but her face has been caught in motion, her features blurred as she laughs. I can't see her outfit because her body's hidden behind Y2K, but she's White, with shoulder-length brown hair, half-up, half-down in butterfly clips. I swear I've seen her somewhere. Opposite them, a boy in a beanie with bloodshot eyes is slurping a piece of spaghetti he's stolen from the pot, his fingers tomatoey. This must be Keith, a rollie tucked behind his ear. Toby's standing beside him, not looking at the camera but smiling to himself as he passes plates around the table, his shirt splashed with sauce.

It was uploaded by Nairong, who captioned it:

msnairong_qín Thank you @tobiasinthebooth for feeding me my first nutritious meal since moving to Bristol. Get yourself an in-house chef as a housemate. @k.blundell06 and @veronicafknfarrington, you're alright too 🐌

This feeling of fluffy-blanket-softness unfurls in my chest as I imagine living with these people. I want to be there in that picture. I skim through Nairong's and Keith's profiles, careful not to accidentally like anything, wishing I could snoop at Veronica's too but not wanting to follow her private account until we've officially met.

I go back to scrolling Toby's tagged pictures until I get to another of Nairong's posts and—

Wait, *what?*

I zoom. Nairong's up close, taking a selfie, a pair of neon headphones clamped to her ears, but Toby's full-length behind her, holding hands with Poppy's friend, Bella.

The fifth toothbrush in the bathroom. *Bella* is Toby's ex?

msnairong_qín Hard third wheelin' on @tobiasinthebooth and @arabellaella.knight's silent disco date lool. Feeling like their adopted child. @veronicafknfarrington where are you!??

Through about ten minutes of intense cross-app stalking I learn that *Ara*bella is in fact Toby's newly-ex girlfriend. And if Bella is the kind of girl Toby's used to dating, then I was right to trust my gut earlier. Seeing him with her confirms that Toby was just messing around with me in the moment, not flirting for real. Or maybe not even flirting at all; maybe I'm so starved of positive male attention from someone other than my brother that I got entirely too in my feelings about it all and started making assumptions.

In one swift motion, I lean off the bed, grab the box of truffles, and flop back against the headboard. Cellophane off, I don't even hesitate, just stuff one into my mouth. As the salted caramel goo in the centre oozes over my tongue, I hear the front door go downstairs.

'Alright?' Otis calls. I hear him jogging up the stairs as I unwrap another truffle, and then he's knocking at my door, opening it before I tell him to come in. 'Alright?' he says again. His work fleece is done up over his upper lip so the supermarket logo stretches long, his nose wet from the cold. My eyes flick to his cornrows, fuzzy with flyaways, his baby hairs wisping from his temples, but I don't comment on it, I already told him yesterday. Tutting, he spit-licks them down with his fingers. 'I'm getting it done tomorrow, man, chill?'

'I didn't say anything!' I laugh. 'You ready to get your bake on?'

He pinches the bridge of his nose, sighing with a weary laugh. 'Yeah, I suppose. Can't believe I'm committing to an eight-tiered Vicky sponge.' He breathes deep, then unpins his managerial name tag and pockets it. 'I am ready, I can and will do this after a ten-hour shift.'

'She's gonna love it.' I smile at him, full-faced. Otis is a really good dad, much better than the one we grew up with. 'What have you got her again? I've found some glittery welly boots but I wanted to get her a toy too.'

'Oh, the boots will be enough. I found this retro wooden xylophone in a vintage shop on Gloucester Road. Harrison's taking me to pick it up tomorrow.' Otis's mouth curls around his boyfriend's name in that moony, sugar-glazed smile of New

Relationship Land. We met Harrison just before Christmas – me, Mum, and Rue. I like him, in his quietly charming way. He's nearly thirty, reserved, and a little mumbly, the exact opposite of Otis, which is why they'll work out. Harrison's everything Otis could've asked for in his first boyfriend since he came out as bi. 'What?' he says.

'Nothing, that's cute, you guys are cute.' He bats my leg and shushes me. 'Oh, and I found a room, by the way. A five-bed in Stokes Croft. Come February, I am gone.' I swallow as the reality of that hits home. This is it, the start of everything I hoped this year would bring.

'*Yes*. Rejoice!' Otis says, raising his palms to the ceiling. 'What? Did you expect me to cry? Send me pics.' He gets up, heads for the door. 'I need to start preheating my oven, man, or I will not be getting my Paul Hollywood handshake before we see in the next year,' he says.

'Not you leaving 'cus you got tears in your eyes,' I tease.

'You wish. I'm gonna do your room up for Rue, slowly because redecorating's expensive, but I want to really make this her home when she's here, you know.' He glances around my room, dreamy-eyed. 'And don't moan, I already asked Mum about it.'

'I wouldn't. She'll love it, Otis.'

He smiles. 'You don't fancy helping with the cake at all, no?'

'I can't, sorry. I was going to, but I thought you'd be home earlier. I've got reading to do.' Technically true. My eyes land on the *Love and Technology* book we're supposed to be discussing chapters one through five of in tomorrow's seminar. But really,

I don't trust myself to resist the temptation of licking icing off spoons, and taste-testing golden baked sponge. I've already done damage with the truffles.

'And how is uni?' Otis asks unexpectedly. 'You keeping up?'

'Yes, Dad. Fine.'

'Don't do that. I'm asking because I care.' He clears his throat. 'I thought the whole virtual attendance thing was only an option. I hear you participating in class all the time from home. Is there a reason you don't want to go in?'

'OK, I'm lazy, sue me. I'm good with learning the same shit from my warm bed, rather than a freezing cold lecture hall, thanks.' I try to laugh, but I can tell Otis isn't buying it. 'Plus, I got lucky – sort of – with my timetable, I've got one lecture and three out of my four seminars all on Tuesday, which is admittedly pretty hardcore, and everything else on Thursdays,' I add truthfully. Otis's hand falls away from the doorframe. He studies it, not meeting my eye. 'Come on,' I say, 'it's first year. You know how it is, all I've got to do is pass.'

'Is that all you want to do though? Just *pass*?' he asks quietly. 'You're so smart and—'

My face falls. I swing my legs out of bed, put my hand on the door. 'OK, goodbye. Thanks for your concern. I feel like shit now.'

'Saff,' he says, sticking his foot in the jamb.

'Whatever.'

I force the door closed, taking the warm glow of the landing with it, the door always left ajar at night so I can hear Otis's soft snore and Mum's white noise playing from the other rooms. Alone again, I climb into bed.

Trying to forget Otis's look of disappointment, I tap into Reveal. Only I don't want to log in as me, where it doesn't matter how clever I am, or funny, or good at chat. That's all rendered worthless as soon as my appearance is Revealed anyway.

I just want a bit of futureless fun and flirting I don't have to second-guess. I open up Sydney's matches. Nolan. The name is unsettling headed above pictures of Jack's face, a face I've laid nose-to-nose with, that hovered above mine when I lost my virginity. A face I also saw screwed with disgust when I wanted to tell my best friends we were together. But sickeningly and despite all that, it's familiar.

Sydney Hey. Sorry for the slow response, ugh, liiiiife

. . .

Sydney You're so fit though. 10/10 would Reveal again

Sydney Are you there? Tell me about these cult movie marathons mentioned in your bio. I have very strong opinions on some fan faves.

. . .

Nolan Hey. Yeah I'm here x

'Happy birthday to you, happy birthday to you.' Rue's face is aglow with the four candles on the cake Otis stayed up 'til 1 a.m. baking last night. Eight-tiered, rainbow sponge, vanilla icing, and sprinkles. Google estimates 300 calories a slice. I want to be here, in the moment, smiling along to everyone's out-of-tune singing. But I'm staring at the cake, at the grit of the sugar in the buttercream, the bloody ooze of the jam. 'Happy birthday to Ru-ue, happy birthday to you!'

Rue blows the candles out, and we all cheer.

'Don't tell anyone what you wished for, OK, angel?' Mum cups Rue's face, her thumbs smoothing her cheeks. 'Even if it is a new man for Grandma,' she murmurs out the side of her mouth, making Tina snort.

'Mum.' I roll my eyes as she falls about laughing on the sofa.

Crowded in our small living room are me, Poppy, Otis, Harrison, the birthday girl, Mum, and Tina.

I feel like Rue's mum should be here for this too, but I didn't dare bring it up. I know Clara will be doing her own cake for Rue later, but it'll be just the two of them, and Rue will be sleepy and celebration-spent by the time Clara picks her up after work. If we'd have invited her, maybe she could've asked her boss for a half day. I know her and Otis didn't exactly end on the best of terms, and Mum still won't have her name mentioned in our house, but Clara doesn't really have anybody else.

Before Otis cuts the cake, I snap a picture of it and send it to Toby. I'm kidding myself it's purely to prove that I didn't make up my reason for leaving yesterday, and that I'm not just looking for any excuse to text him.

Saffron

OK. Hands up, something came up so I can't take one iota of credit for how this turned out – except conceptually. But how good did my brother do!?

I swallow, knowing that the 'something' was catfishing my catfisher until gone 2 a.m.

I glance around the room, at the people nibbling cake clutched in kitchen roll, sipping cups of tea, reminiscing and sharing, crumbles of sugar on their fingers. Mum and Tina have the tiniest of slivers, excusing its calories by deeming it their sole Sorry of the day. (*Sorrys* being SlimIt's daily allowance of calories consumed as treats. Biscuits, chocolate, crisps.)

'Anyone else for a slice?' Otis calls from the kitchen as Harrison sidles off to join him.

Rue strides over to where me and Poppy are sitting on the floor, our backs to the pouffe. She's pretending to be me at work, going round the room writing everyone's cake order on a little flip pad. She hands Poppy a plate.

'Your cake.' She beams.

'My God, that looks so good.' I groan, pinching a shard of flaked-off icing from the side of Poppy's plate. 'Have you had some yet, Birthday Girl?'

'Can't,' Rue says, tapping her pen to her notepad. 'Working.'

I hide my laugh behind my hand, nodding seriously at her. 'Of course.'

'Thank you so much,' Poppy says, pretending to pay Rue for the cake. 'Um, how many Sorrys a day do you get then?' She directs the question at Mum, examining her slice.

'Fifteen,' me, Mum, and Tina say at the same time.

I flick the icing off my finger.

'Yeah, fifteen.' Mum nods, half her cake gone in one bite. 'It's roughly twenty calories a Sorry, so . . .' She peers up at the ceiling, doing quick diet maths. 'With a slice about this size, this is basically our lot today, innit, Teen.' Tina pulls a pretend sad face, licking her fingers.

'It'll all be worth it in the end, when we're on the beach in our tiny bikinis, won't it?' Tina jokes, nudging Mum playfully, but for a second, I catch her expression iron flat with desperation and I have to look away. Is that what I sound like?

'Yeah, you know it.'

'Wish I could afford to just take Ozempic though.' Tina laughs.

'Really?' I say, my eyebrows shooting up.

This is the first time I've heard mention of the drug outside of the internet. From what I've seen regurgitated on social media, traditional media's coverage see-saws between fearmongering and praise for the costly weight loss wonder drug. Even if I could afford it, I wouldn't. I don't do unnecessary needles. I've always been a baby about vaccines and insist the nurse keeps talking as I look out the window and she surprise-jabs me. It's wild to me that so many people are breaking the bank to inject this stuff without knowing its long-term effects. Hearing it come out of Tina's mouth is jarring.

'Nah. That's cheating. And don't you get any ideas about it, Saffron,' Mum says, typing something on her phone. 'Honestly though, Pop, you don't have *a thing* to worry about. Does she, Teen?' Mum tilts her phone screen so Tina can see. 'You could go on *Love Island* with a body like that. You should take our Saff to the gym with you, do a little induction session. It's the machines that put you off, right, Saff?'

Oh my God. 'Mum,' I hiss. I turn to Poppy, but she's suppressing a smile. Her eyes are bright, watching them watching videos of her.

It'd hurt me if Mum hadn't been pitting me against Poppy since we were eight. In primary school, her comparisons started with things like, *'Don't you want to wear a dress? I bet Poppy's wearing a dress,'* offhand, like it didn't matter to her whether I refused to change out of my karate gi for the party or not. Then as we got older, and Poppy grew lean while I grew dumpy, Mum's comments got more body specific. *'I think with your boobs, you're going to need an underwire bra, you can't get away with those little bralettes Poppy wears.'* By the time we were approaching secondary school, thanks to all those micro-judgements and the wider depiction of body image in movies (hello, *Bridget Jones*, Mum's fave romcom and at *least* biannual pick for duvet night), I understood that the world viewed my body as bad, and Poppy's body as ideal. At ten, I told Mum I was no longer accepting sandwiches for my packed lunch because I'd heard bread made you fat, and I didn't want to look fat on my auntie's wedding day. She'd nodded, smiled, and hung my too-tight flower-girl dress in the kitchen for inspiration. And thus, my first diet began.

It wasn't until I was seventeen that I became an official member of SlimIt though. Up until then, Freya and I hadn't had a reason to branch out into a friendship of our own, both of us happy with the dynamic of our trio with Poppy, who was still very much the glue. We were all on prom prep, determined to hit our goal weights before the end of sixth form, ready for beach season. But when we realised that prom prep for me and Freya was a much more serious business than it was for Poppy, I asked Mum to sign us up. Back then, it felt womanly for us to be joining SlimIt, a grown-up club where I'd force my legs to cross at the knee because that's how everybody else sat.

In every way Freya was a SlimIt success story. So much so that when I started to put the weight back on over summer and she didn't, the jealousy nearly devoured me, and the excuses for why I couldn't see her began piling up.

My phone vibrates on the floor next to me. I peer at Toby's reply.

Toby

Bro is talented! Cake looks so good. What flavour is it?? Bet it tastes insane

I bet it does.

Rue clops over to me in the new glittery welly boots I bought her.

'Cake, Auntie Saffy?' she asks. Lost in thought, I shake my head.

'Look at how much she can deadlift! A girl as dinky as her,' Mum's saying, gazing lovingly into her phone screen.

I stare at the cake in Rue's hand. Its calories would be a stain on my otherwise sugar-free day, but I'm out here salivating. I'm only eating 800 calories now, because I keep slipping up and the scales are barely budging. And FastOff proved itself to be *the* biggest waste of money. I had one this morning, hoping to purge the chocolate I ate last night with its 'dynamic body cleanse' like the label promised, but nothing.

My eyes land on Mum's plate, her last bite discarded.

Should I rejoin SlimIt? Let's face it, the New Year New Me mantra isn't proving to be enough; maybe I need the shame of public weigh-ins to hold me accountable.

'Pressure builds progress,' I've heard Mum say to her groups before.

'Auntie Saffy?' Rue says again.

'No thanks,' I tell her, hugging a cushion over my belly. Her long lashes blink, blink, her pen stilled over her notepad. I order an imaginary water instead, and wait until she's out of the room before I say, 'Mum, can you sign me up? I think I wanna join SlimIt again. What I'm doing isn't working.'

february

January, and especially February, in the hospitality industry is tough if you need to pay rent. Yesterday, Pop said the opening cook at Jemima's was sent home by eleven with only three hours' pay. If I didn't have my student loan in the bank, and the guilt money from my dad, I'd be stressing at these early cut times. But I can't lie, when it's this quiet, I love getting paid just to scroll. I welcome being able to sneak out my phone during shift, to hide one AirPod behind my hair and listen to my Daily Mix. Which is exactly what I intend to do today.

I speed-walk up Gloucester Road, kind of late, and trying to get my steps in while I sip my FastOff shake through my travel cup. Was it a dumb idea to drink this on my way to work given the side effects? Potentially. But after its disappointing 'evacuation' results the other week, proving FastOff to be just another gimmicky, post-Christmas cash grab, I decided it was safe enough to get my money's worth.

Phone in hand, I see a text from Poppy come through.

Poppy

Are you on your way??? You're gonna be late af. Hurry up, it's dead, we've only got two tables and I'm so bored I might pass away

Saffron

ETA 2 mins. Was trying to do this soft matte look with my eyeshadow, had to start over twice!

Not to quote one of those middle-aged, wine mum memes that say shit like, *makeup is my warpaint*, but I do pride myself in having a flawlessly beat face. I'm *that* girl, the one you ask to finely flick your winged eyeliner, to glue your lashes on straight, to faux-freckle the bridge of your nose. Early into secondary school I realised that if I wore makeup, I was less likely to be prodded in the belly *'to see how long it jiggles for'* or ranked last in a list of girls Billy Ferris wanted to shag. Makeup allowed me to blend in, or at least be ignored. So I spent the summer I turned thirteen watching endless tutorials, perfecting the art of camouflage. But the better I got at it, the less makeup became about masking. It's the self-care, the theatrical flair, and the creative expression for me. I love it.

Poppy

Doug's supervising

Saffron

OK OK, I can stop running then? He won't care

Poppy

Yeah, how nice for you! I've been on my own with him for the last two hours. HELP

Saffron

Shit. Coming

Doug's a creep. At this point, we warn any new female waitstaff that he'll likely subject them to a combined total of three whole minutes of perving per shift. It's subtle enough that the one complaint made about him by a former employee got dismissed as a witch-hunt, but obvious enough to make everyone he interacts with uncomfortable.

Just as I hit the stretch of road where the vintage shops end, and the storefronts are replaced by pubs and places to eat, my guts twist hot like they've been grabbed by two hands and wrung. I crumple in on myself as FastOff's laxative effect grips my insides. Oh my God, I've got to *go*. Like now. Where was all this *before*? Somehow, I make it the rest of the way to work, my movements restricted by my whole-body clench, so I don't shit myself on the street. I skulk into Jemima's six minutes late, about to diarrhoea in Poppy's section.

'Sorry I'm late,' I blurt, not stopping.

Behind the bar, Doug flips his phone face down when he sees me. He slurps a long audible sip from his coffee, his eyes sliding down my thankfully baggy jumper as I amble towards him. 'Go on, get changed. And go splash some water on your face, you look sweaty.'

I make it, just about, collapsing on to the toilet as the stabbing in my stomach finally subsides. When I emerge, I feel weak, the curls at my temples wet with sweat, bent crooked like I'm recovering from a long illness.

I grip the edges of the sink, stomach still roiling. You don't see this side of FastOff in the influencer promotions. Only artfully arranged shots of powder being whizzed up in the blender with sliced banana and oat milk, then silkily poured into a Mason jar.

Even more tragic is that I can't believe I *paid* for this experience. Is this really what's being sold as a better option over simply existing in a bigger body? I change into my uniform, trying to shake the questions disquieting my weight loss plans, then head to the front of the café.

When I'm sent on lunch at twelve thirty, I take a picture of my black coffee and undressed salad and send it to Freya.

Saffron

> Bet you miss lunches like these. You gotta be SlimIt to win it, babyyyy. Sadly I'm back in the red books again. Got my first meeting Friday eve. Also moving into the new house, which should burn some extra calories before weigh-in lool. Hope you're all good??

Texting her is easy. It's only when I'm confronted by her thinness in person that my jealousy overrides everything else I feel for Freya.

Freya

That is the saddest salad I've ever seen in my life. Just lettuce and tomato, u OK!? At least cucumber. AT LEAST. So exciting you're moving. Remember when me you and Pop used to say we were gonna live together in one of those flats above the river opposite castle park? School feels like forever ago

Freya

Also let's actually meet up and go for a less depressing lunch please? Like actually

Saffron

Yes yes yes yes. Free the cucumber!!
When is good for you?

Freya types, making the three dots dance, and coward that I am, I avoid making concrete plans with her again. I tap out of our thread and switch apps to message Nolan on Reveal.

We've been exchanging first gigs and favourite bands, films we rate 5/5, and ranking *Friends* characters, a comforting casualness already established between us. A tangle of pea shoots dangles off my fork as I read his dissection of the dumbing down of Joey's character by the end of the series. I laugh a warm exhale out of my nose, and think about how impossible this accidental twist of kismet is, and how over the last few weeks, I've grown quite attached to this stranger pretending to be my ex. If Nolan's account was all some set-up to procure nudes, they'd have asked for them by now. Same thing with my bank details or any other personal information that could be stolen from me. Which tells me I must be talking to someone who also feels like their body doesn't belong in some way or another. I know that this can't go anywhere, but I guess the security of knowing he's never going to ask to meet up has kept me talking. And the attention's been too gratifying to give up, so for selfish reasons, I've stayed. I'm not feeling too bad about it because the morals of this situation are murky as hell. 'Nolan's' lying to me too.

Sydney Also, I know it's kinda millennial to like Friends, and Ross is officially cancelled, but I can't help it, it's my comfort show

Nolan Know what you mean. It exists in its own little world. Imagine being a waitress and able to afford the rent on that apartment in NYC.

Sydney Telllll me about it, although I'm a waitress and I did just find a room to rent in the centre for less than 700 quid, all in. I'm in my Rachel Green era I think, except I don't even speak to my dad, let alone live off his credit card

I drop my phone into my apron and get back behind the bar. Not that Doug could ever say anything to me about texting on shift, his Screen Time must be nearing double digits, I swear. It's so quiet, he's sending Poppy home early with half a day's holiday pay, leaving me to run the floor on my own. She sits at the bar for a while, waiting for her bus, then leaves to go get her lashes laminated with Bella.

'Bye,' I call. I feel lonely for a moment, before my phone vibrates. I smile, knowing it's Nolan, knowing I have someone to text like this now. His replies are fervent, never leaving me on read.

For the rest of the afternoon, I allow myself to get caught up in fantasies of this turning into something real, ignoring the fact that it categorically can't because we're both pretending to be someone completely *un*real.

'I don't know how I still have stuff left to pack,' I say, standing in the mess of my room the next night. 'I've been at this for weeks.'

'You're a hoarder, that's why.' Otis launches my old broken karaoke machine into the box for recycling and catches me yawning. 'Busy day?'

'Yeah, it's Thursday, remember? My busiest.' I occupy myself with clearing the shelf above my desk, hoping he won't ask me if I *physically* attended classes today. I was going to, I swear, but I made the mistake of trying on a pair of jeans. Otis spares me though, probably remembering my reaction last time he asked and wanting to keep our 'last night' vibes chill.

Which they are. So far, he's kept things light and not too sentimental, trying to make up for how gutted I am that my last night at home falls when Mum's away for a company-wide SlimIt marketing meeting first thing tomorrow morning.

After I stack the purely sentimental Blu-rays I couldn't get rid of (*Mulholland Drive*, *Spirited Away*, and *Eternal Sunshine* – all 5/5s, of course) into a box, I swipe a wet cloth along the shelf, and something drops on to the desk. A costume ring Jack bought me spins like a totem top. In his boxers, on one knee, he'd presented it to me in his bedroom, the only place our relationship was allowed to live. It was a keep-sweet gift after I'd threatened to tell Billy Ferris, who I sat next to in Maths, that Jack did in fact have a mole on his dick, and I knew, because I'd seen it. His eyes were watery with desperation, not at the thought of losing me, but at the thought of them finding out. I'm reaching for it when Otis shouts, 'Aha!' and I jump, sending the green-tinged piece of tin skittering down the back of the desk.

He backs out of the wardrobe holding a faded copy of the issue of SlimIt magazine that Mum's transformation was featured in. Otis flicks to the middle spread and reads, '*From Morbidly Obese to Motivational Queen*. Bin, yeah?' I nod as he drops the magazine into a black bag and gets out his phone. 'Bless her. Did you see one of her SlimIt groupies tagged Mum in an article she's managed to get into *Chat* magazine?'

I squeal, beckoning him closer. 'No, tell me.'

It's a little bit hilarious, the niche sliver of fame Mum has in Bristol and the surrounding areas. Being SlimIt's Supervisor of the South West, she gets the nod from a middle-aged woman going round Tesco at least once a month and she *lives* for it.

Otis shows me his phone, open on a Facebook post by someone called Debra Wilkes.

He reads aloud, '*I want to thank my most supportive SlimIt sister,*

Dionne, for being the padlock over my fridge this last year – like, no hint of irony, the *padlock* over her fridge.' I swallow, not saying anything. It sounds ridiculous but sometimes that's the attitude you need to get results. And given my weak attempt at sticking to the Military Diet and how loosely my New Year's resolutions stuck, I'm glad I made the decision to rejoin. '*I couldn't have gone on my weight loss journey without her fierce group leadership*, blah blah blah. But look, *look* at the title of Debra's article,' he says.

'*How I swapped Pot Noodles for passion and shagged myself skinny with the help of my … SlimIt pals!?*' I read, my voice whooping up at the end like a slide whistle.

'I know! I mean, I know Debra obviously means she's been shagging her—' He squints to read the small print as I throw my head back with laughter. '*Healthy hubby, Len.* But, come on, who signed off on that?' He shouts the last words through his rising laughter. We lean against each other, silently dying, me more laughing at his insane cackle than Debra's desperate post.

When we're sighing it out, I look at Otis, beaming stupid like we're eight and thirteen again, not eighteen and twenty-three, packing up my childhood bedroom.

'Speaking of noodles …' he says, biting his bottom lip in a grin. My smile sags. 'Oh, sorry, you're trying to be good, aren't you?' I deflate, as I do every time someone makes the implication that what I was doing before made me bad. 'I just thought 'cus it's your last night, you know. Never mind.'

I think of the alarm I snooze every morning urging me to go for a run, of my phone alerting me to my daily average of a thousand steps this past week. I know I should say no to a takeaway, but as I watch Otis peering at the mess of boxes and bags between us that mean our growing up together is done, all I want is to be with him under blankets, shouting at the TV, sharing a plate of beige with him for the last time.

'Fuck it. I'll start tomorrow.'

'Sweet.' Otis taps at his phone before tossing it into my lap.

Deliveroo's already open on our usual Chinese restaurant, Mr Chen's. 'You had your order already in the basket?'

He shrugs. 'Well, you take forever to choose and obviously you were gonna say yes.'

'Right.' *Obviously.*

I choose my food and my mouth pricks with saliva.

As we wait, I get a text from Toby asking what time I'm planning on bringing my stuff over tomorrow.

I tell Toby we're aiming for late morning, and he responds with a selfie in front of the cleared kitchen cupboard space for me.

Toby

House is ready and waiting for you. Us too

I really need him to stop being so sweet. Pining after the hot housemate I have no chance with isn't going to keep me focused on my goals. Tonight's food choices are already enough of a setback.

When the food arrives, we eat it on our laps in front of the TV, but the nostalgic glow from earlier has dulled and we mostly stay silent, my hand moving mechanically between my mouth and

76

my plate. Before half of it's gone, I feel full, the glut of fried food sitting heavy in my stomach, slumping me down against the sofa. But still, I keep eating, because it would be a waste of a treat not to.

After a wakeful night, the white sun streaming through the windshield feels like blinking at a migraine. My phone vibrates from where it's wedged under my thigh. Mum.

Mum

> Good luck today, hon. Sorry I can't be there 😕 Let me know what your new roomies are like later, I'm so buzzing for you ... PS don't put that new bedding straight on, you'll need to wash it first!! Xx

I text her back, telling her not to worry, then lock my phone, too nervous to be distracted by it.

Otis has his seat adjusted so he's straight-backed, his elbows locked up tight to the steering wheel to fit all my stuff in the back. At a red light, he sways his head to a girl singing in cursive. He's doing me a massive favour so I forfeited any decision-making I might've had on the music, but what is *this*?

I swallow against the indescribable ache in the back of my throat that feels like if I speak, I'll cry, just to say, 'Your taste is questionable at best, man.'

'What's that now?' Otis turns to me and slides his sunglasses up over the silk scarf I lent him, his braids finally fresh. '*Thank you, Otis, for driving me and my ass-load of crap over to St*

77

Paul's during Friday-morning traffic. Why, you're very welcome,' he says, turning up the airy acoustic whining louder. 'Pleasure.'

A laugh loosens my grip on the sob I'm holding back. I clear my throat, cough over it. 'Whatever.' I pick at a hangnail, my voice wobbling. 'Seriously, thank you though.' As we set off again, I squint as the wintry light gleams off a block of office windows still strung with Christmas lights. A tear wets my cheek. 'You got another pair of sunglasses in here?' I ask, thick-throated, kind of wanting him to notice I'm on the verge, kind of not.

I'm already opening the glove compartment when he says, 'No, no—'

And a kite tail of condoms flutters into my footwell, a tube of guava-flavoured lube landing in my lap. Otis stares at the road, signalling left, his lips clamped against a laugh.

I sniff, jostling the lube on to the floor with my legs as I swiftly wipe the tear off my face. The indicator tick-tocks as we wait to be let in. Our eyes slide to each other, and I break first. 'Here? In this very seat?'

'Girl, one, it's my car. Two, me and Harrison both live with family,' he reels off. 'I have needs. And three – yes. Yes, right there in that very seat.'

'*Ewwww.* Ew, ew. *Ew.* Let me out. I'm getting out at the next red light, I swear.' I'm laughing, and it's the knit-belly, threat of pins and needles kind of laughing I always get with Otis, but still tears keep leaking out of the corners of my eyes. 'What is this?' I say, acknowledging my confused outburst, because it's obvious I'm upset and tussling with my emotions right now. 'And *guava*!? Otis, guava?'

78

'Yes, guava ... like I guava fuck about what you think.'

And that dissolves us into silent laughing, so we're both wheezing, rocking in our seats. Laughing this hard with my brother settles a sense of belonging in me. But there's also a sadness knowing I won't wake up to that feeling anymore. It makes me cry harder, makes me want this car to keep driving and driving, though I know I have to do this.

'I'm a mess,' I say.

When the laughing's all sighed out, Otis says, 'Yeah, are we gonna talk about what's going on with you? Why are you crying?'

I shake my head, lip quivering as I lean against the window. 'I don't know. I guess I'm sad about moving. And leaving you. But a lot of other stuff too. And it feels stupid even saying this, like I'm twelve or something, but things are so different between me, Poppy, and Freya now, we barely see each other. I miss us, but like the old us.' I roll my eyes, listing my flimsy first-world problems off on my fingers. 'Things are complicated with this boy I'm talking to – I can't even get into it. And I've only lost two pounds since January, even though it feels like I've been dieting for half my life.' Fresh tears pour as I realise that exaggeration is actually entirely true. 'Everything just feels a bit *much* right now.'

'Life's always too much,' he mutters, crawling along the road looking for a parking space. 'Remember how much you want this, Saff. Your own place, your independence. I'm gonna miss you like crazy but you'll have the best time living with friends.' He smooths his lips together, shiny with balm. 'I'm sorry about Poppy and Freya. I'm sure you guys'll talk and air it out, but if things are tailing off –' he shrugs – 'that's OK too. I don't speak to any of my friends from school anymore. Sometimes people just grow apart. People are either in your life for a reason or a season.'

'Ooh, I like that,' I say, flicking the visor mirror down to blot at my smudged eyeliner. 'I just never thought it'd be true with Poppy and Freya.'

Otis nods, craning his neck around to parallel park. 'You'll be good soon enough. And Saff?' I look at him expectantly. 'I'm just gonna say it. You're not losing any weight because your body is in starvation mode—'

'I know, I'm not doing that stupid Military Diet anymore.'

'Military what now?'

'Some diet I found on the internet, don't worry,' I say, slicking a thin winged line over the one I did earlier. 'I'm going to lose weight healthily now, I'm going back to SlimIt tonight.'

'OK? SlimIt is toxic too, and you know it. There's nothing healthy about obsessing over what you eat. Don't go tonight. Throw that little red book all the way into the bin, *eat*, and be kind to yourself. Please.'

I swallow to keep down another sob. He's right, it is toxic, but what else can I do? I hate my body the way it is.

As Otis's phone lights up on the dash and I see myself on his home screen, I pause, realising something. It's a group photo of me, Mum, Otis, and Rue at a family party last May, back when I was a size twelve and in the habit of allowing full-body pictures to be taken of me.

Haven't I *always* hated my body? Didn't I still, even when I was at my lowest weight last summer? What if SlimIt actually works again and I get back to my goal weight, only it's *still* not enough? What then?

Interrupting my thoughts, Otis says, 'Ready?' and I pack away my epiphany into a box at the back of my head, to be dusted off and examined when I don't have to heave all my worldly possessions in real-life boxes up to an attic room.

As he cuts the engine my brain catches up and I say, 'Wait, what are you doing, we want Wilder Street, this is nowhere near.'

'This is Stokes Croft, baby. Nowhere near is close enough.'

We walk for five minutes in February's ever-spritz of rain and find the newly cut key under the terracotta pot on the doorstep like Toby said it would be. He was overly apologetic that nobody would be here to greet me because Friday's the day the whole house is timetabled on campus. I'm kind of relieved no one's home, I need to mentally prepare myself. Especially before I see Toby again. This time, I need to keep my head, no getting breathless or losing myself in baseless daydreams about kissing him. Despite all that, I still feel a flutter as I picture the moment we'll come face to face again later.

I go to let myself in and Otis grunts, hefting a box higher up his hip, his eyes narrowing, looking from the key in my hand to the upturned plant pot.

'Uh, never do that again. You're literally begging to be robbed.'

'Yawn,' I say, carrying my bags of bedding inside.

It takes us forty-five minutes, eight trips back to the car, two cups of tea, and nine climbs of the three flights of stairs to get everything into the attic. I feel faint and fuzzy-headed as I schlep one of the last bags up on to the landing. My body's fuel light is flashing red, having burned through the last reserves of the noodles I had for dinner last night. The bag tumbles from my arms and I drop cross-legged to the floor, my head rushing from all this physical activity on an empty stomach.

I stay down for a minute, breathing away my dizziness. I check my phone, double tap a message from Nolan.

Nolan Isn't today moving day? Hope everything goes smoothly!

I take a picture of the endless bags and boxes spilling into the room and write:

Sydney Thank you! Big yikes though. Very overwhelmed

A few steps behind me, Otis staggers into the room with a box of books. 'Haven't seen you read a single word of these the whole eighteen years we've lived together, but OK.' The box thuds to the floor and he stands in the doorway, hands on his hips, surveying the cardboard box towers. 'Now as much as I *wish* I could stay and help you with all this unpacking, I have to go. It'll take me twice as long to get to work from this side of town . . .' I see his gaze land on a framed photo of us ten years ago. He peers up at the ceiling. 'But you know I'm always at the end of the phone, OK—'

'Stop, you're gonna make me cry again.'

82

'—And you can always, always come home.' His voice breaks and I stumble across the pile of everything to get to him, hugging him tightly. 'Not that you're going to, you got this. I'm so proud of you, Saff. Please don't let anyone make you ever feel less than, OK?'

'OK,' I say.

'Now can we not say bye because I'm really not handling this at all well.' He sniffs.

'What'll we say then?'

'How about, I'll see you at home? Whenever that may be.'

'OK,' I say, choking up. 'Dramatic as ever, but I'll see you at home.'

He blows me a kiss, pulling the door to.

Drained by the emotion, I stare vacantly at all the disarray, listening to Otis's footsteps fade on the stairs. I lean closer to the cracked door at an exchange of voices downstairs, a greeting and then a slap of palms.

The front door slams and immediately I get a text from Otis.

Otis
Don't shit where you eat

Otis
(But by GOD would he be good to eat)

'Hey,' Toby calls from the landing below, jogging up to the third floor. As he approaches, I feel like shaken-up lemonade inside, fizzing with nerves and anticipation. And then he's there in the doorway, and I'm transported to the last time I saw Toby, reliving our conversation on the bed, tender and playful, close but unpromising. Before I bolted. But looking at him now, his face creased with happiness at seeing me, I wonder again if I made a mistake dismissing the spark I thought I felt flicker between us. 'I just met your brother,' he says. 'Nice guy.'

'Oh yeah, that's Otis. He's abandoned me to deal with this on my own,' I say, throwing my arms out.

'Savage. What can I do? What's your tactic? It's just me here until tonight, everyone else is still on campus, but I'm yours 'til three.'

My heart yelps at *I'm yours*, and I let out a laugh, relieved. 'So, this might be mad, but I was planning on just getting everything out of the boxes, on to the bed and then tidying from there. Because right now I don't have a clue where anything is.'

Toby's gripping his chin, nodding slow as he assesses the room. 'That is a mad idea, yeah. But if that's the way you work, let's do it. Oh, and what are you doing later, do you have plans?'

'I do for a bit, yeah.' It's too embarrassing to admit to Toby that I'll be at a SlimIt meeting, so I keep it vague, saying, 'I have this thing my mum wants me to do, only for about an hour though. I'll be back by seven. Why?'

'Cool.' He cracks his knuckles, eyes sweeping the room like he's nervous too. 'Just, um, don't eat anything. Oh, wait – would you want to eat with us? You don't have to.'

I smile, though the thought of meeting my new housemates for the first time while internally battling the anxiety of eating a

84

meal in front of four strangers has me reeling. Still, I say, 'Yeah, that'd be nice,' because I have to try to get comfortable with it.

'Cool, I'll aim for seven then.'

'Oh, I have something of yours.' I dig in my backpack and take out Toby's hoodie, freshly washed and folded. 'Here you go.'

'Thank you. I meant what I said, you could've kept it.' He runs his hand through his short brush of hair, a smile in his voice. 'Red looks good on you.'

'Oh? Thanks.'

Smiling, I duck my head, because that's definitely the colour of my face right now.

When I leave for my SlimIt meeting at five, my room is in post-tornado levels of chaos. Even though Toby helped until he had to get ready for basketball practice, we didn't make a dent, and there were a lot of stretches of quiet where we weren't talking, just solidly unpacking. Maybe only I was feeling it, but it was awkward at first, the eye contact fleeting.

But when he texts me now, there's an easiness, our first face-to-face after his unconfirmed flirting done. I decide to mess with him.

Toby

Wait, you're not allergic to anything are you?

Saffron

Umm . . . what are you making?

Lemme check the ingredients

Toby

Tagine? It's got onion, garlic, sweet potato, chickpeas, bare spices . . .

Saffron

Oh, only literally everything you just listed 👉👈

Toby

Dickkk. But be for real now, I need to check you're not serious??

Saffron

Relax chef, I'm winding you up. So profesh you checking though, thanks

Toby

Wouldn't look good if I poisoned you on night one

As the bus crawls uphill, I press the bell. I'm typing the address of the church hall into Maps when I get a reply from Nolan to the picture I sent him of the moving day madness earlier.

Nolan Ah, that looks like a lot. Anything I can do?

As I step off the bus, it strikes me that in the three weeks we've been messaging, Nolan hasn't asked to meet up once, and *I* know why that is of course, but isn't he suspicious that I haven't asked either? Should I just confront him with the fact that I know what he's doing and confess to my own catfishing right after? Or would that put an immediate end to our talking, which has become a comfort I'm not sure I'm ready to let go of yet?

I need to vent to someone about this, if only to offload my thoughts. I message Pop.

Saffron

Can we FaceTime later?

The moment I hit send though, I'm already second-guessing confiding in her. It'd be so on brand for her to make the conversation about how betrayed she feels that I could keep a secret as big as Sydney from her. But who else am I gonna tell? Even if my envy hadn't put distance between us, Freya's too sweet and unassuming to burden with my catfishing drama. And too much of a sugar-coater to get any decent straight-talking from. At least I know Poppy won't bullshit me. You don't get through ten years of girl friendship without exchanging the raw, brutal honesty of sisters when one of you is doing something stupid. And, believe me, I know how stupid it is to still be talking to Nolan.

Cold to my bones and shivery with anxiety, I hurry out of the wind and rain and into St John the Baptist's church hall.

I take a cup of the sugar-free orange squash from the fold-out table in the foyer, studying the wall dedicated to 'inspiring' members. Pinned Polaroid pictures of mostly women forcing smiles as they stand on the scales. Rounded, bubbly handwriting underneath each picture exposes members' start weights and goal weights. *Karen, 42, 20st, is slimming to 12st 10lb. Sonia, 37, 14st 3lb, is slimming to 9st.* The board begs to be seen as positive and progressive, like the company's just a happy weight 'management' group that offers support and advice. But I don't remember it that way at all.

I flash over a decade of no cake on Mum's birthday; of chemically sweet soft drinks, low-sugar and low-health; of starvation Sundays before Monday's weigh-in, where Mum would be snappy and too cranky to help me with homework; of Monday night's celebratory binge, when me, Mum, and Otis would order an extra-large pizza and a tub of Ben & Jerry's to share. But by the time we got to dessert, I'd watch as Mum would pinch her belly in disgust, calling herself a greedy pig who didn't deserve ice cream. In silence, I'd eat mine, wondering what that made me.

I slump into one of the hard plastic chairs and while I wait for the rest of tonight's attendees to shuffle in, I check Instagram. Poppy's Story shows a row of wine bottles, the labels ripped off, captioned #budgetwinetasting. So that's why she hasn't replied yet. Poppy's always on her phone. I flick it away and scroll down.

At the top of my feed, Freya's posing next to a neon-pink bar sign that says, *Save water, drink champagne*, laughing at somebody behind the camera. Her belly button peeks out from a strapless satin top, her legs long and thin in tailored trousers. The caption reads,

freyalinkleyloves #throwback, can't wait to do it all again tomorrow! ♥ date nights with u >>>

Imagine this is her, wearing clothes like that, engaged *to be married* even, when here I am a year later, fat, single, and about to record my start weight all over again.

It won't be like my last SlimIt stint without Freya in the seat next to me. We'd go for walks together and send each other screenshots of our calorie trackers. I think that's why SlimIt works when it does, because you're being processed through the diet culture factory with friends and familiar faces. The smiles, the nods of encouragement, the rounds of applause.

If I'd realised then how the results of these meetings would end up making me feel about Freya, I wouldn't have suggested we joined together. SlimIt thrives off the competitiveness society forces upon women, and it's fucked up but that's why I'm back. I'm desperate and need this to work.

I remember the first time I said her name and it tasted sour. I saw her across the garden, tucked into a gingham minidress at a family barbecue her parents were hosting. Jack was there with his whole family, his mum and Freya's mum almost identical but unbelievably not twins. I was begging Jack to be more open about us now school was over, but he was adamant. I observed his mum from across the lawn, longing for him to *want* to introduce me to her.

Everything was on the cusp of change last summer. Poppy had just got the job at Jemima's and kept telling me I should submit an application. She was on shift that day. Freya was working at the bank and had met Tom by then, so already we were meeting up a lot less. We were unmooring, the three of us. It'd been a while since Freya had stopped coming to SlimIt meetings, her Goal met, pounds shed, and I wanted to be happy to see her, to compliment her dress, but I wasn't, and I didn't. Smilingly, I seethed.

'Frey!' I'd said, plucking at the smock dress I hoped was hiding my weight gain.

She held an untouched paper plate of salad, and gushed endlessly about Tom, how they'd met when he accidentally walked off with her coffee instead of his own at work. She kept floating untethered suggestions of double date ideas, wanting to set me up with one of his friends, and I'd nodded noncommittally, watching Jack turning over the charred meat on the barbecue.

I've only seen Freya once since.

And it was one of the last times I saw Jack too. We broke up not long after. He was off to study Physio in Brighton in September and said he didn't want to try long-distance because it'd be too hard for him to be away from me for so long. This was obvious code for: I want a free pass to shag about at uni, so we're done here.

I was hurt, and eating felt like comfort, so again, I got bigger.

As the circle of chairs slowly fills around me, I scroll to the next post on my feed. It's a Reel from Molly Mills, titled Wedding Dresses I Tried on, but I Knew Weren't the One and Freya's liked it. In the first frame, Molly's posing on a plinth in white bridal lingerie that she makes sure to tell everyone she has a discount code for in the caption. Every shot after is her looking radiant in various skintight dress designs. I go to the comments, about to vote for number four as my favourite, when I notice another comment from that influencer, Bliss Adeyemi, I came across a couple of weeks ago. It's popping off with close to five thousand likes.

bodiedbybliss Molly, you look stunning. Always do. Which is why I'm so confused you felt the need to use a body altering filter in this video without disclosing this information to your followers?? (I'm sorry ms editor, mistakes were made, look at the warping of that plant leaf by molly's left hip!!!) I just checked your audience analytics and the average age of people viewing your content is 19, girl. Considering that 40% of teenagers surveyed during MH awareness week (peep my bio for links) said content they'd seen on social media made them worry about body image, don't you think your young audience deserve to know that what they're seeing is NOT reality? I know it might not seem like it, but I say all this with love, angel. You do not need to be playing with this kind of fakery online. You are BEAUTIFUL and you are ENOUGH xxx

I watch the Reel again and spot the obvious manipulation. That peace lily is looking decidedly unpeaceful. I like Bliss's comment because she's right, influencers need to start being held accountable for the trickle-down effect of their unspoken use of filters. But I can't help but feel bad for Molly. If Miss Lingerie Brand Deal feels insecure about her body, what hope is there for the rest of us? In a reply to her own comment, underneath a storm of backlash from Molly Mills fans calling Bliss jealous and a clout chaser, she writes:

bodiedbybliss Also I'll say it louder for the @molly_mills stans at the back, if you think my calling this out on a public domain is problematic, you need to re-evaluate your definition of the word. More than a third of British teenagers STOPPING EATING because of negative body image is what's problematic. It's an epidemic!! Apologies for all the heavy stuff – come over to my page if you need a little positivity boost. This week's #slimitsurvivor story set my heart soaring y'all

SlimIt *survivor*? Curious, I go to Bliss's profile and tap her latest post. The carousel opens with an image of an apple-bodied woman smiling in a straw hat and sundress. Bliss introduces her in the caption as Grace, a proud size twenty and a pharmaceutical microbiologist.

I glance up over my phone and see we're still waiting on a few seats to be taken.

Bliss goes on to explain that Grace had been an on-and-off-again SlimIt member her whole life. Periodically, she'd lose a ton of weight too quickly, only to yo-yo right back up again once she stopped adhering to SlimIt's extreme restrictions. Hard relate.

bodiedbybliss Sound familiar? It wasn't until Grace was hospitalised after fainting at the top of a flight of stairs while following SlimIt's Super Speedy plan (big effin yikes) that she decided diet culture could get in the bin. Grace you are a LI-TER-AL #slimitsurvivor. I'm so glad you're OK, and you're at a place of self-acceptance now. So, please everybody, join me in the comments in welcoming Grace, stay safe (and away from flights of stairs if you're starving), and remember to dress like you're blessed –Bliss x

I double tap the post and follow both Bliss and Grace, swallowing the misplaced sense of betrayal I feel consuming Bliss's anti-diet content literally waiting to be handed my SlimIt starter pack.

I pocket my phone as the last person in shuts the door, echoing round the dank church hall. She turns around, flustered and obviously running late, and my eyes meet Clara's. Clara, as in Rue's mum, Otis's ex-childhood sweetheart, who looks like she did *not* want to be recognised. She lifts a hand in a meek hello, her eye contact faltering as she quickly finds a seat, all the way over the other side of the circle.

While the group's leader introduces herself as Cathy and runs through an update to SlimIt's calorie-counting app, I sneak out my phone and text her.

Saffron

Excuse me, are you lost?? What are you doing here?

Clara

Well shit. I came all the way to the Keynsham group to avoid you Saldanas. Your mums not here is she?

I catch her eye, shaking my head. Clara bites her lip, both of our faces fighting smiles because texting during this silent circle time set-up feels like we're breaking school rules.

Seeing her in person, I realise how much I've missed talking to her outside of logistical childcare chat. She and Otis got together when they were in year seven, so she always felt like an honorary big sister to me. They surprised everyone when they stuck it out all through school, rightfully earning their prom king and queen titles. Of course Clara got voted queen; she's teen comedy, high school pretty, Dionne Davenport pretty. She'd be cast as the head cheerleader every time. I looked up to her. And I guess maybe that's why I was surprised that they made it through two years of doing their relationship long-distance when Otis went off to uni. Clara could've had any boy she wanted, and yet she stayed faithful to my lanky, bed-headed brother. When they reunited over that summer break though, they both brought their own Big News™ with them. Otis had figured out he was bisexual, and Clara was almost three months pregnant.

I watch her now, raking her fingers through her relaxed hair, like she did when they broke the news to us at the kitchen table. Though I in no way condone the way Clara treated Otis after he came out to her – most notably, not letting him accompany her to the twelve-week scan – I do believe her heartbroken and hormonal actions shouldn't define her forever. Clara was nineteen and hurt and scared.

She bows her head as she writes another text, then slips her phone into her bag.

Clara

> And bless you but look at me, surely you can see my reason for being here! It's been 4 years (😔😔) and I cannot shift this mfing baby weight!! Let me tell you this 'mum tum' is not compatible with my want to wear something other than leggings and an oversized T-shirt. Anywayyy I'm feeling like Cathy's bout to put me in detention or something. Talk to you after

My arm drops to my side. That's what she's wearing now, old, bobbled leggings and a black slouchy tee printed with Prince's *Purple Rain* album cover. Even in millennial mumwear, I still think of Clara as having the ideal body. Slim but hourglass, a size ten in some shops, a size twelve in others. She does not need to be here.

As I look around the circle of attendees, it occurs to me how many of these people I'd never have guessed were unhappy with their bodies. On the outside they look perfectly at one with society's standard of beauty. And yet I'm still seeing women chewing their nails and fidgeting in their seats because they're worried the scales are going to confirm what they already feel about themselves: that they are not good enough.

I glance at Clara. And if all these women are feeling like the babies they've birthed, or the careers they've built – whole pharmaceutical microbiologists, for God's sake – are less definitive of their worth than what they weigh, will we ever be allowed to feel like we're enough?

Interrupting my thoughts, Cathy invites us all to line up behind the scales. As I join the queue, I don't seek out Clara, purposely dawdling until there's enough people between us. My mind's still newly processing the entire SlimIt enterprise as a deceptively sinister operation and I want time to think on that.

I wonder how many of these women are someone's idol, like Clara was mine. And with fresh horror, I wonder what the decision to be here is unconsciously telling those little people who look up to them. I picture Rue with her flip pad in hand, wanting to do the things that I do already, and remember denying myself a slice of her birthday cake in front of her, how preoccupied I was with policing my food.

And if Clara's this open about her body shame to me, I can only imagine the negative self-talk she might let slip into her conversations with Rue.

The queue shuffles forward.

'We've got a special guest observing us tonight, everyone,' Cathy says, gesturing to the back of the hall. Following Cathy's gaze, I'm unsurprised to see Mum, waving with a clipboard in her hand. Clara glances over her shoulder at me and I shrug, shaking my head apologetically. Interrupting herself to note the weight of the first woman on the scale, Cathy says, 'Fourteen stone eight, Gita, that's ... half a pound up from last week,' she tuts as Gita snatches her diary back from the volunteer jotting down her weight. 'We'll talk through this week's food choices in a minute, find out what went wrong. Now, our lovely guest, Dionne, otherwise known as SlimIt's South West Size Supervisor, isn't here on business today, so you can all stop sucking in your tummies.' A ripple of forced, polite chuckling passes down the line. Anticipating Cathy's next words, I wince. 'No, Dionne's here to support her daughter tonight, who's rejoining SlimIt after a bit of time off-plan. Saffron, your mum tells me you need the support of the group, is that right?' Cathy nods and it's patronising.

All I can do is nod back, internally squirming from all the stares, like prodding fingers, pointing into the problem parts of me.

'We've all been there,' Cathy coos. 'But you're here now and won't everyone join me in welcoming Saffron.'

'Welcome, Saffron,' the group zombies, trudging ever closer to the scales.

One by one we step up, jackets shrugged off and shoes kicked aside to make ourselves as light as possible. Toes splay, heads bow, our weight recorded like prized pigs at a county fair. Tuts and sighs and shaking heads. And then it's my turn.

The soles of my feet blanch cold against the scales' black surface, sending a shiver up my spine.

I try not to think of all the people who have stood here before me – in a literal sense because standing in the imprint of all these people's feet is sending me – but also in a bigger, societal sense.

'So, your starting weight, Saffron, is sixteen stone and five pounds.' Shame sludges into the pit of my stomach at hearing my weight called out to a room full of people. My eyes find Mum's at the back of the room and she stares me down. She nods sharp, as if to say, *Let's do this*, giving more overinvested personal trainer than disappointed mum. Cathy asks, 'How does that make you feel?' Like shit. When I don't answer, she says, 'It should make you feel determined to get this weight off, to meet the new you.'

'. . . I do want to change,' I find myself saying, despite how revelatory tonight's been.

'And you will. With our Super Speedy plan, we'll have you good as new in no time.'

The same Super Speedy plan that saw that girl, Grace, lose consciousness and fall to her almost-death. As I'm handed a red SlimIt food diary with my name and *16st 5lbs* scrawled on the front cover, I imagine her falling, her mind a blackout, no power over her limbs as she nosedives.

I take my seat in the circle, feeling tens of tonnes heavier.

I thought I wanted the pressure and the threat of humiliation to hold me accountable, but now that I'm faced with the reality of those feelings, I hate it. Hate everything about it.

'Wow, Vicki! You're five pounds down this week, making you this week's SlimIt Saint.' Cathy moves over to a board decorated with cotton wool clouds and glitter-glued stars with group members' names written on them. She moves Vicki's star from below the clouds, where the background is stuck with black tissue paper, and right to the top, where yellow pipe cleaners are fanned out to look like rays of sunshine. 'Can you share with the group anything you did differently?'

'Well,' Vicki says, beaming at her name tag's new celestial status. 'Our Harry brought a stomach bug home from school. It was horrible, don't get me wrong, but when I felt that first twinge of nausea, I did think, at least I'll get a big loss this week.'

The room laughs and *applauds*, and I feel utterly sick.

Members of the group file past me as I wait for Mum to finish talking to Cathy, a biting wind whipping through the entryway. Feeling numb after the events of my first meeting back, I get out my phone to look more into Bliss's SlimIt Survivor hashtag, when I see a text from Clara.

Clara

Sorry I rushed off. Felt like I was about to die I was so hungry. Had to skip my lunch break to be able to leave early enough to be here today. And ngl I kind of got spooked by your mum!!

Dark. More fodder for my internal diet culture collapse.

As I stand staring at her message, wishing I had the right words to defuse the tension between her and Mum, the toilet door opens beside me, and I move out of the way to let two girls pass.

'Oh my God, it's freezing,' one of them says, letting her backpack drop from her shoulder.

I watch as she digs around for a jumper and pulls it over her head. She turns to see her reflection in one of the plexiglas display boards, and my jaw drops, clocking the jumper's embroidered school crest. The uniform instantly ages her down to about thirteen, drawing my attention to the braces on her teeth. And the thought of her coming here after school, going from science class to Diet Culture Indoctrination 101 is beyond disturbing. She should be doing homework or hanging out at the park, not listening to Cathy preach about her insane food 'hacks'. Making cheesecake out of Weetabix and quark, and spritzing toast with Fry Light instead of butter, are not eating habits anyone needs to adopt, let alone a thirteen-year-old.

Maybe last time I was a member I didn't take in how truly noxious SlimIt's programming is because I had Freya beside me. We were too busy whispering plans for our first girls' holiday – a holiday that never happened because she met Tom, but one that was exciting and distracting to daydream about.

Seeing how self-conscious the girl in front of me feels in her school uniform is the embodiment of all the doubts that have surfaced here for me tonight. Mum appears, not registering anything wrong with the girl's age as we follow her out the door, and I silently *swear* to never come back here again.

After asking Mum how her big meeting went and assuring her I brought enough cutlery to the new house, we fall into a stilted silence. I'm still inward, working through how I feel about this evening. Still, the white noise of the wet road is occasionally punctuated by her saying things like,

'Grapefruit. I ate a grapefruit a day in the beginning.'

'Switch to green tea. Matcha green tea.'

When I get out of the car I wilt with relief. As the engine dies and I see her unbuckle her seat belt, I rush round to the driver's side.

'Mum, do you mind if I give you the tour next time? It's just, my new housemates are doing a dinner thing, and I think they're waiting—'

'Say no more, hon,' she says through her rolled-down window. She chuckles, not a bit put out. 'I won't come in and embarrass you. We'll have a cuppa next time. Anyway, I've got a date! I'll tell you all about it when I see you.' She reapplies her lipstick in her visor mirror, then blows me a kiss. 'Well done for today, Saff, proud of you.'

I wish her luck on the date, wondering which app she met this one on, and wave her off.

As soon as the car rounds the corner, I return to my disillusionment. There has to be a better way to do this whole diet thing. To lose weight without the ritualistic displays of disparagement, and the creepy cult vibes. I shudder, reliving the cognitive dissonance of the group *clapping* Vicki for puking and shitting her pants so bad all week she couldn't eat, being undernourished equated to being saintlike as her cardboard star was lifted to the top of the leaderboard.

From the street, the kitchen window emanates warmth, and I put all thoughts of SlimIt out of my head for now. The glass is wet on the inside from condensation, a yellow light glowing from behind. Voices lilt and talk over each other, and I find myself smiling as I let myself in.

I watch the scene from the kitchen doorway, remembering these people from the photo I saw Toby tagged in, everyone acting exactly as I imagined. Nairong still looks like she stepped right out of 2001. She's wearing another pair of baggy cargo trousers that she keeps having to hike up over her hips as she lays the table with mismatched cutlery and napkins from the falafel stand down the road. She nudges a packet of baccy out of the way to lay down a knife and fork. The boy who must be Keith grins at her and apologises, then returns to picking buds off a knot of weed and lining his paper. Toby stands with his back to them, stirring a pot on the stove, subtly nodding to the bass from the wireless speaker on the worktop. He turns, jabbing the spatula in his hand to the beat, and just as he notices me, I feel a hand on my shoulder.

'You're here, hi! Can I hug you? I'm a hugger.' I laugh, spluttering out a yes, and as I face whoever it is, she throws her arms around me. 'So good to meet you, I'm Veronica.' When I pull back, I notice the same butterfly clips glittering in her hair from the photo. And I *do* know her. Or rather, recognise her from around campus. In my head, I refer to her as Bodycon Girl, because every time I see her, she's always wearing something in a material and fit that bares the shape of her body rather than hiding it, unlike most of the slouchy plus-sized clothes I own.

'Hey,' I say, glancing in turn at everybody else in the room. 'I'm Saffron.'

As Veronica steps past me to peer into the pot, I confirm what I always thought about her from afar, that body-wise, it's like I'm looking in a mirror. Same big boobs, wide butt, thighs that touch down to the knee, her waist rounded and soft. But it sits so assertively on her, hugged by her denim minidress.

'*Yessss*, you went for the tagine. Thank you, chef.' Veronica clasps her hands in prayer and bows to Toby. 'You are in for a treat, he's such a good cook,' she says to me.

I only laugh, still nervous.

Someone taps me. 'Hey, I'm Nairong, nice to meet you,' she says in a Mancunian accent, lightly embracing me. She smells of mint and eucalyptus.

'Hey,' I say.

Over her shoulder I watch as Toby finishes washing his hands, flicking out his fingers to dry them and splash Veronica at the same time. The two of them laugh. She flinches, her body bunching, belly rolling, and I can't take my eyes off her. She's fat in every way society tells us not to be. Unflinchingly but nonchalant with it, the most positive representation of fatness I've seen. Sure, I've searched through the 'body positivity' hashtag on Instagram, but I never see bodies like mine, real bodies with cellulite and back bulges. In my experience, #bopo's less about normalising bigger bodies and more about disguising fatness to look like thinness. All the algorithm had to offer me was endless waist trainer ads, miracle bodysuit try-ons, and shapewear recs by mostly midsize influencers. Bodies like mine, like ours, don't sell.

But Veronica? She's serving size sixteen-to-eighteen realness, her confidence flaming, igniting a glow in the pit of my belly.

I look back to the table, to Nairong, now sat and patting the seat between her and Keith. I drop down, my smile easy.

'Yo. Keith.' Keith tucks the joint he's finished rolling behind his ear and offers me his hand, the skin rough and red from winter.

'Hi.'

Veronica bounds over to the table, the stack of plates in her hands clattering against each other.

'Mate, calm down. They were my nan's plates,' he says as Veronica sets one in front of each of us.

She marks herself with the sign of the cross before blowing a kiss up to the ceiling. 'Soz, Keith's nan.' My laugh splutters as she turns to me. 'So, Saffron – do people call you Saff? Did you move here? What are you studying? Tell me everything—'

'Hang on, hang on. Don't start without me.' Toby carries the pot to the table, then leans between me and Nairong to place it in the middle, just as it was in the photo I wished I was a part of. As everyone says how good it smells, he crouches slightly, putting his lips to my ear to whisper, 'You sure you're OK with this?'

Warmth washes down my back as I realise the reason he's asking is because he remembers me telling him I don't like to eat in front of people. It's soothing, being cooked for, considered, remembered. It feels like bathwater being cupped over your head as a kid.

'Yeah,' I whisper back. 'Thank you.'

Toby takes the seat opposite me as Veronica ladles tagine on to my plate. I thank her, thank him, and find that for once I'm not itching to get out my phone to google the calories of each ingredient. I'm letting the tendrils of its heat curl up into my face and breathing in its Moroccan flavours. I taste it, the harissa hot on my tongue, the sweet burst of tomato pips as I bite one whole. And as I eat, I'm listening, able to take in facts about my new housemates because I'm not obsessing over my meal. Veronica's studying English; Nairong, law; and Keith – surprisingly – computer science. I'm noticing the details. How Keith's spoon lolls between his fingers, bouncing and flicking sauce as he talks with his mouth full. Nairong does too, but daintily, behind her hand, taking small slurps from her spoon that she lets rest in the bowl during intervals when she's the one telling a story. Veronica's an active listener, *mmm*ing and nodding with great feeling whenever I answer one of her questions, which are always specific and interesting.

And when I look at Toby, he's watching me with a warmth I want to stretch out in.

Perhaps I did judge him too harshly, tarring him with the same level of disrespect as Jack. And with how his breath on my neck made everything shiver, can I let myself believe that he feels this too? That maybe he does have an honest attraction to me, and maybe his flirting was sincere the day we met.

I watch him too, considering this.

The meal sprawls long, maybe an hour, and I lose myself in the togetherness of it.

When everyone's finished, Veronica gets up to make tea and Keith steps out to smoke. My phone vibrates in my pocket. It's a notification from the SlimIt app, reminding me to log what I had for dinner. I cringe, imagining asking Toby to list the ingredients he cooked with so I can submit it to my digital diary and get my meal rated. In two taps, I delete it.

As I put my phone away, another one starts buzzing.

'Someone's phone,' I say, but Nairong laughs loud at the same time.

The conversation started off with debating the deservedness of some of this year's Oscar nominations, which I confidently spoke my piece on. But when Toby googled the nominees for best supporting actress, and read aloud the title of an article that came up about the widespread use of Ozempic in Hollywood, I went quiet. I'm certain of how I feel about it on a personal level, but I'm still on the fence about my general opinion on its use. Nairong's condemning it as a weight-loss drug, citing the supply issue for the people with type two diabetes who actually need it. This was in response to Toby – *stressing* his position of devil's advocate – mentioning that morbidly obese people were now being prescribed it by their doctors. I'm not getting involved because I only know what my socials have been showing me, which is conflicting and inflammatory information, and the topic makes me uncomfortable. With one scroll I'm seeing sensationalised horror story side effects, and posts exposing famous people for having 'Ozempic Face'. And then I'll refresh the page and it's being casually joked about in interviews, or defended by hollow-cheeked celebrities whose glaring use of it is a visual open secret on their faces. I'm not in a position to confidently debate the morality of how the drug is used and who for.

All I know is, Ozempic gets a hard no from me. Seeing videos speculating on its use by celebrities I consider body-perfect was enough to send me spiralling last year when the hype first hit my algorithm. It was actually one of the catalysts that got me to sign up to SlimIt in the first place.

'It's literally wiping out the already dire exposure of diverse body types we see on screen,' Nairong's saying.

'You sound like an essay,' Veronica says, not looking up from stirring the teas. I'm wondering if she's ever considered taking it, despite her outward body confidence, when she makes her opinion known, loud and clear. 'Ozempic is bullshiiiit, we know this. There, discussion done.'

A phone rings again. Its vibration dies then instantly starts up once more.

'Guys, I think one of your phones is ringing,' I say.

Toby sighs. 'It's mine.' He gets his phone out on the table and silences the call.

Not letting the topic drop, Nairong says, 'I wonder if it'll become one of the things the people *not* doing it start getting called brave for, like the smattering of actresses in Hollywood not having Botox so they can still emote.'

'Probably,' Toby says, distracted, his eyes straying to his phone as it goes off again. I sit up straighter, chancing a glimpse at his screen. Bella, it reads. 'Fuck, I should probably answer.'

'Um, no?' Veronica slides our mugs in front of us, shaking her head. 'You shouldn't.'

'She'll keep calling.'

She juts her neck forward. 'Block her?'

'Who is it?' Obviously I'm already fully aware, but I'm curious about what answer I'll get.

Toby and Nairong speak at the same time.

'No one—'

'—His ex.'

'Exactly. No one. Back in a bit,' Toby says, avoiding my eye.

It's silent as he leaves but when the landing floorboards creak above us, Veronica mutters, 'God, I hope they don't get back together. What is she doing, calling like that?'

'They didn't end on good terms?' I ask, blowing ripples across my tea.

'She cheated on him,' she says, glancing at the ceiling, to Toby's room. 'Like nothing physical happened, but emotionally. He saw the texts. What is he *doing* even entertaining this shit? I can't stand that girl.'

'Maybe he's forgiven her.' Nairong shrugs. 'I know we wouldn't, but nothing *technically* happened.'

'Please.' Veronica rolls her eyes. 'That would hurt. He better not be inviting her to the party tomorrow.' She gasps.

I look between them. 'Party?'

Nairong sighs.

'I can't believe I gave it away, I'm sorry.' Veronica looks at me, clapping her hands over her mouth. 'It's not a *party*-party. Just pre-drinks, like, in your honour. To welcome you, and so you can meet all the side characters in our lives. Is that OK? We bought you a ticket to Motion as a moving-in present.' She laughs. 'Did we mess up? Do you hate surprises?'

I laugh, nervously.

'You can invite whoever you want,' Nairong adds.

Like who? I know from her Story Freya already has a date scheduled with Tom tomorrow, which leaves Poppy. And honestly, do I want her there? Do *I* even want to be there?

'No, um.' I swallow a gulp of tea. 'Thank you. For thinking of me. You've both been so welcoming, so lush.' I drum my nails against the side of my mug. It *is* thoughtful and such a nice gesture, so why do I feel so apprehensive? 'I don't have anything to wear,' I say, realising that the apprehension comes from not being as far along in my self-improvement journey as I thought I'd be by now. Tonight's SlimIt shitshow and meeting Veronica has thrown my perspective on body size at the wall, and I'm still trying to piece my thoughts on it back together. But regardless of how I feel about my weight, I'm stuck with the same self-doubt and lacklustre wardrobe.

'Girl, I got you.' Veronica's lips press together smugly. 'You can borrow something of mine.'

'Really?' I say, leaning towards her.

And God, I don't expect it to, but it feels so validating to have someone I can share clothes with. I feel like this whole evening has altered my brain chemistry for the better. Not only did I renounce SlimIt, but I comfortably ate dinner with four of the nicest strangers I've ever met. I didn't once convince myself I was inferior or question whether I belonged at the table with them. I didn't detect a hint of judgement for how much I ate, or what I was wearing. With them, it didn't ever feel like what I was saying was overshadowed by what I looked like, like my insecurities had me fearing it would. I rest my hands on my belly, watching Veronica.

'Look at this top,' she says, showing me a picture of her in a crop top. 'You wanna borrow it?'

Everything about how she moves in her body is assured. And it makes me wonder if maybe I can get there too.

I take the phone, picturing myself wearing that top as proudly as she does, and slowly, I nod.

21:48

Saffron

Hey, dw about calling. Decided I'm actually going to my 9am tomorrow so I'm gonna get an early night. Have a good one x

. . .

In bed, I watch the typing dots bounce then fade, bounce then fade. I imagine Poppy clumsily thumbing her phone in between shouts of laughter around the kitchen island. I'm not longing to be there with her though. I feel full from the food Toby cooked, content from the company, and cosy in my new bed.

I'm actually low-key relieved she forgot about FaceTiming me.

Poppy

OMG SOSOSOO SORRYYYY

Poppy

I forgt!! It was the cheap sauvy b. Gone tomy head Saff!!!

I let the screen go black and consider the reality of inviting her over for drinks tomorrow. Inevitably, it'd become The Poppy Show. And instead of getting to know my new housemates and their friends, I'd be fielding questions like, *Is she single? Did she get a boob job?* like some paid representative.

I tell her to sleep well and reply to Nolan's earlier message, settling in for a long convo, when his reply pings right back.

Remembering Bella's name lighting up Toby's phone, I decide to lean into the blissful ignorance of what I have with Nolan – a low-expectancy, zero-pressure situationship without real-life consequences. I don't need to worry about Nolan getting calls from his stunning ex-girlfriend, or whether he's only flirting with me to one-night me. I never need to stress about what to wear on a date with him, or if his friends are making fun of me. Because Nolan's not real.

Sydney Hey! Missed you today, what did you get up to??

*

Sitting cross-legged in front of the mirror, I feel the floorboards thrum with bass from the music downstairs. I've had to redo my eyeliner four times because my hand keeps shaking. The front door rattles open and closed as more people arrive, bringing shouts of laughter and clinking bottles. It sounds like everything I've been missing out on, the life I watched Poppy living through my phone and yearned for. So *why* am I hiding up here then?

My phone goes off as I'm aggressively spritzing finishing spray over my makeup.

Toby

Veronica says hurry up lol

I glance around my new room, my fairy lights strung, my posters pinned, and people downstairs waiting to meet me. But my palms are sweating, and the waistband of my trousers digs too tight. I'm twitchy with nerves, worrying that Veronica's crop top is too short. The urge to micellar water away this makeup, do my skincare, bundle up in my dressing gown, and pick up where I left off in my *Friends* rewatch is strong. Appreciate the party and all, but I don't know if I'm ready.

I could use a calming presence, and Toby's consideration last night at dinner makes me want to see him. I reply to his message.

Saffron

Can you please come up actually

Twenty seconds later he's knocking at my door. 'You ready?' he asks when I open it a crack, like I'm afraid the party will spill in.

I drag him inside. 'No?'

'What's up?'

Oversimplifying, I say, 'I'm nervous.'

'Don't be. I get it, but everyone's buzzing to meet you.'

'That's the point, what are they buzzing for? I'm not ...' I trail off, feeling him looking at me, like really looking. 'What?'

'Is that Veronica's?' I nod, and his head tilts, taking in the whole fit. 'You look nice. Like, *really* nice.'

The word floats, falling featherlike and landing soft. Nice. It's the vanilla, the margarita, the ready salted of compliments. *Nice* could be perfectly platonic, but the way he's looking at me hazes the lines.

'Thank you.' A real blush deepens my powdered-on one. I glance in the mirror at my high-waisted khaki cargo trousers and Veronica's white baby tee with a double cherry on it. It's fitted, which means I'll be fighting the urge to stand up the whole night, or else cross my arms over my belly rolls, but I think I look good. Like, as good as it's gonna get. I point to my Adidas Gazelles by the door. 'Can I wear shoes inside? Is that weird? It's just this is the whole outfit, you know?' I say, already putting them on.

He laughs. 'Does that mean you're ready to come down?' I take a deep breath and tell him yeah. My eyes widen at his outstretched hand, and I take it. His fingers slot through mine.

As we linger by the bottom of the stairs, he says, 'Look, I know you're stressing but I promise all these people are chill. Let me give you a little preview.' He shoulders us through the crowd into the living room and surveys the people crammed in here. 'Those are some guys from my team, all real ones, but that one there –' he points to a boy with a topknot – 'he's probably gonna try to rizz you.' My mouth falls open and I laugh. 'That couple over there are Luke and Kashvi from my Genetics class, both great individually but between you and me, on the verge of breaking up—'

'Goss,' I cut in.

'Those girls are Veronica and Nairong's little gang, all studying different things, but they get lunch together most days. You got nothing to worry about there, you'll fit right in. They'll love you.' His eyes catch mine and he holds my gaze like he wants me to think on that last part, his smile slow, unfurling. I glow, taking in each of the girls. All different shapes and sizes, but each striking and individual. I see blue hair, shaved sides, thigh-high boots, a leopard-print catsuit. And Toby thinks I fit in there too. 'Come on,' he says, squeezing my hand. 'There's a spot.'

He hustles us over to take the sofa space of the Genetics Class Couple who look like they're getting up in search of drinks.

'Catch up with you later,' he says, slapping Luke's palm. Toby nudges me, nodding to the break in the crowd where the couple walk through. 'Look at Keith, talking up that girl he doesn't know is ten times out of his league. Bless him.'

I follow Toby's gaze and my face drops. What the hell is Poppy doing here? Keith's leaning in close, topping up her drink from a hip flask.

'I know her,' I say. 'And in fact, if she's here ... Toby, that's Poppy—'

'You know Poppy? She lives with my ex.'

'Yeah, I know. So, if Poppy's here, so is—'

'Bella,' Toby shouts through cupped hands. He waves her over and she bounces on the balls of her feet, waving back, her dress clinging like a second skin over her body, milk white and gossamer. 'Veronica's gonna kill me,' he says out the side of his mouth as Bella picks her way over to us.

My stomach sinks. 'You invited her?'

'I said she could come over to pick up some stuff, forgetting we had this pre-drinks arranged, and when I went to rearrange with Bella, she said she had tickets to Motion too. Kind of made sense at the time.' He shrugs. 'I was gonna see her there anyway.'

Her dress hugs her tan, gapped thighs as she walks over to us, and the closer she gets, the more cemented my cynicism about Toby liking me becomes. I can't compete with Bella. I categorise his *Nice* comment firmly as platonic. She stands over me, angularly, runway beautiful, her long chestnut hair tumbling over her bare shoulders.

The three of us exchange hellos, the atmosphere stilted, uncertainty over who knows who and how. Before anything can be clarified though, Kashvi from Toby's Genetics class comes back looking for her bag. Toby digs down the back of the sofa cushions for it, while I stand with Bella.

'What are you doing here, Saff? I thought you didn't have any friends at UWE?' she smirks. 'I thought that was why you were so obsessed with Poppy. No offence.'

Behind her, I notice Poppy being tickled by Keith as the two of them crash up the stairs.

I fold my arms. 'I live here now.'

What I want to say is, *What the fuck is your problem?* but her behaviour's not deviating from the norm, she's always this casually baiting, so I let it go.

'Small world,' Bella says vacantly, eyeing Kashvi before returning her gaze to me. 'I just thought you might've mentioned your little party to Poppy, seeing as she always used to go out of her way to include you in everything back at the start. Even though you never came, lol.'

My thumb clicks as I clench my fist. Toby's deep in conversation with Kashvi, who's laughing and dusting off her bag. What *is* this bitch's problem? I open my mouth to tell her to say what she *really* wants to say to me with her chest, when Nairong's slender fingers close around my wrist.

'There you are,' she says, dragging me away from Bella's display of peak passive aggression.

She leads me over to the few people in the middle of the room brave enough to be dancing this early on in the night. Over my shoulder, I catch Bella's haughty face transform as she sidles in next to Toby, laughing mechanically at whatever she's pretending to have heard Kashvi say. My anger dissipates when the arm of one of Toby's teammates is slung around my shoulders, dragging me into the dancing. Of course Veronica's here, her hips twisting, bum jiggling, thick thighs zipped tight as she coils her body, snake out of basket style, to the afrobeat song playing. And I'm hypnotised, truly.

'Where were you!?' she says.

Nairong gestures over to Toby and Bella. 'Just saved Saff from third-wheeling the least anticipated getting-back-together chat of the century.'

'*No.*' Veronica peers over my shoulder. 'He hasn't, has he?'

Subtly, I act like I'm fluffing my hair, then sweep it off my shoulder, turning to catch a glimpse of them hugging. I sigh. 'Indeed, I think he has.'

Veronica steers us to the sofa in the opposite corner of the room, sandwiching herself between me and a boy she doesn't care about spilling some of herself on to. Nairong perches on the arm next to me and I fill them both in, feigning surprise at realising my friend's friend, Bella, and Toby's ex, Bella, were one and the same.

While the two of them make bets on whether or not they'll have make-up sex tonight I get out my phone to quickly text Poppy. Bella's snide comments have made me feel guilty for not inviting her. But I pause to read the message from Nolan, waiting on my screen.

Nolan Hey, how's your night going??

I'll reply later. Instead, I go straight to my chat with Poppy.

Saffron

Hi, you're in my house! And you're getting off with my new housemate, Keith, wtf haha?? I'm downstairs

'Oh, here they go, look,' Nairong murmurs.

My head snaps up to see Toby being led out of the room by Bella. His eyes lock on to mine, his expression, his intentions, unreadable.

As I sit and talk to Veronica and Nairong, the pre-drinks does its thing and unravels inhibitions, guests getting gigglier, spilling drinks. One girl cries on her friend's shoulder, a couple kiss in the corner. Occasionally, someone'll come up and join our huddle and introductions will be made. More hugs and smiles, and getting to know people.

I'm so mad that I wanted to stay upstairs tonight. Mad that I'd convinced myself certain spaces and scenarios weren't meant for me because of the body I'm in. And that Jack and the suffocating sameness of school made me believe that if I were to be myself at uni, I would be instantly rejected. It's what made me desperate to cling on to Poppy's friendship. I've been denying myself *new* friendships, and parties, and cute tops, and for what?

Mostly it's just been me, Veronica, and Nairong all night, conversations bubbling up before we've finished the last one. Earlier we all spoke about our heritage – Veronica's Scottish and German, Nairong's Chinese, and my Trinidadian and English – which led on to families and siblings, and I got to gush about Otis for a bit. All night we haven't run out of questions to ask, shows to recommend, exes to complain about—

'What about you, Saffron? What was your longest relationship?' Nairong asks me now, dabbing under her eye from where she just got teary telling us about how she and her recently-ex girlfriend couldn't make the long distance work.

I gulp the dregs of my third vodka cranberry and Veronica immediately refills my cup. 'Technically five months, but I'm not sure if it counts if only you knew you were going out?'

'What do you mean?' Veronica asks, switching her crossed legs, the bare skin of her inner thigh dimpling like rippled milk. She doesn't acknowledge it, and I let the cushion I'm holding against my stomach slip.

I relax back into the worn sofa. 'What I mean is, we did everything that couples do for five whole months, but nobody knew we were doing it. He told me not to tell anyone.'

She gasps. 'Like you were his dirty little secret?' I nod, not able to look her in the eye. 'Prick. How dare he! Look at you, you're *stunning*, Saff,' she says in that gushing, love-lipped way girls talk to each other in club bathrooms.

'I can't believe somebody did that to you.' Nairong shuffles off the arm and next to me, laying her head on my shoulder. 'I'm sorry.'

'I— Thank you.' That's the first time I've ever told anybody about our relationship. Or had the cruelness of it acknowledged. A tear drips down my cheek and Veronica and Nairong take my hands. 'There has to be a reason someone doesn't want to be seen with you. I wish I could be like you, Veronica, you're so—'

'I am *not* brave for wearing a miniskirt, girl, don't.'

My face boils. 'I wasn't going to say brave, though *to me* you are. I'd never have the confidence to wear something like that. That's what I was going to say – confident, not brave.' Actually, I was going to say brave. 'I wish I didn't care what people think—'

'But I do care.' She sniffs.

'Yeah, totally,' I stammer. 'Ugh, sorry. I'm saying all the wrong things.'

'No.' Veronica smooths her thumb over the back of my hand. 'You're saying all the things Big Diet and Big fucking Beauty wants you to say. That we're so brave and, *Oh, look at you in a skirt, good for you, I could never.* They're so reluctant to normalise us. They *want* to other us, to discourage more of us from being happy the way we are. Because if we were, then we'd stop buying their stretch mark creams, and their waist trainers, and their fucking Ozempic.' I stare at her, her words effervescing up new thoughts, like a fizzy vitamin dropped into a cool glass of water. 'I wish when people looked at me the first thing they thought was just, *I love that top, where'd she get it.* But it isn't, it's more like, *Wow, I can't believe* she's *wearing a top like that.* So, yeah, I do care that being fat is the big definer for me. I just choose to care about me more. I care about liking the clothes I wear, and about how my body feels when I move it.'

Veronica blinks at the ceiling so her tears won't fall. Her hand that isn't holding mine grips the sofa cushion like it's all that's keeping her from punching through to its spring innards in frustration.

'She's not mad at you, this is just how she talks,' Nairong stage-whispers.

'No, I'm not mad at you.' Veronica's voice softens but the tension's still there in her jaw. 'I'm mad *for* you.'

For a beat, we say nothing, and as the party happens around us, I'm reminded that I'm here, happy, making friends and experiencing everything I felt I wasn't worthy of because of what I weighed. Which is when I feel Veronica's rage bleed white hot into me.

'I should be mad.' I down my drink. Fuck you, Jack Day. Fuck you, FastOff, and SlimIt, and too-tiny slivers of cake. Fuck you, #thinspo, gym bros, and body goals. Fuck all of it. 'I know we have to go soon,' I say, checking the time on my phone. It's twenty minutes 'til entry to Motion, and even if we leave now, there'll be a queue that snakes back about a mile long. 'But can we all please get up and dance, just for a bit.' I drag my new friends up off the sofa. 'I think that'd make me feel immediately better.'

The girls' yeses hiss like Medusa snakes as we twine together, dancing in the middle of the living room. I don't care if people are looking at me, judging me for winding my waist or shaking my bum, because being in this moment with my friends is so much more *fun* than thinking about that. As I twist to the music, I spot Poppy in the doorway, lurching towards me, her phone in her hand.

'You do live here!' she cries, throwing her arms around me.

'Hey! Yeah, these are my housemates, Nairong and Veronica. Guys, this is my—' I blink at Poppy, and instinctively thumb the smudged lipstick off her chin. In a moment of bittersweet clarity, I realise that *best friend* doesn't feel accurate anymore, and it doesn't hurt as much as I thought it would to admit that. 'My oldest friend, Poppy.'

'We've known each other for ten years,' she screeches as Veronica and Nairong try to say hi. We all laugh, and then Pop throws her hands up. 'Oh my God, I love this song!'

Nairong drags her into our circle as Veronica threads her

fingers through mine and twirls me round and round. Laughing, I spin like an unwound thread, 'til it feels like I'm flying, unbodied, weightless. I'm empty ...

... so empty in fact it feels like there's nothing in my head, out of energy to make thoughts. The edges of the room swim in a blur of unfamiliar faces, and it feels like all my body's blood has pooled in my trainers.

I'm light as a feather, floating.

Nice, Toby called me.

And it is nice, my eyes shutting against the blur, an ebbing of a hot blackness behind my lids. Yeah, it's nice here in my new house, with my new friends.

So nice, until I hit the ground hard, pinned by my own weight.

I wake in a disoriented swirl of nausea and hunger. Cavernous, gnawing hunger that hurts. It takes me a minute to familiarise myself. My stuff is all here but the room's all wrong, bed too big, ceiling too low. As I blink up at my own reflection in the skylight instead of my peeling constellation of glow-in-the-dark stars, I realise I probably had way too much alcohol.

I grab the glass of water on the floor next to a pack of paracetamol. I'm still dizzy as I sit up to drink, thinking back. I was dancing and then my vision started to smudge, and I fell. I clutch my stomach as my hunger burns and writhes. I didn't eat enough, and I fainted, just like the SlimIt survivor Bliss featured, Grace. What if I'd been at the top of a flight of stairs like her, or alone and hit my head?

One wholesome house meal together and the *intent* to better my relationship with food hasn't undone the years' worth of damage diet culture's done to me. I still woke up today and chose not to eat the toast. Chose to only eat soup before putting on this outfit, so I wouldn't look bloated. Four freely poured vodka cranberries in the space of two hours on watery instant soup was not a smart decision. It was dangerous. After tonight, I'm no longer putting my body's needs second to its appearance. I'd rather be waking up with belly bloat than a rushing head and exhaustion delirium any day.

I push my hair off my face, realising everyone must've left for Motion and I wasted my ticket.

I pat around for my phone, trying not to prang out too much as I skim-read the notifications that have piled up.

22:43

Otis

Mr Chen's hits different without you, little sis. Hope you're settling in OK 🖤

Poppy

Howd I end up in YOUR HOUSE wtfff. You live with Bellas 'ex' boyfriend loool. Messy. Love your other housemates though, esp the boy in the beanie oop. Omw to Motion with the two babes you live with. Sory you couldn't come text me when you wake up xxxxxxxx

Veronica

Hey Sleeping Beauty. Please don't hate us – we're on our way to Motion. If you wake up and feel better, PLS come. We'll pay for your uber!!! But if not, we left you in the capable hands of Tobias and we'll see you in the morning 🐚 and don't worry, we'll look after Poppy!

Toby

Hey. I didn't feel like going out in the end, so I'm downstairs. I set you up with paracetamol and water but give me a shout if you don't feel well, or you can't sleep. Or you need anything at all

I double tap Toby's message and send back a collage of heart and flower emojis to Veronica, smiling because it feels like I've known her and Nairong forever. No way am I going out now though. I think of the three of us earlier, posted up on the sofa all night, our talks deep and heart-raw. That was where the night peaked for me.

I send back an *I miss you* to Otis and pan my camera around my mostly decorated room to show him I'm OK, that I'm making this space my own.

Finally, I go back to Poppy's message and tell her to drink some water and stay with Veronica and Nairong.

Still tipsy myself, I make my way downstairs to settle my stomach before bed. A slim shaft of light shines from under Toby's door. I go to knock, to thank him for staying, but then I hear her

I hover on the landing, listening to the soft murmurings of his and Bella's voices. Even though hearing them together makes me kind of sad, I'm also relieved for the clarity. At least I can extinguish any romantic feelings for him once and for all and focus on our friendship. Because who's spending time in their bedroom with their ex at 11 p.m. if nothing's going on?

I pour myself a bowl of cereal and tread lightly on the stairs.

Back in bed, I find my attention straying to Reveal. Nolan's status says he hasn't been online for over an hour, but I send him a message coded with thinly veiled neediness anyway, hoping he'll ask what's wrong and a girl can indulge in a little wallowing. I stare at the screen, willing the text bubble to tick Seen, but it doesn't. I'm suddenly wide awake with no one to talk to. Otis will be asleep, Freya's with Tom – their date night documented all over her Instagram – and Poppy's with all my new friends, who unwittingly now have front-row seats to The Poppy Show. I cringe at an embarrassingly childish thought: *What if they like her more than me?* I dismiss it, cherishing my earlier chats with Veronica and Nairong. They're still not here now though, and before I know it, I'm sifting through profiles on Sydney's account. I'm bored – and forget *fearing* missing out, I know I'm missing out.

Aaron, Freddie, Samuel, Jake, Connor, Brodie, Hamza, Cain.

No. No … No. OK, yes. No. Yes. No—
Oh my God.

Toby, 19

Cactus dad. UWE Jets point guard 🏀 I like cooking good mood food.

On auto, I swipe right before my brain catches up, then look at my finger like it's not mine. *Why* did I do that? I blink up at myself reflected in the black skylight, like my bed's floating in space. It's fine, I don't have to do anything, this doesn't mean I'm going to talk to him. Not every boy who comes across

Sydney, 18

virgo girly, funny by accident, tbh I'm just here for new memes

will be interested in her. But when I look down at the notification on my screen, a twist of illicit glee steals my breath.

It's a Match!

The majority of Saturday is spent nested in the living room with everyone, hungover and bingeing *Always Sunny*. I sit with the girls on the sofa, while the boys stretch out on a blanket at our feet. Toby in front of me. I'm in denial that Sydney and he matched on Reveal, swerving messages from Nolan so I don't have to open the app. Toby's name will be there and I'll be confronted with my baffling impulse to swipe right.

Every time he turns to talk to me, he rests his head just above my knee, sparking this current of electricity that travels all the way up my leg and between my thighs. And then he'll turn to watch the TV again, and I'll see him text Bella with his phone held close to his chest. Instant power outage. I've never had to deal with getting mixed signals like this before, but I'm not loving it. Not hating it either when those signals look like holding my hand at the party last night or making sure I'm comfortable eating in a group situation. I stare at the back of his head, wishing there was a way to know what he was thinking without, you know, having to ask him.

At three, I leave for my closing shift at Jemima's, every minute of which drags, until I come home and collapse into my fresh bed. Mum's sent a picture of her pulling a pretend sad face, snuggled up on the recliner, her features blue-lit by the TV.

Mum

First solo duvet night ☹ missing you, hon. Hope you're settling in alright xx

We FaceTime and she catches me up on how her date went the other night. She doesn't give up any of his personal details, and I've learnt not to ask so early on, but I'm glad she had a good time. Then I tell her all about the party and everybody I met, and about the little bit of exploring I've done round the neighbourhood. The falafel stand down the road, the matcha latte place round the corner, and the gluten-free bakery on the high street. But mostly, I talk about how at home and accepted I feel here, until at some point, I fall asleep.

On Sunday, I unpack my cookware and return Toby and the rest of the house's welcoming kindness by cooking a huge pot of pesto pasta. Before calling them down, I make sure to rinse the jar labelled *reduced fat* and throw it in the recycling.

As Keith serves himself seconds and Veronica swipes her finger round the oily, herby smears left on her plate, I glance round at them all.

'I hope it was OK, sorry it was a bit basic.'

'That wasn't basic. You should've seen the level of basic I was eating before Toby stepped in.' Veronica pauses to bow to him, laughing as she does it.

Toby stacks his plate on top of mine. 'Anyway, basic doesn't mean bad, pesto is peng. Thanks for cooking.'

'Yeah, thanks, Saffron,' Keith says through a mouthful.

I relax against my chair, genuinely happy and so grateful, as the girls echo the sentiment.

'Oh.' Nairong checks an alert on her phone. 'Tomorrow's the twelfth! What're you doing tomorrow?' she asks me. 'Are you on campus?'

When I tell her no, she reminds the others that they said they'd watch Toby's basketball game together, and insists I come too. Toby grins as he gathers up the rest of the plates and takes them to the sink.

'It's only a friendly. You don't have to come,' he says over his shoulder. 'But it'd be cool if you did.'

I grin right back, blowing a loose curl off my face. 'Yeah, I'll be there.'

So, the next day, I don a red lip and classic black eyeliner to match the team's colours, then meet Veronica in the kitchen, also in a red-love-heart-patterned jumper. It's just us. Nairong and Keith have classes today, so we're meeting them there. Before we leave, I spy Toby's UWE Jets hoodie on the drying rack and bite my lip. He *did* say I was welcome to it. I shove it over my head as we go out the door, catching Veronica raise an eyebrow at me.

'Go team? What? I want to be supportive.'

She winks. 'Whatever you say, girl.'

She links her arm through mine as we walk to the bus stop, her warmth buttery and suffusing. I melt into easy conversation with her and realise how much I've missed the unambiguity of a friend showing you they really want to be your friend. No teasing or showing off, no backhandedness or uncertainty. Just nonstop talking and interest in what I've got to say.

On the court, the benches are abuzz with students laughing and chatting, their voices echoey and giving the illusion of a bigger crowd filling the sports hall. We find Nairong and Keith saving us spaces in the front row, and then the team are jogging on to the floor.

'There's our boy!' Veronica shouts through cupped hands.

Toby gives us a two-fingered salute as he runs past us to get to his position, his biceps taut and defined. He does a double take when he sees me, plucking at his vest in reference to his stolen hoodie, and laughs.

I've never been to a sports event, never felt the swell in the atmosphere, the tension before the whistle goes. And then it does, and my eyes are pinned on him, the way his muscles work, the determination hardening his features, my breath caught in my chest.

When he shoots the first basket of the game eight minutes in, Nairong, Veronica, Keith, and I jump against each other, cheering and screaming. And I feel every bit as connected to this moment as anybody else here, just another body in the crowd, hoping for the same outcome. I feel a part of something. From the middle of the fray, Toby's eyes find mine across the court. Just like how it felt with Veronica earlier, as he smiles and thumps his fist in the air, I feel sure he wants me to be here.

march

I'm walled in shoulder to shoulder in the queue to the club, Toby behind me, the girls flanking me, Keith on the outskirts. Am I the drunkest again? Is that why I'm in the middle?

I love it when the whole house is out. We're coming up on three weeks since I moved in but it feels like these were never not my people.

Finally, the front.

'Five of us.' Toby. His hand resting in the scoop of my back just above my bum. The closeness between me and him came fast, magnetically so, but I still find moments when he touches me confusing, conflicting with the amount of time he spends with Bella.

After showing the bouncer our IDs, we careen into the club, the others in front, my skin alight when his fingers touch where my top's come untucked from my skirt at the back to steady me. Veronica spins, walking backwards down the black, drapey corridor to the main part of the club, Nairong trailing her hand along the wall, Keith between them.

We spill through the door at the end of the corridor and the room shakes with reverberating bass.

Drunk Veronica wastes no time and leans into Toby, shouting loud so I hear. 'What's going on with Bella then?'

'Nothing.' Defensive, retreating, his back against the sweating wall.

I fall into a chair beside them, gaping up. Definitely the drunkest.

'We're getting drinks.' Keith gestures to the bar.

Nai smooths my curls off my forehead. 'I'll get you a water.'

I nod, smile gingerly. Look back up. Veronica's anger is tender; she's frustrated with Toby, who I've come to learn is her best friend in the world, even if she hasn't noticed it yet.

'No, not nothing. Who hangs out with their ex on the weekly? Why don't you just admit you're back together. I can go back to pretending I don't hate her, I really can, I just don't like to be lied to or seeing my friends get hurt.'

Toby folds his arms. 'Why are you so mad about this?'

'Because.' Veronica flutters her strip lashes toward me, coming unstuck. I open my mouth to tell her there's lash glue in my bag when she says, 'I think you can do better.'

'*Stop*,' I mouth.

My face flushes. Is it that obvious I like him, can't stop liking him, no matter how many times I try to talk sense into myself, or how often I bump into Bella coming out of his room?

'Bella's a friend, Veronica. And even if she wasn't, like this is how I'd wanna tell you we were back together.' Toby propels himself off the wall, pressing into the bodies packing the dance floor just as Nairong appears with bottled water.

I get out my phone for something to focus on as the room blurs.

00:59

Nolan How's your night going??

Sydney I kne w tequila was a bad. Idea ffs

The next day, I trudge down to the kitchen in my dressing gown as soon as I wake up, hoping to bump into Toby before his game. My memories from the club are hazy. I fell asleep in the Uber, so I'm not sure how he and Veronica left things. But I want to apologise for being a mess. He stayed sober because he's playing today, and I hate that he probably felt responsible for me. I can't believe he willingly let us drag him out last night anyway.

Me, Nai, and Veronica were already out, but we wanted to make it a whole-house thing. Toby and Keith met us at the bar we were in, then around midnight a round of tequila shots showed up at our table that nobody would admit to ordering. Someone suggested the club, and the rest is a bad headache.

In the hallway, Veronica's hobbling about with one shoe on, searching through the chaos of the shared rack for the other.

She sees me, and a smile lights then leaves her face so fast it's a strobe effect. 'You're up early.'

'So are you,' I say through a yawn.

'Why'd you delete your Story? I loved that photo of us.'

I slump, not wanting to admit the nastiness of what I did. 'I literally told my friend yesterday morning I couldn't meet up with her because I had to do coursework.' Sliding my hands up into my hair, I let my fingers drag the skin of my face taut. 'I feel so bad, I haven't seen her in ages. I just— I don't know why I'm avoiding her.' I do, but I won't admit how sabotaging I've let my envy of Freya's weight loss become. Least of all to Veronica. It's not like I'm even in that headspace anymore, of wanting to change. Instead, I'm trying to accept myself, to reach a point where I feel neutral about my body. And I'm getting there, slowly. Over the last few weeks, I've gotten to a place where I'm not meal skipping, or routinely weighing myself, and I have more good days than bad on the body-checking front. It's probably irrational, but I'm afraid that seeing Freya will send me spiralling right back into my old restrictive habits again. 'Anyway, where are you going? No hangover?'

'Yeah, I'm dying inside,' Veronica monotones. 'I'm supposed to be on my way to sweat the vodka out of my system but—' She waggles her socked foot at me. 'Also, don't be a mean girl. Be honest with your friend. And send me that pic, please.'

My stomach sours imagining Freya's face as she noticed my haloed profile picture at the top of her screen. Flicking through my Story that wasn't uploaded from my bedroom surrounded by stacks of books while I studied, but *out* out. I picture her thumb holding my selfie in place as I smiled, drunk, clutching another friend when I told Freya I couldn't see her, realising that in actuality I just didn't want to.

I refresh my profile now, reassuring myself it's gone. I consider texting her to clear the air, but cringe at the thought of acknowledging it. I *will* text her, today. I'm feeling better about myself mentally, so I need to have faith that when I see Freya, the progress I've made with my own body image will translate into good feelings about her too.

'I'll send it now,' I say, scrolling through my camera roll from last night. Veronica convinced me to pose for a full-body, and I don't ... *hate* it. We look so happy, it's hard to conjure up any feelings of negativity when we're smiling like that. Which is how I've felt ever since moving in here to be honest. I pocket my phone, properly taking in what Veronica's wearing. 'Sorry, *where* are you going?' I ask again.

Her outfit's screaming nineties rave X Gymshark, with her lime-green cycling shorts and neon-pink sports bra.

'Aha,' she says, shoving her foot into her found shoe. 'Thanks for all your help, by the way.'

I laugh, rubbing my eyes. 'Sorry. I am struggling today. And like, is where you're going a secret, or?'

'Sorry, I was a little distracted by my one-man search for my other shoe, bitch.' I crease up, hinging forward giddily. 'I'm going to a dancercise class at this wellness centre in Clifton.' She stands up, planting her hands on her hips. 'After putting myself through years of being stared at as the fattest girl in the gym, I vowed that the only exercise I'd ever do again would be the kind where I could throw it back to Beyoncé – hey, you should come!'

'Oh, I don't know.'

'I do. You'll love it, Saff. *Please*. But be ready in, like, thirty seconds.'

'There's absolutely no way that can happen. Don't look at me like that, I'll come next time,' I say, having no intention of actually going. 'Maybe.'

'I'm holding you to it.' Grinning, she thrusts a pointed finger out at me, backing up towards the door. 'See you later.'

'Bye. Oh, yeah,' I remember. 'The tequila shots last night. You, right?'

'Yeah,' she says, shrugging matter-of-factly.

'Thought so.'

Once Veronica leaves, I make myself a cup of tea, trying not to be disappointed it looks like I've missed Toby.

Since moving in, mid-mornings have offered up this spoonful of time where it's usually just us. Now that I'm actively participating in my course and going on to campus on Tuesdays and Thursdays, I'm committing to doing all the reading. Which means I've had to drop some hours at work so I'm spending more time here.

Nairong's one of those astonishingly organised people who leaves for the gym at five and then heads straight to campus to settle in for the day. Keith's a serial alarm snoozer and always sleeps in. And Veronica is just *Everything Everywhere All at*

Once-ing life, so I never know her schedule. Today it's dancercise, yesterday it was plate throwing, tomorrow she could be abseiling the suspension bridge.

But Toby, I always find him here around 9 a.m., methodically planning his meals for the day. Filling the compartments of his lunch box, blending a smoothie, chopping vegetables for the slow cooker to work on while he's gone. I usually sit on this counter, sipping my tea, and we talk. Occasionally he offers me a taste of what he's making. A glass of pulped pears and greens, almond butter and banana on rye. And my mouth moves comfortably, finding words with ease. I don't feel threatened by food anymore, wary of its nutritional value to me.

It's made me realise I have a lot of healing to do. Though I'm not sure where to start. So much of the information I've been fed about cooking and meal prep has been poisoned by diet culture.

And I'm not just talking food morality – simply that there are good foods and bad foods – I'm up against undoing the idea that all consumption is something to be feared. Because I ate so much of that belief system *up*. Feasted on it. From movies, from Mum, the magazines she always left lying around, from conversations with more or less every woman I've ever known, and near enough every minute of media I've ever consumed. But at the time it tasted sweet. Aspartame. Sucralose. Thin was morally superior and it was OK to want that.

I'm not sure how to rid this ideology from my system for good, or if I ever will. But sharing my mornings with Toby is helping. Sometimes I think he likes me too, as he brings a teaspoon to my lips for me to taste the pepperpot stew he's made. But then the phone will ring and it'll be Bella. Always Bella.

My phone buzzes now.

Toby

Missed you tryna get in on my snacks this morning ha. Hope you slept good.

Saffron

Liessss. You can admit you love showing off your food prowess in front of me, it's OK. I did miss my morning smoothie though ngl. What time did you leave?

Toby

Early. Well early for us. Was at gym for 7. Elijah, your predecessor, decided to spring a surprise flying visit on me, so I had to make time to chill with him today. Miss that guy

Toby

Also, smoothie in the fridge for you 😊

As I'm beaming at my phone, I hear footsteps on the stairs.

'Good morn.' It's Keith.

'Morning,' I say, and offer him a tea.

I pour the water as his bare feet pace the linoleum behind me.

'So, Poppy's your friend, right?'

'Yeah, we were at school together.' I turn, handing him a mug.

'What's her situation? I keep trying to see her again after, you know, whatever happened *happened* between us that night we had everyone over.' He's digging around in his pockets while he talks, dropping lighters and lint on to the worktop, his eyes roving the floor. 'But she's always busy or leaving me on read. Like, we made plans, and she was talking like she really wanted to do something again. I don't get it.'

I sigh and Keith's face drops. 'I can't speak for her, but I think her actions do. I don't think she wants anything serious, Keith. I'm sorry she gave you that impression.'

'Ah. One of them ones, is it? OK. Well, thanks for being honest.' His hands move mechanically as he starts to roll a smoke. I try to catch his eyes, but he just raises his brows at me like a nod, signalling he doesn't want to talk anymore.

'OK, well, I need to get ready for work.' I back up, fearing a *nice guys finish last* sentiment coming, and I don't want a reason to dislike Keith. I head for the door, calling, 'I'll see you later,' over my shoulder.

Somehow late again, I take the stairs two at a time, but pause to reply to Toby.

Saffron

Thank you for the smoothie! That is so kind wtf.
Why do you take better care of me than me??

I run up Gloucester Road until my lungs can't squeeze back breath anymore, bare-faced and still in my comfy clothes. I was supposed

139

to be front of house, ready to take my first order one minute ago. With no time for breakfast – which I now understand truly is the most important meal of the day – I'm gulping back the smoothie Toby made me from my travel cup. If I'm remembering right, it's made with chia, flaxseed, hemp, an avocado, and banana, ingredients that taste wholesomely sweet, and that will energise and keep me full. Not a combination of artificial flavourings and chemicals that drain me and make my stomach cramp, like those FastOff shakes I inflicted upon myself.

Doug's nowhere to be seen and Poppy's busy seating a table, so I sidle past to get changed into Jemima's hideous uniform: a shapeless, boxy yellow T-shirt and slouchy brown slacks. Quickly, I do my brows. As I pencil in an arch a bit too thick, I repeat the mantra, *sisters, not twins* and fight the urge to start over again. I mean, they're giving third cousins twice removed but OK, today we move with distantly related brows, there's no time to redo.

Do not love when my brows are lacking though.

When my phone goes off in my pocket, I fully expect it to be Doug, telling me my lateness is coming off my break time, but it's not. It's the kind of quiet, considerate 'thinking of you' message I haven't received since the early days with Jack.

Nolan Hope you had a good night last night, and aren't too hungover for your shift today lol. Remember WWRGD

Nolan And we know Rachel Green would do the bare minimum but look hot doing it

I smile, though the familiarity he has with my real likes and dislikes, and even my work schedule, makes me lower my phone in a moment of unbearably stark clarity.

What am I doing? What the fuck am I doing playing around with this shit? I have *no idea* who this person really is. They could be a serial killer, or a Trump supporter. Where's MTV? Come with the cameras and find me out, put a stop to all this delusion.

'Saffron, where are you?' Doug calls from up front. 'Customer.'

'Coming! Sorry,' I shout back.

I grab an apron from the peg and then immediately collide with Poppy in the hall on her way out of the stockroom, head bent over her phone.

'You! You're here.' She drops her phone into the pocket of her apron and links her arm through mine, her blonde hair thrown up in an annoyingly perfect yet messy high ponytail.

'Who're you texting? Keith?' I ask.

'No, should I be?' Remembering how crushed he looked this morning, I want to say, yes, give the boy some closure, but I've got to get through the rest of the shift with her, so I just shrug. 'I'm actually chatting to this girl I met on Instagram, Lola Rae. She's *verified*. And she shared one of my leg day workouts. Got nearly 250k views.' Poppy flashes her screen at me and I see a blur of tanned, blonde gym thirst traps. It could've been this girl, Lola, but I also could've been looking at Poppy's own profile, the content is so similar.

'Oh, nice.' I glance sideways at her. I'm genuinely at a loss for words. It's been a while since we've seen each other, and how little I cared about everything she just said was jarring.

'Ladies.' Doug nods as we approach the bar. Arms folded, he bulks himself up and refuses to make way for us, so one way or another some part of us is going to have to brush past him. He's naturally broad, someone who would've been encouraged to play rugby at school but has become more of a spectator than a participant since his teenage years, developing a hard barrel of a beer belly. My eyes stray to the yawning gaps between his shirt buttons. Isn't it mad that we don't hold men to the same standard of thinness as women? Sure, there're gym bros gloating about their gains on Instagram, but I never saw a man on the Special K cereal box, or in the before and afters on SlimIt magazine covers. And I've never seen the internet flooded with applauding think pieces written about fatter male characters paired with thinner women, like how everyone swooned over Penelope Bridgerton's 'mixed-weight relationship' (hideous). Because we see bigger men with skinny women all the time on screen. Even in fiction, men don't get held to the same standards as us. 'I'll be in the back doing rotas and emails as it's so quiet,' Doug says, bouncing his phone on the flat of his palm. 'I'm trusting you two with the floor, alright?'

He might as well have said you four because he was blatantly addressing our boobs.

'Cool,' I say, both of us shaking our heads as he walks out of sight. 'Freak,' I murmur at the same time Poppy whispers, 'Pervert.'

Our eyes catch, and just as I open my mouth, about to ask,

Coffee? Poppy twists loose the portafilter from the machine and bangs out the used grinds. 'Are you allowed milk today or are we being mean to ourselves?'

I frown at her judginess. 'Just black, please. What?' I say as she glares at me, pretending to be pissed. 'I like it black.'

After she makes it, I take a sip to prove it, but as I swallow its acrid bitterness, I realise I don't. Did I ever? Or was taking my coffee black another one of those small but insidious sacrifices my brain was propagandised into thinking I wanted. The sachets of 'skinny' coffee by the kettle, the watery, zero-fat milk in the fridge that made cereal taste like cement.

Without saying anything, I take the carton of oat milk from underneath the bar and top up my mug.

'See—' Poppy's about to smug it up when the girl sat at our only table clears her throat.

'Can we order drinks, please?' she says, pointedly placing her menu down, her voice echoey in the empty café.

'Sure.' I grab a notepad off the side and approach the couple sitting at the table in the window, looking all romanticised against the rain-streaked glass. 'What can I get you?' I say, glancing up.

They let go of each other's hands as the guy flicks a curtain of dirty-blond hair off his face, and shit – it's Tom. Freya's Tom. Tom, who I've never officially met but of course have exchanged hundreds of messages about while he's been dating Freya, whose photos I dissected in the group chat when she said she'd met someone at work. I know next to nothing about him, except that he has a six-pack, a penchant for taking post-shower thirst traps, and an inactive Facebook account from 2019.

He meets my eye, furrowing his brow. Surely, he must recognise me too, from tagged photos, from the collage of photos Freya's had on her wall since school.

Do I say hi?

'I'll have a skinny chai latte,' the girl says, 'some water for the table and, babe?'

Babe?

Wait, they were just holding hands, weren't they? Is he—

'Are you—' I cut myself off. If this is what I think it is, then this is Freya's confrontation to have. 'Ready? To order?'

The girl flips her sleek hair over her shoulder. I feel her gaze feather up and down my body in this sack of a uniform that sags and clings in all the wrong places.

She looks between us. 'Tom?' she says, her lips jammy with a thick layer of gloss.

'Uh, I'll have the bush tea, please.' Nodding, he pulls a tight smile at me. 'Alright?'

Is he saying alright, as in hi, admitting he knows who I am? While he's on a date? Being served by his *fiancée's* best friend.

'Yeah?' I say, caught way the hell off guard. 'You?'

Confused, he gathers the menus and hands them to me. 'Yes. That's it. Just drinks.'

Weaving through the tables back to the bar, my shoulders sag with guilt. Because what kind of reaction to getting caught *cheating* was that? Nonchalant and unbothered, taking his side piece out for brunch on a Wednesday. He clearly didn't know who I was. I know there's more at stake here, but did Freya take the photo booth strips of us off her mirror? Tear down her collage? I knew she wiped all photographic evidence of her size sixteen self from her socials, but if she's gotten rid of the physical photos now too, that means every photo of us is gone.

Her fiancé doesn't even realise I've caught him cheating on her because he doesn't know who I am.

I'm sad at how far I've let us fall out of each other's lives, our friendship only tethered by likes and message reacts, the elusive, ever-moving suggestion of meeting up, and moments our phones tell us we should be reminiscing about through slideshows soundtracked with sombre piano music. *Freya Spring–Summer 2022.* I mean, how can I have not met the man one of my oldest friends has – maddeningly – chosen to marry? We've been lulled into a false sense of intimacy by social media.

After tapping their order into the till, I beckon Poppy into the short walkway between the bar and the kitchen and catch her up.

'*What?*' she says, pulling her phone out of her apron. 'Oh my God, that *dick*head. This was her Story literally a few hours ago.' She shows me her screen, a photo of Freya and Tom's entangled legs lying in bed, hers draped over his, a tented book on the duvet, a mug of coffee in his lap. *Morning cuddles with this one.* 'Poor Frey.'

I stare at the phone, shaking my head. 'Men are wild. How do you go from pure domesticity and sharing a cafetière and shit, to immediately taking another girl out for coffee? Side note, the man needs to watch his caffeine intake,' I joke. Poppy giggles, telling me to shut up. 'And it was definitely a date, she *babed* him. You've met him before, right?'

'Once. When Frey's parents were in Spain and she had a party. You said you were ill.'

'I *was* ill.'

I wasn't. I saw what I looked like from the back and decided not to go.

'But apparently I was so drunk, I tried to show him my surgical scars.'

'Surgical scars,' I scoff. 'So, your boobs then?' Poppy runs her tongue over her top teeth, flipping her middle finger up at me. 'Shit, you'd better do their drinks,' I say.

'Shall I spit in it—'

'—Don't spit in it,' we say at the same time.

Drumming my nails against the till, I watch Poppy froth the milk for the girl's chai latte.

'We need to tell Freya,' I say in her ear, using the blare of the machine to disguise my voice. Pop nods emphatically. My instinct says immediately, but also that this isn't the kind of news you want delivered over text. 'In person.'

'Yeah,' Pop says in a way that sounds like she really means *Obviously*. She places their drinks on a tray, and I go over, setting them down on the table, getting nothing but a mumbled thank you.

Back behind the bar, I nearly trip over Poppy, crouched on the grimy floor, thumbs scrabbling over her phone screen. She tugs my trouser leg and I duck down with her, glasses tinkling as my bum knocks the shelves. Gesturing for me to get out my phone, she taps send and my apron vibrates.

Poppy

Are you free tonight??

I nod and she starts frantically typing to me again.

Poppy

Shall I send her this – Hey babe, how are you! Me and Saff on shift together today and decided last minute to go for drinks tonight and it's been TOO LONG since the three of us have been out!! Won't be the same without you! Can you come? xxxxx

Saffron

Yeah but the kisses are excessive, she'll think something is wrong

Poppy rolls her eyes, but backspaces on the kisses and sends it to our neglected group chat. In less than a minute, Freya's eager reply comes through, and I'm swamped by guilt yet again.

Freya

Ahhh yes! Tell me when and where and I'll be there, cannot wait!

Freya

Jeans and a nice top vibes?? Xx

'Always,' Pop says out loud.

As the cafe winds down for closing, me and Poppy end up getting cut at the same time. We agree to go home, change, and meet at the bar fifteen minutes before we told Freya to arrive, so we can work out how to break it to her.

Makeup and hair done, I've only left about ten minutes to pick an outfit, and I'm stressing. I'm standing in front of my wardrobe in my bra and pants when someone knocks at my door.

'Can I come in?' It's Veronica. I hesitate, arms instinctively folding in front of my belly. But it's *Veronica*; if I can't be in my underwear in front of her, how will I ever wear a bikini on the beach in this body? I open the door, backing away shyly as she takes me in from the shoulders up. 'Ooh, you look so pretty! How did you do that to your face, you're an artist. Shut your eyes.' I close them, smiling my head off. 'You need to show me how to do eyeshadow like that.' Veronica sprawls on my bed, licking cheese dust from her fingers, an open packet of crisps in her other hand. 'So, what are we wearing? Where are we going? And by we, I mean you. I'm just killing time 'til my pizza arrives.'

I fill her in on today's scandal at work and mine and Pop's plan to expose Tom's cheating to Freya tonight.

She gasps, scrunching her packet of cheese balls. 'Pure goss.

I love drama I'm not in any way associated with. OK, show me the outfit.'

'It hasn't exactly materialised as of yet. I want to go for something like this,' I say, grabbing my phone from where it's on charge. I show her the Get Ready with Me for Drinks with the Girls video Imogen Shawcross posted the other week, showcasing a bunch of outfit ideas of the jeans-and-a-nice-top variety. I hold up my one pair of tapered jeans. 'Here's the jeans, sans nice top. It has become apparent I don't own a nice top.'

'OK.' Veronica takes my phone, watches the video again. 'I see your jeans – your very cute jeans, and I'll raise you— One sec.' Scrambling off the bed, I hear her bombing it down to the next floor, and in thirty seconds she's back and holding out a dress to me. 'One black sequinned bodycon.'

I recoil, the material twinkling in her hand. 'Nope. No way.'

'Try it on.' She shakes it at me. 'Try ittt.'

I huff and grumble, hoicking it up over my body, but when Veronica spins me to face the mirror, my resistance immediately falls away.

'I look . . .'

I can't say it yet, so she says it for me. 'Beautiful.'

The dress looks like star-flecked charcoal, hugging mid-thigh, slinking over my hips and waist, not cinching it in but holding the shape of me just so. I never would've dared to think my body belonged in a dress like this, but I feel like it was made for me. It doesn't hide or billow, swamp or cover. It only adorns what's already there.

I twirl, peering at myself from all angles.

'Wait, wait, I have an idea.' Using a star-shaped spot sticker on the outer corner of each eye, I stencil over it with a silver glitter shadow, leaving a shimmery star outline on my lids.

'Love. It,' Veronica says.

'Thank you.' I hug her tightly. 'Thanks for making me put this on.'

She looks me up and down, beaming. 'Jeans, nice top who?' I shush her, laughing, my eyes straying back to myself in the mirror. 'I fixed your feed, by the way. Your fat fashion girlie representation was weak, near non-existent actually.'

'When, you sneak? What did you do?'

'When you were pretending you didn't wanna try on the dress. I injected a little body diversity into your phone, followed a few accounts I love that help give me ideas to dress *this* body, instead of making me wish I had theirs. At least, that's how I used to feel when I solely followed people like Imogen Shawcross. Bless her. You were off to a good start with Bliss Adeyemi but your algorithm was *thirsty* for relatable content. Check out posibodybecky, she does a bit of fashion stuff, but she mostly posts about intuitive eating. I think you'll ... connect with it,' she says pointedly. 'And Heather Kellogg is *hilarious*, you need to watch her *shit people say to fat girls* series.'

'Right.' I smile down at my phone as Veronica hands it back to me, open on the profile of a user named @kelloggsforbrekkie. I double tap her latest post, a photo of her posing in her bra, showcasing her latest tattoo, a snake winding all the way across her rolly stomach. Then I gasp noticing the time. 'Seriously, thank you – for all of that – but I should've been gone six minutes ago.'

I shove my boots and coat on and hug her again.

'The dress, watch the dress!' she says, splaying her orange-tinged fingers out and away from me.

We say goodbye and then I'm down the first set of stairs, twisting round the banister and—

'Whoa, whoa.' Toby's hands hold me in place, after catching me about to collide with him.

'Shit, sorry,' I say, as we sidestep round each other. 'I took too long getting ready and now I'm so late!'

'Well, it was worth it.' He says it fast, without thinking, and I catch his gaze wandering down the length of the dress. He shakes himself, hitches the strap of his gym bag higher up his shoulder. 'You look incredible. *Incredible*,' he repeats, scoffing at himself. 'I mean, you look really nice – better than nice, ah—' He drops eye contact as his cheeks redden. 'Just have a good night, OK?'

My hand falls away from the banister, and all I can do is smile at him, hoping it radiates some of the gratitude I feel glowing on the inside.

'Night,' I say, as Toby retreats into his bedroom.

As soon as he's out of sight, I descend the rest of the stairs two at a time and I'm out the front door, out into the world, feeling naked but clothed, wearing a *bodycon* dress.

The bar Poppy picked is in a listed building, themed like a gentlemen's club. The ceilings are arched, high, and swirled with Renaissance paintings, the décor all polished mahogany and fringed table lamps. I'd be lying if I said I didn't feel a bit Hollywood slinking through in my shimmering dress. Confident, even. I'm about to sit on one of the stools by the bar to wait for Poppy when my eye follows a waiter carrying two drinks on a tray to a table in the back corner. She's already here, sitting with someone in a backless top, the neat ends of a bob just brushing their slender shoulders. As I approach, I hear Poppy thank the waiter, and then I see her see me, her eyes popping wide.

'Oh my God, what are you wearing? What happened to jeans and a nice top?' she says. Stopped cold in the middle of taking my coat off, I shrug it back on to my shoulders and take the seat between Poppy and her friend, tucking myself away under the table. I guess she's shocked because she never sees me in anything other than loungewear or our uniform these days, but damn, that stings, and Poppy knows it. 'Sorry.' She touches my hand. 'It's just so not you, but like in the best way. You look great.'

If her gut reaction to seeing me in a bodycon was to baulk at me, what must everybody else be thinking? It's like all those positive affirmations I felt looking into the mirror with Veronica didn't travel with me into the real world. Or they did, but vanished as soon as I was perceived.

'Literally glamorous.'

My head whips round. 'Frey!' She's the other girl I didn't recognise from behind. 'It's you, I didn't even realise – oh my God, you cut your hair.'

As we get up and embrace, I notice how I seem to be mostly

152

holding my own arms. Freya's body is birdlike against the trunk of me. She's even skinnier than before, practically unrecognisable. I'm both relieved and saddened that seeing this version of Freya doesn't feel anything like I feared it would though. I'm not burning with jealousy, bitter that she fits the body standard and I don't. Mostly, I'm upset at how different she looks – the hair, the muscle definition, the *ring* on her finger I haven't seen up close yet – all of it signifying how long it's been since we last saw each other.

'I'm so happy to see you,' she says.

'Me too! And you're so tiny, you look amazing,' I say. Because she does. Her outfit falls effortlessly in all the right places, her figure sleek and hard like that of a mannequin, maybe as small as a size six now. I almost forget the reason we're here and go to reel off a list of catch-up questions. *How's your mum? How's work? Is your supervisor still a massive twat?* But then I take in the crumpled napkins in front of her, the watery smear of mascara under her eyes. 'Wait, why are you crying?'

She lets out a harsh laugh, strangled by a sob. 'You know why I'm crying.'

I shake my head questioningly at Poppy. 'You told her without me?'

'Well, you were late. I couldn't sit here and make small talk knowing what I knew.'

'Not even for ten minutes, it was eating you up that bad?'

'What do you want me to say, Saff? I'm an empath.'

The way I roll my eyes all the way into the back of my head. 'OK, Miss Empath,' I mutter.

'Anyway.' Freya sniffs, squeezing my hand. The bangles on her arm sink to her wrist. 'I do know now and even though on the inside I'm freaking out and want to cry and cry my eyes out, at least I know. This could've carried on for months if you guys hadn't caught him.'

'For real, that would've been crazy, 'cus who knows how long he's been at it already,' I say, realising I should shut up. I take a sip of Poppy's espresso martini to do something with my hands. 'Don't feel like you have to stay out, Frey. If you need to be alone, go home—'

'No way. I'm OK. Or I'm not, but I will be. I'm not letting Tom ruin the first time I've seen my besties in forever.' I can't help but exchange a guilty glance with Poppy. It's not just Freya's appearance that's changed, she's acting different too. Her Swiftie, golden retriever energy has gone, an energy that was once infectious. We were always fitfully giggly when we were together. She seems older, worn out by an adult kind of tired. Maybe it's the bob, or working nine to five, or the engagement. All I know is I'm glad to have her back in my life again, even if this feels like a reintroduction. I've missed how being around her feels like you always have someone rooting for you – that's still there. Elbows on the table, she smooths her hair behind her ears. 'Plus, I think I'm numb, you know. It hasn't sunk in yet, and the longer I can distract myself from the reality that Tom's met someone else the better.'

'Get that,' I say.

'Totally.' Poppy nods. 'Whatever you need.'

Freya presses the backs of her wrists to her eyes and gives us a wobbly smile. 'Drinks?'

It happened again.

One minute me and Pop are sharing a bottle of wine, the next it's sambuca shots and standing in line to get into some club where the DJ's butchering noughties anthems with house remixes. I noticed Freya nursing the same watery Diet Coke the whole time we were at the first bar, and thought about telling her it's OK to let loose, that if she's holding back because she's worried she'll end up calling Tom, I'll confiscate her phone. But I thought better of it. I don't think she wants us to know how cut up she is, and Freya's a sad drunk, like, been known to cry at missing-cat posters kind of drunk.

Inside, it becomes obvious Poppy's had way more to drink than either of us when she makes a show of stripping her jacket off at the cloakroom, and nasally singing the opening bars of 'Man! I Feel Like a Woman!' Then she promptly turns and rolls her ankle at the top of the of stairs leading to the dance floor. Freya and I catch her by either elbow, glancing at each other as she dissolves into giggles.

'Jesus, Pop. How hard did you pre-drink?' I shout over the music, hoisting her up.

'Maybe, sorta, might've been on a date before, OK?' As we amble arm in arm down the rest of the stairs, she must feel vulnerable, embarrassed about us having to help her walk. Before I can ask her how the date went she heaves her chest up and boasts, 'Lola says she's gonna make my glutes workout go viral, you know, and then I'll be famous and *then* who'll you be to judge me? I've handed my notice in at Jemima's. No more dodging stares from Desperate Doug. I'm gonna put my all into my fitness content, it'll be the first step towards opening up the gym. Lola's going to help me.'

'I'm not judging you, Pop. Sorry.' I know I didn't do anything wrong, but I want to keep the peace. I don't want our first night out with Freya in months to be cut short. 'But wow, you're quitting Jemima's?'

'Yep.' She wrestles her elbow out of my grip.

'Right.' I thought I'd feel sad when me and Poppy eventually stopped working together, but is it bad I'm a little . . . relieved? It's hard forcing things to talk about with someone you see weekly but have decreasingly little in common with. Maybe more time apart is the thing our friendship needs. 'Where'd that come from? And who's Lola again?'

'Lola *Rae*. My verified friend from Instagram. I'm gonna go up to London and see her.'

'That'll be nice,' Freya says, biting back a smile at Poppy's pouty behaviour.

'Waitressing was only getting in the way of my real dreams, you know.'

'Right,' I say again. '*I'm gonna get her some water*,' I mouth at Freya, who nods, struggling to steer Poppy toward a table.

The bar's packed. I mould my body against the crush of people waiting and reach for my phone out of habit. But I'm too tipsy and distracted by my surroundings to reply to the message Nolan just sent.

Nolan How was work? What you getting up to tonight?

After about five minutes of mindless scrolling and not moving any closer, I angle my path toward the bartender on the left side, who seems to be thinning the crowd faster than the other two servers. A couple of women wearing jackets emblazoned with 'Pink Ladies' decide to ditch the line, and I rush into the gap they leave in front of me. Somebody else has the same idea, and I end up wedged shoulder to shoulder with this boy who's wearing the same cologne Jack used to wear. The Dior one, fresh and peppery. He's Black, darker skinned than Mum, with a headful of thick twists, set in curtains that fall just past his ears. Side-eyeing me, he catches me staring at him and smiles wide.

He leans close, tucking my hair behind my ear to speak into it. 'Wanna make a deal?' His proximity ramps up my heart rate.

'What kind of deal?' I say, the sambuca shot from the last bar hitting me right on time. I remember the dress I'm wearing and let the crowd push us closer together, forgetting about my hopeless crush on Toby and my unworkable relationship with Nolan. Instead, I focus on this boy right in front of me with the deepest brown eyes I've ever looked into.

'You get to the front before me?' he says. 'And you tell the guy to serve your friend next.'

'Who's my friend?' I ask coyly.

'Me.'

His grin smooths out as he takes me in. All of me. As his gaze slips down my body, the combination of the dress and the alcohol make me bask in his perception, knowing he's seeing me the way I saw myself in the mirror earlier. I feel self-assured, finally on the receiving end of that wanting look I always see cast over Poppy. I forget about her shitty reaction to the dress and instead focus on the one that matters. His. *Mine*.

Then he does that thing, pointedly looking from my eyes to my lips.

'I don't know,' I say, doing it too. 'I've got pretty high standards.'

'Who are you here with?'

'My friends. Over there somewhere.' I turn to look for them, but all I see is the scrum of people behind us, my vision bleary from the sambuca and the strobe lights. The boy steadies me as I sway off balance, and his beautiful face comes looming into focus again. I don't even know his name. 'What's your—'

'What can I get you?' It's finally my turn and the bartender's desperate smile says, *Hurry the hell up*, so I tip myself over the bar to shout in his face for a water and a Diet Coke.

'Hey, can you serve my friend next?' Grinning, I look for the boy I was talking to, but he's been served by someone else, and is already tapping his card on the machine. 'Never mind.'

I watch as a red-faced boy comes up behind him and plants a thick pair of hands firmly on his shoulders.

'That'll be two seventy-five, please.'

I turn back to the bartender, pay, and catch the boy being led away by his friend, without even a glimpse over his shoulder to see if I'm still here. For a second, I'm gutted nothing happened, but as I walk through the crowd carrying the confidence his attention reminded me I should have, I'm beaming. I catch myself in the mirrored wall, and I swear, I almost don't recognise myself. I watch her, shining in her dress, walking with purpose to a throwback song the DJ says is by some girl called Liberty X. She's owning the room. She smiles like she knows how hot she is.

And that's *me*.

I love this dress, and I love this song, and I love my friends.

I spot the back of Freya's blunt bob over one of the booths lining the dance floor where the music isn't so loud, arriving at the same time as a waiter carrying a tray of Jägerbombs. Freya looks bored, practically falling asleep staring at her phone, and Poppy's draped over a boy in a bright blue Ralph Lauren polo, her arms wreathed round his neck. As she pulls back, I get a look at his face and my heart stutters.

Jack.

'Look who's home for a few days,' Poppy cries, gazing at him like she's starstruck.

I take in his stubble and the smattering of shit tattoos up his arm, adrenalin threatening to choke me.

'Looking good, Saffron,' he smirks, staring blatantly at the fit of my dress.

Does he think I look good? I don't know how to feel about that. What is he doing here? With her.

'Fuck off,' I mumble.

I slip into the booth beside Freya. Sitting across from Jack, I'm instantly transported back to how I felt skulking the school hallways when nobody knew we were together. Feeling invisible, his silence much louder than the insults his friends used to hurl at me.

'These aren't ours,' Freya's saying politely to the waiter, but Poppy pounces on the tray. 'How did you even order these?'

'There's an app.' I point to the QR code on the table, clenching my fist when I see my hand shaking.

Jack's mouth's moving over words, his eyes on mine.

'What?' I say. I feel *sick*.

'I said how's uni?'

'Good. Fine.'

It's been so long since I've been around both Jack and my friends at the same time, the whole-body lie I have to perform not to expose what we had has me twitchy. It's hard having to alter your body language, your eye contact, everything about how you interact with a person, so as not to betray how intimately you knew each other.

I could just tell them, could just blurt it out now. But I won't.

Poppy rambles on about the four of us doing this more often, not getting a read on the room at all. Jack's been watching me the whole time. And under his stare, I realise *why* I still feel the need to lie for him. For some fucked-up reason his opinion of me still holds weight with my self-worth. If I confessed our relationship right now, to hear him deny that it happened or that it all meant nothing to him would break me. Me keeping his secret is me still desperate to believe that everything he said about me when we were together could be true.

I *want* to out him, to scream about his weird little mole and the *Wreck-It Ralph* figurines he has on his windowsill, but my jaw feels wired shut.

Again, I wonder what's going on, why he's suddenly here with Poppy. I scan the room, looking for people he might be with, but don't see anybody, so I doubt it's a coincidence he just happened to be here and they ran into each other. Is this who she was on her date with earlier? My eyes prick with tears. I never told her anything about me and Jack, so she doesn't owe me anything, there's no girl code to break, but it hurts all the same.

'You look good, doesn't he look good? Not you, Freya, I know he's your cousin, but—' I stop listening. Poppy places her hand on his chest, and I know what's coming. 'Here. You're welcome.' She slides two shots across the table in our direction. Freya's eyes widen, hiding a yawn behind the back of her hand. 'To old friends,' Poppy says, clinking her glass against Jack's, 'and missed opportunities.'

I feel frozen, watching everything unfold in a paralytic state.

'Your mum didn't say you were coming home,' I register Freya saying.

But they ignore her. I watch in horror as something unspoken passes between Poppy and Jack and their mouths suction together. She kisses him, sloppily and hungrily, while my heart cracks.

She peels apart from him to sink one of the shots, but by the time she's bringing her head back down, she's already spluttering it back up, followed by a spume of bile down the front of her top. Revoltingly, Jack laughs, and then everything happens on fast-forward. In a second, I'm up, yanking him out of his seat by his shirt.

'Get the fuck out of here.' I shove his chest, forcing all my pain into it, not caring if Poppy and Freya are watching.

He staggers back. 'That's not a very mature way to treat your ex, is it?' he says, low enough so only I can hear over the music. Spinelessly, he leaves, prowling back to whatever corner of the club he came from. I take his place, shielding Poppy from view as I rub her back.

Freya leans across the table, helping her take sips of water. 'I'm gonna get her in a taxi, make sure she gets home,' she says before I can.

It makes sense Freya takes her because Wilder Street's in the opposite direction to Poppy's halls. I'm relieved because I still need to process seeing her all over Jack, and I don't trust myself not to say something I don't mean right now.

After they leave, I slump down into the booth and stare at the Jägerbombs, considering downing the five little plunge pools of amber. The moment I drink one, the boy with the twists appears by my side, his smile slung like a hammock.

'I was looking for you,' he says, his hand resting low on my hip and making his intentions clear. I wonder if he can feel me trembling. I turn my head, holding his gaze, trying to remember that I am wanted, I am desirable, exactly as I am. 'And now I've found you.'

I wordlessly hand him a shot and we throw them back.

We look at each other for a second and then he grips my jaw, his thumb gently opening my mouth as he puts his lips on mine. I push my tongue against his, tasting of the cinnamon liquorice of the Jäger. The kiss disintegrates every thought I have in my head about Jack and Poppy, and I melt into him.

'You OK?' He pulls back, maybe sensing my mind's a hot mess right now. In answer, I arch my hips into his and kiss him harder, our teeth accidentally clicking. 'Hey, what's your name?' he asks.

I stare at him, wanting so desperately to channel the girl I felt like earlier, sparkling and strutting and *wanting* people to look at me. But I'm still shaken from seeing Jack. Saffron's the girl you don't want your friends to know you've been sleeping with. And kissing this boy now feels like I'm out-of-body, pretending to be someone else, the lines only getting blurrier as those last two shots hit my bloodstream.

So, when he asks me again, 'Your name. What's your name?' it slips off my tongue so easily.

'*Sydney.*'

Because I don't feel like being Saffron right now, she overthinks everything and isn't confident or sexy. Sydney's a name, an idea I can embody just for tonight.

I squint one eye open, my head splitting, registering the itch of the sequins from the dress I slept in. A squeal from downstairs makes me flip on to my front. I'm not at the house, I'm home. *Home*, home, looking up at the ghoulish green of my glow-in-the-dark stars, listening to the patter and shriek of Rue running around downstairs. My room's been painted a frosty blue for her, and Otis has been exercising his fine art skills, a stencil of a fairy-tale castle on one wall, unfinished. I check my phone, confirm I drunkenly ordered an Uber to drop me here, and reply to worried texts from Freya and Veronica asking if I got home OK.

My stomach twists sick as last night comes back to me, and I relive the moment Jack and Poppy kissed. Briefly, I unblock Jack and stalk his recent posts. Close-ups of his clichéd tattoos, posing with his suitcase outside his dorm, captions that say he's missing his yellow lab back home. No mention of Poppy, no incriminating third-party tagged photos of them together. Not that she's done anything wrong; Poppy has every right to date Jack. But I wonder if she knew what he was really like, whether she'd still want to. Part of me wants to accept this as a subtle sign from the universe that it's OK to let our friendship go, but I can't sit back and let her get involved with someone like him. I get out my phone.

Saffron

Hey Pop. Hope you're not dying too hard today. I never want to see another espresso martini in my lifeee. But anyway, last night was . . . interesting! I don't know what's going on with you and Jack, but I'd feel like I was letting you down if I didn't say something. Are you sure this is what you want? To get involved with someone like him? He is a fuckboy through and through, you know this!! You remember the things he said to you in school, making fun of your boobs, and how he treated Ava Minchin in year 9, and god knows how he treated all the girls he was with that we didn't know about. I want you to be happy, I swear, and if that's with him OK . . . but I think you could be happier

As soon as I send it, I feel my muscles unwind. She'll get it. She'll see through his attempt at reinventing himself with the tattoos and the facial hair and remember what a dick he was.

Sipping the water on my bedside table, my lips feel tender and raw. I flash over how the night ended, kissing that boy at the back of the club. I check my contacts, friend requests, and new follows for any sign we exchanged details, but nothing. I don't think I even got his name, and if I did, I don't remember it.

Feeling deflated at the blunt full stop to anything happening there, I take the dress off and step out of it, leaving it glinting on the ground like a puddle of spilled moonlight.

My phone goes off and I hear Mum yell, 'It's me!' from the bath, her voice echoey against the tiles.

Mum

Morning hon . . . or should I say Good afternoon!!! Seeing as you're here, will you stay for dinner? I've met someone and I want you to meet him. No pressure though xxx

I roll my eyes so hard it throws my head back. I'm too tired and hungover for this shit. For another dead-ass dinner with a man she's known two minutes, destined to be deleted from her phone within the week. Ever since Mum lost the weight after Dad left, she's been rebounding her way round every middle-aged dating app available for download. And yes, five years later, it's still a rebound, because she hasn't sat with her loss long enough to process it. Instead, she's dressing it up as the unrealistic expectation that this next man's going to fill the hole that a husband of twenty years left.

Damn it, I have to stay, don't I?

After throwing an oversized T-shirt of Otis's over the cycling shorts I had on under my dress, I pad downstairs and push open the door to the living room. Rue sees me, her smile like a sunrise buttering an open field.

'Hello!' she says, jigging on the spot, her little socked feet shuffling against the carpet. 'Can we play waitress? I want to be Auntie Saffy again and you're the customer.'

I reach my hands out to my mini me. 'Anything you want.'

I haunt the house all day, smiling sleepily through drawing, hiding, and play pretending with Rue and Otis. Mum's out all day sourcing ingredients for tonight's dinner at shops with names like Seedling and Harvest.

At three, I video call with my tutor, Vanessa, for Modern Kinship and Belonging. I try my hardest to sound enthusiastic delivering proposals for the assessment coming up worth 50 per cent of our final grade, but it's just not there. I thought when I started to capital-P participate in my studies, I'd feel the same passion for my course I see fired up in Nairong about *constitutional law*, for God's sake. But the thought of committing five thousand words to the ethics of surrogacy, or a study on polygamous relationships, or even the rise of the matriarchal family structure fills me with dread. Sure, I'd watch a documentary on any of those subjects, popcorn in hand, but I don't feel compelled to make *my* opinions into several P.E.E. paragraphs.

And this is only year one. I'm expected to produce tens of thousands more words on social anthropological issues. I close my laptop and sit in silence, overcome with the sinking question of *What am I doing with my life?*

Drained, I take a nap, and at five I trudge to the corner shop to buy a carton of fresh orange juice because that's what my hangover is craving. The other day, I watched a video by one of the creators Veronica recommended, posibodybecky, titled **De-Demonising Sugar**. She talked about her own experience of fearing consuming sugary treats to the point of complete avoidance. I related *hard* as she confessed that every period of restriction would result in her bingeing an entire pack of biscuits, or half a cake, and then the cycle of shame and control would start all over again. It was only by leaning into eating intuitively and allowing herself to have these foods that her obsession over them levelled out. Eventually, she found she only wanted them in moderation anyway.

So, I guess if I want orange juice right now, I'm having orange juice.

Back home, I let myself in, nose wrinkling at the stench of boiled cabbage. Through the inside door's frosted pane, I watch Rue stretching on to her tiptoes to reach the handle. She cackles under her breath, surprised yet triumphant, when it snaps down and the door opens.

'You're back.'

'I am.' Otis appears behind her, holding a bundle of silverware, looking miserable. 'What is it?' I ask him as Rue skips off to the kitchen, a tea towel folded over her arm like she's working a Michelin-star gig.

But as I hear Rue ask, 'Can I get you another drink, *sir*?' I remember Mum's text and Otis's expression starts to make sense.

'Mum's friend's here?'

Otis nods, miming stabbing himself in the heart with his clutch of cutlery. 'I don't know if I can handle another *friend* dinner.'

'Who knows, maybe this guy might be the one,' I say sarcastically.

At this, Mum peers around the archway at the end of the hall. 'What are you two whispering about?' she says. 'Come here, I want you to meet someone.'

'Your table is ready.' Rue appears again, taking us both by the hand, and me and Otis look at each other with a dry sense of resignation.

I peer round Mum and take in the manboy sitting at the head of the table. He's wearing a suit that doesn't fit, and he still has his AirPods in. His hair's a quiff of oily black on top and a sharp fade round the sides. Very precise. But that suit, so loose and shabby, and a total mismatch to the manscaping. Make it make sense.

'This is Philippe,' Mum says, holding me by the shoulders.

168

'We met online, in the comments under an Eddie Abbew video.' She clears her throat, nearly shouting as she leans towards him. 'Saffron's here, Philippe.' When he holds up a finger, she taps her earhole, referring to the AirPod rudeness, and says, 'He's a businessman, always has about a thousand voice notes to listen to from the team.'

'Oh right.' My eyes cut to my brother. Otis ain't having it and neither am I.

Philippe places his phone face down as he gets up. 'Hello, Saffron. I am so pleased to meet with you,' he says, offering me a hand to shake. I grasp it, and with a thoughtful intake of breath he says, 'You know, I don't see it,' in what I realise is a French accent. He's gesturing between me and Mum, his wrist rolled, fingers curled towards the ceiling. 'You say she look like you, but not to me. And your figure, it is better. You –' he points to her, shrugs matter-of-factly – 'are beautiful.'

Too stunned to speak, I drop down into the chair next to Rue.

'Uh—' Mum's gagged, looking wordlessly from me to Philippe. For a second, I see her internally despairing that *this* is our introduction. Despite his obvious rebound status to us – to Mum, he's someone she really likes and wants our approval of. She regains composure. 'Now I know, I *know* you mean that as a compliment, Philippe, and that what you're saying ... what you're saying is that Saffron's beautiful in her own way. But you can't say shit like that. That was rude.' Mum blows a huff of air up into her red face. She palms back the flyaway hairs at her temples, following the grooves of her box braids twisted atop her head in a bun.

'Yes, Saffron is beautiful, of course,' Philippe says with a micro-nod, seemingly unbothered. 'With a mother like you, how could she not be? But she is not as lovely as you, *mon petit chou*. You say all the time that she look like you. I simply say, I don't see it.'

My mouth falls open.

The memory of how I felt yesterday, so insignificant as I watched Jack openly kiss Poppy, threatens to keep me quiet. But actually, I'm done with feeling like because my body takes up space on the outside, I should compensate for that by being small on the inside. Being fat shouldn't shrink me, or make people think that they can talk to me – talk *about* me, *in front of* me – however they want.

'Are you for real? Like, nice to meet you, bro, but what is wrong with you?' I say, not believing I've said it out loud until it registers on Philippe's ignorant face.

Otis scoffs, giving me a nod of approval, and Mum makes a clattering distraction of banging her stirring spoon against the pot.

Philippe grips his chin, sucking air through his teeth. 'Sorry, sorry. I say the wrong thing.'

'Yeah. You did.'

'OK, rewind.' Mum laughs nervously and tugs on one of the gold huggie earrings me and Otis bought her for Christmas, the other hand tracing her clavicle. This is how she self-soothes, giving herself little touches of reassurance. I give her what I hope looks like an encouraging smile, trying to communicate that I'm willing to start over, I don't want this to be hard for her. She exhales with a strained smile. 'I'm making pelau!'

'Are you? I would not have guessed that by the, um, smell,' Otis says.

'Well, it's a SlimItified pelau. Sugar-free and super green, cleansing and full of fibre.'

He gasps, fingers splayed against his chest. Because this is his kitchen really, we just microwave in it. When Otis cooks, the air is heavy with turmeric, cumin, and garam masala, lingering because he finds the extractor fan overstimulating, but filling the house with memories of Nana Cleo, whose Trini dishes of buljol, and saheena he's always trying to replicate. He's a *good* cook, natural with it, no measuring or recipe reading, it's all in his hands and on the tip of his taste buds.

'But the whole base is caramelised sugar.' Bereft, he sweeps himself up from the table and peers into the pot. He blinks, two, three times. 'You've done the art of Trini cuisine dirty, I fear. This is not pelau.'

Mum flushes as Otis drops some truths about the dangers of the Westernising effect in altering cultural cooking to adhere to diet culture rules. I tune out of his favourite TED Talk and get out my phone, eyeing Philippe. He's trained on his own screen again, not at all concerned with even giving off the pretence that he wants to get to know us.

No reply from Poppy to me warning her off Jack yet. But Instagram says she's online.

I fidget in my seat, uneasy as I read through a stack of unanswered messages Nolan sent last night, creeping into the early hours of this morning. The latest one, sent a few hours ago, reads,

Nolan Ah, I feel like I'm annoying you!

I recoil with guilt. Nolan didn't enter my mind once when I was out with Poppy and Freya, sipping, laughing, sparkling in my dress, or wrapped around the boy with the twists. Nolan, who's become my constant during these last few months of uncertainty, an ever-presence in my phone when I missed Mum and Otis, or heard the braying laugh of Bella coming from Toby's room. Always there, like a sentient Siri.

Somewhat apprehensive but wanting to reassure him, I reply,

Sydney Not at all! I was out, sorry. Dying today. Hope you didn't miss me toooo much. Looks like you had a late one though, what did you get up to?

Opening a message from Toby gets an utterly different response, however.

Toby

Hey, me and Nai had tickets to hate-watch the new Nick Cage film tomorrow night (not an ounce of hate from me tho, I've got all love for the Cage). But she just found out her mum's broken her ankle, so she's gone back home for a few days to visit. You up for it? Starts at 7.

Yes, yes, yesss. Longtime Nick Cage stan over here. Con
Air is unironically in my top 10!! Thanks for thinking of me!

I can't keep myself from grinning, but Otis doesn't notice as he
sits back down beside me, his face utterly grief-stricken watching
Mum ladle out her hotchpotch rice dish. Toby just invited me to
the cinema! He could've asked Veronica, or Keith, or *Bella*, but
he chose me.

Otis catches my eye and mouths, '*What the fuck?*' nutting his
head toward Philippe, who still hasn't looked up from his phone.

'*The AirPods never came out*,' I mouth back, which sends us
into soundless hysterics.

I stare intently at the food as Mum serves us each a bowl of pre-
portioned pelau. Having dinner with my housemates nearly every
night since I moved in, I thought I'd be over my fear of eating in
front of people, but I'm getting major fat girl anxiety. Probably due
to Philippe's comments and Mum's insistence on stripping the pelau
of its essential syrupy base. She doesn't seem to know I haven't been
back to another SlimIt meeting since February, and if she does,
she hasn't mentioned it. Shoutout to Cathy for the confidentiality.
I take a deep breath, refusing to spiral here, and remember how
far I've come. I want to show Mum I'm learning to love eating for
nourishment. I take a piece of sourdough bread and butter it.

'Thanks, Mum,' I say, smiling as she watches me chew a big
hunk, her lips pursed.

'Yeah, thanks,' Otis echoes.

Philippe's AirPod case snaps shut as he finally decides to acknowledge us again, his new girlfriend's kids who he's meeting for the first time. For a minute we sit, chewing silently, stewing in our shared awkwardness until Philippe's oversized suit jacket starts ringing and he pulls out a *second* phone.

He glances at the screen and says, 'I must take this. It's Milan.' I laugh, involuntarily. Without waiting for her response, he answers, '*Allo. Oui, c'est moi ...*' and has a three-minute conversation in angry French. When he finally hangs up, he lets out a withering sigh, pulling a smoking tin from an inside pocket. 'I don't want to –' he pauses here to place the filter between his lips and I have to physically fight not to roll my eyes – 'but I have to leave. Zoom call, all departments. The loan has been approved, thanks to you.'

Mum claps giddily. 'Happy to be of help. All that legal jargon.' She bats her hand dismissively.

'This means we have the funding for new advertising efforts I was telling you about. I need our autumn samples to work on pitch for the billboard companies. They are at the office.'

'Honestly, it's fine. I'm so proud of you, go.' Mum smiles, but I see through it. She's disappointed. 'I'll cook you something back at the flat later.'

'No. I eat out. *Au revoir, au revoir.*' He blows us fistfuls of kisses before putting the phone to his ear again. '*Allo? Oui, je pars.*'

When we can't hear Philippe's drawl on the other side of the door anymore, Mum moves her mouthful into her cheek and speaks behind her hand. 'I know that could've gone better, but what do you think?' she asks. 'I mean Saffron, not you,' she adds when Otis holds a finger aloft, gulping to finish his drink. 'You've made it quite clear you don't like him.'

'No, you're wholly right, I don't. I think he is – *'ow you say –'* he waves his fork around, pretending to search for the word – 'a deekhead.'

I clear my throat, aiming for some middle ground. 'He's OK. But he's on his phone a lot.'

Mum's teeth clash against her fork as she takes a bite. 'I know. But at the end of the day, a relationship should be about raising each other up. I want him to be successful, and success for him means being in touch with his team night and day.' She nods, like it's herself she's convincing. 'Philippe's the CEO of his own sportswear brand. Here, look.' Mum taps at her phone a few times before sliding it on to the table.

Otis leans over the top of Rue to see as I scroll through a pastel palette of pictures featuring impossibly tiny women wrapped in bone-hugging Lycra.

'Legger?' I read.

'Léger,' Mum corrects in a French accent.

I'm still scrolling through obvious bot comments on Léger's posts (*Wow, more of this please!!*), when my phone goes off and Mum unashamedly tilts her head to read the notification.

'Ooh, who's *Nolan*?'

'Mum!' I snatch up my phone. 'I don't know who it is,' I mumble, annoyed that I can feel my face going red.

'How can you not know?'

I shrug. 'It's Reveal.'

'Tell me you are *not* using Reveal, Saffron,' Otis says, full-naming me and giving me a heart squeeze of adrenalin. He rests his hand on top of mine, like I've just told him I'm dying. 'It's so toxic. Harrison was on there before he met me and the screenshots I've seen from some of his matches after he Revealed.' Tongue pressed to the roof of his mouth, he shakes his head, pulling Rue's plate towards him. 'So toxic.'

'Why's it so bad? I've never even heard of it. Me and Philippe met—'

'Can we not,' Otis cuts Mum off without looking up from slicing Rue's food to pulp, and I can tell he's in one of those moods he gets in with Mum where it's hard to be on his side. Otis has been housing some therapy-recommended resentment for Mum since Dad left.

Mum carries on talking. 'Is it the same kind of thing, swiping and—'

'We're still trying to forget about Carl, and Tamir, and Robert, and Jahzeil, and Greg.' Their sentences overlap, their voices growing grittier, throatier, each trying to swallow up the other. 'Am I forgetting anybody else?' Otis spits. I hate him like this, taking his hurt over Dad's abandonment out on Mum. 'Why can't you just learn to be happy on your own?'

'Otis, come on . . .' I try, though the last thing he said resonates and finds a deep unconscious crevice of my thoughts to sink into, probably only to resurface when my head hits the pillow.

'Well, I don't need to now, because we're getting married!' Mum picks up her glass and downs the rest of her wine. She doesn't ever shout, just bigs her voice up so it's wide and bassy, like an echo from a dark room. 'I can't believe I cooked this nice dinner for us all so I could tell you – and I was so *excited* to tell you – but you push, and you push, and—' Mum's words are lost as her voice thickens, on the brink of tears. 'The wedding's in ten weeks. Come, don't come, it's up to you.'

Otis doesn't say a word, only swings Rue up into his arms and carries her upstairs. I sit, stunned, no words coming.

I watch Mum pull the chain of her necklace taut across her bottom lip and run the clasp of her locket across it. She *can't* be serious, can she? She's asking me to accept this man for a stepdad she's only known a month?

As we load the dishwasher together in silence, I look for the glint of an engagement ring on her finger as she reaches for the cutlery basket, but she's not wearing one.

We catch eyes and Mum tuts, sweeping the dishwasher door up and bumping it closed with her hip. 'Come here.' She sighs, tugging me by the hoodie into a hug. 'I'm sorry, love. I didn't want you to find out like that, it's just – that boy really knows how to get under my skin, man. He's too like your dad.'

'He can be.' *He's actually too like you*, I want to tell her, but don't. 'Where's your ring?'

'We're not bothering with that because it's all happening so quick.'

'Oh?'

'I'm over the moon, love. I know he's a bit of a workaholic but trust me, Philippe's a *good* one.' How she's expecting me to react positively to that after he pretty much called me fat before heading out halfway through the meal I watched her cook for him, I do not know. 'I haven't met someone who makes me feel like he does in a very long time.' Her phone goes off on the worktop. 'That's him now,' she says, gazing at the screen.

As she answers, I find myself staring at the corkboard on the wall above the snack cupboard, unsubtly crowded with Mum's old SlimIt certificates from before she started working for them. Mum had been a member for years, periodically losing half a stone or so, then yo-yoing it back on. But her big drama weight loss, the one that stuck, was actually a side effect of dealing with the depression that followed her and Dad's splitting up five years ago. It was through sheer self-neglect and becoming a single-income household (not through discipline, determination, and the formation of healthy restrictive habits like she tells people it happened) that she shed the eleven stone that she'd continued to gain after I was born. Mum skipped meals to fill our freezer with the only food she could afford, ultra-processed and twenty minutes on 180 degrees. I don't blame her, but oven pizzas and nuggets on nuggets definitely contributed to the weight I put on in secondary school. Though as the scales went up for me, they went down for her.

I don't know that it made her happy though, the weight loss, I think it was more the subsequent attention she got from men on dating apps that distracted her from Dad. And since then, she hasn't been alone long enough to know if happiness was something she cultivated by changing her body or not.

She hangs up. 'Going to meet him back at the flat in a bit.' *The* flat, not his flat. 'So, this Nolan,' she says, gathering her things. I groan. 'No, listen, my biggest bit of advice to you, Saff, would be to show *yourself* some love first. Because you can't expect anybody to love you if you don't love yourself.' A smile tugs at the corner of my mouth because Mum's giving off something close to progressive. Maybe SlimIt have taken notice of the negative feedback online, now amounting to a 30,000-post-strong #SlimItSurvivor hashtag that Bodied by Bliss has been covering. And maybe Mum's about to surprise the hell out of me by being supportive. 'That starts with looking in the mirror and liking what you see. I know you're not happy.' My shoulders slump. 'I wasn't when I was at my biggest. Signing up to SlimIt was the best decision you could've made for yourself, Saff. We've got the wedding to think of now. I want you to want to be in the photos, not hiding behind people and shying away from the camera, OK? Remember your Auntie Naomi's wedding?'

I wince at ten-year-old me *dieting* to fit into my white satin flower girl dress because Nana Cleo had said I looked like a marshmallow in it. And they all wondered why I hid from the photographer on the big day, scowling in the group photos I was forced to be in.

As I walk her down the hall, I don't know what to say, how to tell her I'm no longer working towards changing my body, and rather towards accepting it. That increasingly, I *do* look in the mirror and like what I see. How do I tell her any of this, when her whole life is dictated by the idea that to be beautiful is to be thin?

In the end, I project what I hope I'll have found the courage to do by then, and say it with my chest. 'I'm not gonna be shying away, I promise.'

'That's my girl.' Slipping her pristine Air Force 1s on, Mum opens the front door and points the car key out into the dark. 'A stone, maybe a stone and a half, is *easily* doable in ten weeks if you really try, love.'

I keep my face neutral and kiss her on the cheek. 'Congratulations, by the way.'

Walking backwards, she beams at me, the street lamps illuminating the cheekbones and the tight-skinned jaw she starved for, that she works so hard to keep. Sweating, restricting, running away from her old self.

As Mum's headlights fade, I lock up, then head upstairs to softly knock on Otis's door and see if Rue's still awake. She is and I go to her.

'Night, night,' I say into her spritz of curls, wondering if we'll have figured out how to have healthy relationships with our bodies by the time she's eighteen, if Rue will ever look at herself in a mirror and cry. I screw my face, force the thought away.

I undress in front of the bathroom mirror, observing myself, finding the soft pouches of skin between my bra and my armpits, the stretch marks on my hips, like pale tiger claws against my brown skin. I work hard to keep my mind blank. Neutral.

I smear away my makeup with oil, cleanse and scrub my face,

and there in the mirror are Rue's brown, almond-shaped eyes blinking back at me. The same eyes that are red-rimmed in all Auntie Naomi's wedding photos, because she thinks she's ugly, that her body doesn't belong in a pretty dress.

How could anyone have made her feel like that?

april

The engine rumbles as I step off the bus back from campus, about to thread my arm through my jacket. On Gloucester Road, the sun still dusts the tops of tables where people are eating outside, the air still warm enough for me to walk home with my jacket tied around my waist.

I'm wearing a vest, and the breeze is nice. Nobody's staring or paying any particular attention to me. The world didn't stop turning because I dared to dress appropriately for the weather.

As I walk, I choose a playlist Spotify's named 'frolic' and check my messages, my bare arms tingling with goosebumps as I pass through a block of shadow. Three messages from Nolan asking if I'm OK, at eleven, two, and again at six. I reply back with a simple, Yeah, good, you? because the constant check-in texts are getting a bit excessive honestly, and it's making me draw back. Next in my notifications is a selfie from Freya to the group chat. She has a box of Tom's stuff tucked under her sinewy, toned arm, her cheekbones cutting, her jaw angular. She looks unreal. In a literal sense. And the competitiveness that flared between us back when we were at SlimIt together isn't there; I don't feel jealous looking at her. Instead, I wonder if she's as OK as she wants us to think she is. It looks like she's taking the breakup hard, like she might not be eating.

Freya
When are we burning this shit ladies 🐒 ♀

I send back,

Saffron
Down to help you get rid of his stuff any time. But how are you doing??

I say any time, but that's not strictly true. Yeah, finally meeting up with Freya forced me to confront the inferiority complex I'd built up comparing myself to her, but we still never have time to hang out. Our schedules clash, her 5 p.m. clock-off at odds with my frequent closing shifts at Jemima's, her strict exercise regime and early nights totally incompatible with my new and earnest effort with my studies. We text more frequently though, or rather I'm better at replying.

Seconds later, Poppy texts the group.

Poppy
Revenge body looks good on youuuuu

Evidently Poppy isn't concerned about Freya's health.

Seeing her name on my phone feels conflicting. I'm relieved but things feel unresolved. I've only had passive interactions with her Instagram Story since that night at the club – my likes, unacknowledged. My message urging her to stay away from Jack got marked as read, and then she went silent. Her last day at Jemima's came and went. I wasn't on shift, but I left her a card and a baby offshoot of one of Toby's cactuses in her locker. I got a simple thank you text and that was it.

Some part of me misses her, but I think it's more that I miss how she used to be and the things we used to do. It took that night for me to realise we don't fit together anymore. And that maybe that's OK. If we did, it'd mean we weren't growing.

There's a bunch of new messages from Mum, as there is any time I pick up my phone at the moment, using me as her personal Pinterest board for flowers, favours, and makeup ideas she wants me to try out on her.

Mum

> OK don't be mad, but I may have picked out the bridesmaid dresses. I know we said we'd look together at the weekend but these are the ones. I saw them by accident, I swear. Ads on insta … Tina and Kel are on board, and once I get your blessing, I'll get them ordered!! xx

She sends through a link to a pearly pink satin dress with spaghetti straps, a sweetheart neckline, and a calf-hugging skirt, all blaring red flags for someone with boobs that are too big to go braless, and a belly satin will wrap around like clingfilm. What is she doing? It might be alright for Tina and Kelly, but that dress wasn't made for me. A black bodycon on a night out and a couple of vest tops are one thing, but the thought of walking up the aisle in a skintight formal dress in front of a roomful of wedding guests makes me feel sick.

Mum

I bet if you just lost a stone it'd fall beautifully on you hon xx

When I turn on to Wilder Street, I'm still searching the website for an alternative style I can persuade her to go for. Inside, I find Nairong loading the dishwasher in her dressing gown, and Veronica straddling a chair wearing zebra-print hot pants, a sports bra, and stripper heels, licking a yoghurt lid.

I'm staring, of course I'm staring.

'You look ... affronted,' Veronica says, jabbing her spoon at me. She waves it down the length of her body, giggling. 'Do I affront you?'

'No, I don't think so,' I say, fidgeting with my phone. 'I don't know what that means. You look extra, obviously, but good extra. Look at those heels!'

How can Veronica be so chill sitting here basically in her underwear, when here I am obsessing over a slip dress. How long do I have to have been *doing the work* before my default isn't to want to hide?

'Just finished pole fitness,' she explains. 'Here, let me give you a preview.'

I burst out laughing as Veronica prances round the dining chair, showcasing an exaggerated run-through of some of her warm-up pole moves, sexily caressing the back of the chair. I lock my phone, forgetting all about the dress.

Just then the door goes, and I know it's Toby by the squeak of his Jordans on the hall floor, the thump of his gym bag.

'What's going on?' he says, strolling in, a sapped smile on his face. It's been a few days since I've seen him, and my body reacts with that jolt of suspension in the deep middle of my pelvis, like when Otis drives too fast over a bridge. Doug's had me on a string of opening shifts with tacked-on extra hours as the days get longer and the café gets busier, and Toby's either been at practice or, according to Keith, out with Bella by the time I get home. He holds my stare, grinning like he's got stuff stored up to say to me. 'Hey, stranger,' he says as he passes me, unzipping his jacket. I catch Veronica and Nairong exchange a wide-eyed look. 'So, what we doing? What are we eating tonight? Because I am famished.'

Nairong's impeccably plucked brows knit. 'Insensitive.'

Toby holds up his hands. 'Correction, I am very hungry.'

'We stopped for falafel on the way home,' she says, gathering a well-leafed book and her laptop from the table. The pastel annotation notes pressed between the pages remind me of the assessment I've about exhausted procrastination time for.

'Yeah, and my leftover flatbread is calling me to come devour it. So, looks like it's just the two of you. Almost like, I don't know –' Veronica saunters past me, heading to the door with Nairong – 'it could be a date.'

I cut a look at Toby as they scamper off, brow furrowed like I don't know what Veronica's talking about. But she's been on at me about asking Toby out since last week when I came down to her unpacking her shopping, face lit by the open fridge door. She'd squealed, holding out a smoothie he'd left for me, a note tacked to the side of the bottle in his chicken scratch handwriting. *Hemp and coconut water in this one. Extra energy. I heard you up a few times last night, thought you might be tired x*

At this she declared him either in love or a psychopath and hasn't shut up about it since.

He laughs it off, scratches the back of his neck. 'What you saying for food then, Saff? Though I haven't been shopping and your shelf in the fridge is looking bleak as always,' he says, drumming his fingers on the side of the fridge door. 'So options are stir-fry, stir-fry, or stir-fry?'

Staring at the ingredients he's taking out, I hesitate, unable to stop imagining the glut of the avocado bagel and pasta I already ate today. The thought of piling another meal on top of that makes me uncomfortable.

'Oh, I'm not eating,' I say, but as I do, my stomach twists with hunger, a physical clarification that I'm being irrational.

'But you just got off work, right?' Toby asks. I nod. 'And you would've eaten lunch like seven, eight hours ago? You're not hungry?' I open my mouth to lie when my belly emits the most embarrassingly loud gurgle. Toby smiles. 'Right, how about you keep me company while I cook? If you wanna eat when it's done, we'll eat. No pressure.'

'Deal.'

As he sautés and marinades, I ask Toby more about his uni course and what made him want to study nutrition. He tells me about his dad who's a gardener and has a greenhouse at the bottom of the garden, bursting with blueberries, rocket, and tomato in the summer. And on the subject of his parents, it feels OK to ask about his heritage, to confess my guessing at his honey-toned skin when we first met. He tells me his mum is mixed, White/Caribbean like me, his dad Caucasian. I laugh when he says his dad encouraged him to apply for *Junior MasterChef* every year from age eight to twelve and learn that when he's at home, Toby helps his dad keep their allotment. He throws some frozen kale from last year's crop into the stir-fry.

I envy his relationship with food, how rooted it is in the bond he shares with his dad. And being let in on Toby's knowledge of its magical and medicinal properties over the last couple of months makes me want to get to a place with my body where I can allow myself to love feeding it.

When the meal's plated up, I find I don't even need to repeat my mantra of *I need to eat to function*. I want to eat, to taste every last bite of what Toby's poured into this.

'You would've won. *MasterChef*, I mean. That was so good, thank you,' I say when we're done. I fold my hands over my rounded middle, just the right amount of full. Not uncomfortably, like how it used to feel necessary to lick the black bean sauce from the plate after a takeaway with Otis, so that the treat was worth it, but suitably, having listened to my body's needs.

'Anytime.' Toby smiles over his shoulder as he takes our plates to the sink.

'I'll do that,' I say, but he dismisses me, already running the tap, and I'm about to insist when my phone goes off. I look at the screen and prickle with irritation. Yet another message from Nolan, sent eight minutes ago.

Nolan Seriously let me know you're OK when you can. Getting worried I haven't heard from you

My thumbs stab at my phone, typing Can you please chill for a sec!!? before backspacing, not wanting to be argumentative when he's obviously having a bad day. Glancing at Jack's face in the corner of the screen where Nolan's profile picture is displayed, I'm reminded that he might not have anyone to talk to about how he's feeling. Maybe I'm it. With a slow exhale, I write,

Sydney I'm totally fine!? I've been in class literally all day, and eating just now. Is everything alright with you?

I stare into nothing, imagining what could've happened in Nolan's life that he's having whole heartbreaks over the internet with people he'll never meet. Toby's phone rings next to me, interrupting my thoughts. Bella's name with a heart next to it.

189

No matter how many times I remind myself that nothing is going to happen between us, seeing her name light up his phone sinks me every time.

'I'm going to bed,' I say, holding out his phone, the intimacy of sitting across a table from him for the past forty-five minutes, sharing a meal he cooked from scratch, tainted. Was he expecting her call? Was he waiting for an interruption the whole time we were talking? Still, I try wringing sincerity into my smile because I have no right to be upset about that whatsoever. 'Night.'

As the *Friends* season seven finale plays in the background, I scroll Instagram. Out of habit, I double tap Poppy's latest post as it appears on my feed; a shot of her and Bella posing in front of a flower wall at a cocktail bar in Clifton. Seconds later, I get a message.

Poppy
Hey! Things are weird between us?? Are you mad at me?

Saffron
No, I'm not mad. Promise

Poppy
I feel like you are mad ... about me kissing Jack. I know you liked him butttt is it my fault you didn't do anything about it in school? Is that fair babe?

> I told you I'm not mad. You do you. Am I
> worried about you being with him? Yeah.
> I'm telling you, he's bad news Pop

I watch the screen as it shows her typing for some time but then nothing.

As I sit and listen to the sounds of my shared house – the distant hum of two different TV shows, the white noise of the shower running – I realise it's the first time I haven't felt devastatingly lonely at the thought of not being friends with her.

Still awake at half past midnight, I get up to pee. As I approach the second-floor landing, the warm, sugary smell of baked chocolate hits my nose. Its sweetness smothers another smell too, something pungent and earthy.

As soon as I see Keith in the kitchen, I realise what's happening.

'Sup,' he says, swiping his finger round a scraped bowl of brownie mix.

'Can't sleep,' I say, peering through the sauce-splashed glass of the oven door. 'When are they done?'

Keith laughs.

Is it that obvious that I'm waiting for an invitation? It'd be nice to slow everything down, have my thoughts spaced out a bit. And with the deep brown syrupy smell of these brownies, I'm not *not* gonna try one.

'Timer went off a minute ago, but I did the knife check. Didn't come out clean, so I'm gonna see how they look now. And yes, you can have some.'

I flounder. 'But – I didn't—'

He shushes me, and when he pulls them out of the oven, I agree that they're done. After waiting for them to cool, we traipse upstairs to our top-floor rooms, brownies in hand. Two for him, one for me.

About to go our separate ways, he pauses in his doorway. 'Wait, pinky promise me you've tried edibles before.'

I link my little finger with his. '*Yes*. God, I promise. This is not you corrupting me— Holy shit.' Through the gap in his door, I catch the opening credits to *Rick and Morty* playing out on a TV screen almost the size of his entire wall. 'Um?'

Keith grins, opening the door all the way up to reveal his room's practically humming with high-tech gadgetry. Underneath the TV is a mounted soundbar, with a sleek side table displaying every kind of games console I know to exist, and on the far side of the room is a triple-monitor computer set-up.

'OK, how have I never been in here, and do the others know you have a VR set? How did you afford all this stuff?'

'Yeah, they know. You should come hang with me sometime. Though once the novelty wears off, the headache doesn't seem worth the VR experience.' He mutes the TV. 'I got into doing some cybersecurity work for an American internet provider. Pay's *good*.'

'So nonchalant about making bank.' I lightly slap his shoulder with the back of my hand. 'Good for you. And yeah, I do want to play VR one day. Not when I'm about to eat this brownie though.'

He laughs, taking a huge bite out of his own one. Careful not to trip over any wires, I head for the door.

'Now, if you don't mind,' Keith says. 'I've got plants to water on *Animal Crossing*, so, I'll see you in the morning.'

'You go water those virtual roses. Night.'

Back in my room, I hit play on season eight of *Friends*. For the longest time I swear I don't feel anything. I'm on the cusp of going to the fridge to sneak another one when this cotton-soft heaviness descends on my whole body like a weighted blanket, both cushioning and pinning me to my bed. It's then that my bunny slippers become the single most funny thing I've ever seen in my life. Did they always look so … so, rabid, with the teeth. Those *teeth*. Who signed off on the design of those hellish teeth, my God?

No-context, I send a picture of these things to Veronica, Nairong, and Otis.

While my phone's open, Mum texts,

Mum

I'll pick you up at 10:40 tomorrow, our appointment is at 11 and bridal shop is about 10 mins from yours. That OK? xx

I reply that it is, and then time blurs, my mind tripping from one untethered idea to the other.

And I feel so floaty and buoyant and stupid, I don't want to be laughing alone. But I want to respect the sanctity of Keith's *Animal Crossing* time. I mute *Friends*, listening for sounds in the house that someone else is awake.

It's eerily silent. No sound underneath me from Toby.

He's who I want to be laughing with. He's not online on the usual app we text on. Nobody is.

I know who will be though.

I go to Reveal and sure enough there's a green dot next to Nolan's name. Then again, is needy, vulnerable, and demanding the vibe right now? Maybe talking to him isn't the best idea. Quickly, I hide my status, so he can't see I'm online, and actively choosing to ignore his messages. On a whim, I decide to mute him too. Maybe we need a break.

There's a green dot next to another of Sydney's matches though.

Impulsively, I tap his name. Toby, who's nineteen, a

Cactus dad. UWE Jets point guard 🏀

and likes 'cooking good mood food'.

I smile, and staring at the blinking cursor in our blank chat box it dawns on me that this is my evidence proving Toby and Bella aren't back together. Some might argue I already had that answer because he *told* me that. But, trust issues. I do, however, trust that Toby would never respond to someone, let alone be active on a dating site, if he was in a relationship. As a friend alone he's loyal, considerate, somewhat of a perfectionist—

Something must glitch in my fog-swaddled brain because one second, I'm staring at Toby's faceless avatar, the next I'm watching my own message bubble on to the screen.

Sydney Hey

What did I just do? Why did I—

. . .

FUCK. He's typing.

Toby Hey, how's it going?

Toby Ngl your name made me think of that sadist kid from Toy Story

No, no, *no*, don't be funny. Don't make me want to talk to you. I can't. I shouldn't. But I definitely will. Though it's wrong, so wrong.

OK, I'll just reply once so he doesn't feel ignored.

Sydney You know how we do *casually soldering Barbie doll*

That's it. My finger hovers over the Unmatch button, ready to tidy this mess, but his reply is instant. It's witty, enticing, and I'm stoned and what is willpower?

*

'Don't touch that,' Mum hisses, head poking out between the changing room curtains as Rue runs a veil through her sticky fingers. Sticky with what, I don't know. I'm currently sitting on the handprint she left on the chaise longue. 'You're meant to be watching her, Saff.' Mum's anxious and I get it, she's a body-obsessed supervisor for SlimIt about to try on wedding dresses. But I wish she'd admit to that anxiety so I could be there for her. This is supposed to be fun. Aren't I expected to shed happy tears in a minute? 'Oh look, the lady's back with my dresses!'

Mum steps out of the changing room in a complimentary silk robe as the shop assistant strides towards us carrying three zipped-up bags in her arms.

If I were to imagine this moment, I'd picture Mum squealing and clapping, excited to see herself in white. The Wedding Dress Shopping Experience is something society has tried to sell to women as a defining moment in our lives for decades. Instead, she's cracking with the pressure of what she thinks her body should look like when she sees herself in the mirror. Something I can't believe *Mum's* stressing about. My size ten mum, who exists solely on kale salad and unseasoned chicken breast, who is a biweekly Pilates participant and Peloton fanatic, and a *literally* qualified thin person. But none of that stopped her from getting this distressed about it.

Prayers for plus-sized brides everywhere, is all I can say.

I try to inject a little optimism. 'You excited, Mum?'

'Rue, that's glass!' My head whips round to see her balancing Mum's empty Prosecco flute on one of the boutique's coffee table books she's using as a tray. It's giving shrill, it's giving high octave, and Rue's instantly on the brink of tears. Checking herself, Mum mumbles, 'God, that Prosecco went straight to my head. I didn't eat breakfast today for this, that's why.' Then to Rue, 'Sorry, love. It's OK, I know you were playing waitress, let's just save that game for at home, OK? Please?'

Regaining her bride-to-be composure, Mum goes to the other end of the shop with the assistant to browse shoes with the right heel height for her ideal dress drop. While we're alone, I reiterate to Rue that Grandma didn't mean it, and explain that she's nervous, though that doesn't make it OK to shout. Eyeing me with her bottom lip thrust out, she stuffs her hand into her pocket. Her features lift with pure delight when she pulls out a fistful of pocket grit and Jelly Tots. Worryingly, she knows not to let Mum see, and I watch as she shuffles off to the side and pops one into her mouth, closing her fist around her sugared treasures.

I wink, but when she returns a conspiratorial grin, I feel guilty for reinforcing the idea that some foods are bad and should be eaten in secret.

Suddenly, the room feels stifling. The pristine white walls, the searing lights, the feathery cushions. And mirrors, mirrors everywhere. Mirrored tables, mirrored doors, hand mirrors, wall mirrors, sliding mirrors. If I stand anywhere in this shop, I'll see myself reflected in at least seven different surfaces, and I can't do that today. I can barely look myself in the eye.

I was up until four in the morning talking to – no, *catfishing* Toby, which means he and Sydney now have a Revelation Status of 49 per cent. It was a weak, intoxicated decision. I can accept matching with him weeks ago was an unconscious oversight, but I didn't have to message him. I didn't have to *keep* messaging him. I suppose I just wanted to know what it'd be like to flirt with him without my head being full of crippling doubt.

With one eye on Rue, I open up our chat again, rushed with adrenalin as I reread his most recent message.

Toby If you're game, how about we meet and do all this in person? I'm not fussed about waiting for the big reveal – ngl this whole percentage thing is weirding me out

Toby No matter where it goes, it'd be nice to go for a drink with someone I can dissect Charlie Kaufman films with ygm

Setting aside how panic-inducing this all is, I can't believe I've been living in the same house as Toby since February, and it's taken this long for us to discover our shared love of cinema. His mention of Barbie last night incited a (regretfully in hindsight) pretty pick-me self-comparison to Bride of Chucky. This led to us both admitting we'd never seen any of the Chucky franchise because we hate horror movies, but are both big film fans in general and go hard for independents. He said Bella walked out of *I'm Thinking of Ending Things* only twenty minutes in because *it was a boring movie for boring people*, and when I said,

Sydney

Literal blasphemy. ITOET is my third favourite film

that's when Toby asked Sydney on a date. And now I have palpitations because this is getting out of hand. I've had my one night of ill-advised fantasy flirting, I need to do the right thing and unmatch him, or better yet, delete Sydney's profile entirely.

'Saffron!'

Mum's snapping her fingers like she's been trying to get my attention. 'What?'

'The veils,' she hisses, poking her head out between the curtains of the changing room. She snaps towards Rue, who has a veil draped over her head like a cobweb. 'You know what, maybe it'd be best if you take her somewhere else for half an hour. She's normal size for her age, right?'

At the jolt in my stomach, I wonder when 'normal', or rather the suggestion of being 'not normal', started to feel like a slur to me.

Taken aback, I say, 'She's actually in size 5–6 bottoms, so I don't know—'

'Is she?' Mum says. I wince, instinctively stepping towards Rue, wanting to shield her, to put my hands over her ears. Oblivious, Mum squints across the ice-white shop towards the dresses tailored for little girls. 'That's big, isn't it?' She doesn't even whisper. Mum must've felt the weight of those words land once, spoken by Nana Cleo. But at forty-three, they probably feel like old, yellowing bruises to her now, that only hurt when you press very hard. Mum tilts her head. 'Now you mention it, I suppose she is a bit ... big.'

Rue lifts the veil from over her eyes and I watch as she finds herself in the mirror, a scowl furrowing her gentle features. She tugs at the hem of her jumper like she's trying to cover more of herself, and my heart breaks.

'I didn't mention it. I would never. She's not big, she's *tall*. And even if she needed to wear a bigger size for whatever other reason, she's *four*,' I hiss, leaning in close to Mum, who's clutching the changing room curtain against her.

It looks like she's cowering. Confronted by the bright lights of changing rooms. And it's then that I feel an overwhelming sense of grief for Mum, and for her mum. I remember Nana Cleo emaciated, her limbs like gnarled roots, a headscarf slipping off her hairless head as she joked from her hospital bed that *at least I'm thin now*. There's a grief for every mum and every daughter shackled by the chains of intergenerational body shame.

I go to Rue and crouch in front of her.

'She's Rue, and Rue wears size 5–6 because she has long legs for climbing trees and bouncing as high as the moon on the trampoline.' Cupping her face, I gently lift her chin. 'For winning races and dancing her little butt off with me. Rue Saldana is exactly Rue Saldana-sized, OK? She's exactly as she should be.' Her smile's like a gulp of orange juice, fresh and so, so sweet. Without looking back at Mum and the assistant, I say, 'I'm gonna take her to the coffee shop next door, text me when you're done.'

I squeeze Rue's tiny hand in mine. I'll buy us both hot chocolates with all the works, and unsubtly note how nice it is to enjoy sweet things sometimes. Maybe we can share those pocket-lint Jelly Tots I saw her hide. I've learnt unsubtlety is key with toddlers.

As we walk towards the door, I hear Mum try to laugh over her awkwardness. 'You don't actually have to leave,' she flusters. 'I'm sorry, it's just so hot in here, and I shouldn't have necked that Prosecco. Don't you wanna see my dress?'

I shrug. What I want to see is my niece smiling, carefree and kicking her little feet as she enjoys something chocolatey. Protecting her body image is more important to me than bolstering Mum's.

'Take pictures,' I say.

Rue leads the way to the café, puddle stomping and squealing with joy.

The next day, I wake at eight underneath a swathe of blue sky, the sun in my eyes because I forgot to pull the blind last night. I stretch, kick the covers off. Below me, the plucky, opening bass of Bill Withers's 'Lovely Day' thrums through the floorboards. I imagine Toby bobbing his head to its mellow, sunshiny opening as he gets ready for the day, and roll over and groan into my pillow.

When I came home last night, I twisted my key as slow as the hour hand of a clock, and held the handle down rigidly as I closed the door again. I tiptoed past the kitchen, guilt-ridden as I heard Toby laugh with the others, his message to Sydney still unanswered on my phone. I went to my room, and didn't unlock it once. Utter avoidance.

Now, I snatch it off my bedside table and shut off the alarm.

My resolve to delete Sydney once and for all is concrete and I want it done immediately. But before I can tap into Settings, the number in the red dot next to Nolan's name stops me dead. 209. I muted contact from him only two nights ago and he's sent me over two hundred messages? Anxiety churns in the pit of my stomach.

Nolan Hey, where'd you go?

Nolan Hope everything's OK with you? When you get a chance, please reply so I know you're alright xx

Nolan ??????

Nolan Just saw you were online.

Nolan Did I do something wrong? We were having such a good time 😔

Nolan Please reply, please don't be like everyone else and leave me

Nolan Well I'll just go and fuck myself then.

Nolan Definately didn't see this one coming

Nolan Sydney???? I see you're online

Nolan Hellooooo aha

Nolan How was your day?

Nolan Ffs will you just speak to me

I scroll through them, a lot of them memes or strings of question marks. Adrenalin floods my chest and the urge to type a scathing response makes my hands shake. But I don't want to get into a back and forth with this person, whoever Nolan really is. He's clearly not OK, one of the catfish that MTV would edit sinister music over. Now desperate to kill communication with him too, I go to Settings and do it, I finally delete Sydney's account. It shouldn't be instant, but seeing the app's blank login page bleaches clean the guilt that's been festering in me since I started doing this.

Bye, Syd, thanks for being a bad bitch when I couldn't.

While I'm at it, I go to my own Reveal account and shut it down. I've been inactive on it anyway since moving in here. I haven't felt the need to go searching. What I thought I needed in a boyfriend – connection, validation, someone to do life with – I found in my new friendships.

I climb out of bed and stand in front of the mirror in just my pants. My hands run over my stomach, soft and grabbable as pizza dough. Reflexively, I twist to the side and suck in, then I sigh, letting my arms fall to my sides. Judgements gather like black clouds, so instead, I picture Rue giggling at the whipped cream dotting her nose as we drank our hot chocolates, or Veronica flouncing around in her stripper heels. My self-critique is learnt, and one day I'll have done all my unlearning, and I'll look at myself in a mirror and there'll be nothing but clear skies, maybe even sunshine. But for now, I think of *good* things, tangible and true, that bring me joy.

Like bumping into Toby before his basketball game; the watermelon I'm gonna slice for breakfast; the spring sunshine pouring through the skylight in my room in a house full of people I love; the monochromatic makeup look Bliss posted that I'm gonna try and recreate.

I reach for my makeup bag, but before I can start getting ready for work, my stomach growls, and I listen to it.

I'm people-watching as I walk into work, head turned towards the sprawl of people along Gloucester Road in warm weather moods. I hear that I'm at Jemima's before I see it. One couple's holding the door open for another so the soulless lo-fi reggae mix curated by Doug swings out into the street. As I reach out to catch the door, another hand gets there quicker, fingertips pushing it closed. I turn sharply to face whoever's out to ruin my own good mood when my lungs go vacuum-packed.

He grabs my wrist. 'I need to talk to you.'

I can't breathe.

'Saff, it's me.' He slides his sunglasses up into his hair, as if I didn't recognise him before. My breath's caught, so I can't speak, can't tell him I don't want to go with him into the alley he's dragging me down. 'How are you?' he says when we're there.

Jack grins, wolfish. His canines crowd the front of his mouth, and I wonder how I once considered his smile cute. It's menacing. And the way he yanked me without a thought about whether I wanted to go with him or not reassures me I was right in my decision to warn Poppy about him. Even if it may have cost me the last shred of our friendship.

'What do you want? Why the hell are you here?' I move like I'm about to walk through him, making him back up towards the gap between the buildings.

'Chill, chill.' His laugh flays at my skin. 'I'm home for a few days for Mum's birthday. I was over the road, at the Golden Lion with Billy and Char. Saw you walking.' He shrugs. 'And I'm still blocked on everything, how am I gonna talk to you otherwise?'

'You don't! You don't *ever* talk to me, and you never pull some shit like you did the other night, coming around me and my friends – kissing them *in front* of me. You just pretend I don't exist.' I jab my finger into his chest. I stare at it, like I can't believe it's my own nail digging into the skin between his shirt buttons. 'You were so fucking good at it before.'

'Jesus Christ, get over it, Saff,' he says, shaking me off. 'It was school, it didn't mean anything. I thought you understood our arrangement.'

'Fuck you.' It doesn't satisfy, so I say it again. 'Fuck. You. What is it? You're making me late for work.'

Jack thrusts his tongue in his cheek, glaring down at me. I guess he's only used to seeing me nodding, sitting, smiling, yessing. He sniffs, tilting his chin up. 'Alright, be like that. Be bitter. I just came here to ask you to tell Poppy we're cool. That you don't care.'

Confused, I scan his face. 'What? Why would she think I care?'

Jack sneers. 'She's gone all quiet on me 'cus she thinks she's *being a bad friend*,' he mocks, 'because you fancied me in school. She thinks you're jealous, and pretending you're worried about her getting with me, when really, we both know you're just pissed off it ain't you.'

'Wow, OK. So, it's not that you were a pushy, controlling, belittling piece of shit the entire time, and I didn't want my longest friend to be love-bombed into having sex with you like I was? Oh no, it's because I'm *jealous*. How utterly unsurprising of you not to take any accountability whatsoever.' In answer, he spits on the ground, my heart pounding. 'You're together then?'

'Not together; I said to her what I said to you, I'm not doing the long-distance thing. But while I'm here, I don't see why we can't keep things casual, a strictly physical thing, you know. Or that's what we were supposed to be doing, before she decided she was running for friend of the year.'

'Hardly,' I scoff. 'She hasn't talked to me in weeks.'

'Just tell her, yeah. That you're not jealous and that you give her your blessing or something. Oh, and I meant what I said the other night, by the way. You are looking good, Saffron.' Jack cups my chin and I crick my neck jerking away from him so hard, but his grip holds. He peels the wet of my bottom lip out with his

206

thumb, staring at my mouth. 'It really tore you up that bad, did it, me and you? We could also have some fun too, while I'm here . . .'

I wrench my face away from him. 'You're disgusting.'

I can only stare at his hands, unnerved out of my mind that they once touched me with something close to gentleness.

At the end of my shift Doug tells me I got two frowny faces on the comment cards we give out with the bill. Honestly, I'm surprised there aren't more. I monotoned my way through the evening, barely able to offer up a smile.

I charge home past pubs and clubs and chicken shops, their doors belching out fried food smells that stir my stomach sick. Before I reach the turn-off for Wilder Street, I pinball through a gaggle of girls waiting for the bus. One shouts, 'I love your eye makeup, babe!' and I thank her, blinking up to the sky, so I don't let my tears fall and ruin it.

But then another one says, 'Cheer up, love? Might never happen,' and they spill over.

Because it did happen, I let it. When Jack held me in place earlier, I felt powerless, exactly how I felt the entire time we were together, because all my worth was contingent on how he treated me. Being sworn to secrecy about your first kiss *by* your first kiss told me I wasn't worth shit. And alone down that alley with him, it hit home that I've never processed any of those feelings with anybody. I have Veronica, and – parasocially – Bliss Adeyemi, as handholds for dealing with my body image issues, but who do I talk to about Jack? Yeah, I drunkenly acknowledged it to Veronica and Nairong the night of my welcome party, but I don't want the only thing I bring to the table to be trauma. Our friendship's so new and they've been there enough for me already. There isn't anybody else in my life – Mum, Otis – that I think could wholly put aside their hurt feelings that I didn't tell them sooner.

Poppy's a no go, and even if we didn't have a conflict of interest right now, I don't feel like we hear each other anymore. And Freya, she has her own heart to mend.

I unlock the door into the dank hallway and burst into tears, missing my family, especially Mum, who I wish wasn't so whirlwinded with all the wedding planning and could just be still, be my staying place again. For all her flaws and trauma-dumping on me, Mum can *listen* when she isn't preoccupied with her own problems. She'll let me go off, uninterrupted, only interjecting for clarity. And she's never the one to let go of a hug first.

But she's on a surprise, adults-only Big Weekend at some budget holiday park with Tina and their other friend, Kel, tonight. Only hours after Mum told us she was getting married, I was added to a group chat called, DIONNE'S 1 DICK FOREVER PARTY 🕊️🍾, and let in on the plan for the hen. It sounded like literal hell to me, so I'm thankful Mum bought my legitimate excuse of having overdue coursework to do.

The switch for the landing light is nonsensically on the second floor up, so I feel my way in the dark. As I reach the top of the stairs, something solid and dripping wet streaks past me and I let out a scream, gripping on to the banister so I don't fall. The landing floods with light, Toby's hand on the switch, a towel wrapped round his waist.

At first, he laughs at us colliding, but my face must be smudged with mascara and eyeliner from crying.

'Oh, shit, what's wrong? Hang on, I'm dripping everywhere.' He hesitates, looking from his door back to me. 'Doesn't matter. Come in my room, we can talk.'

Inside, I sink on to the bed. I blink and it's like I'm only just noticing his nakedness, his stomach flat but undefined, his chest and shoulders broad. He folds his dressing gown around him and steps into a pair of boxers, too quickly for me to realise I should be looking away.

'Do you want to talk about it?' he says, sitting down next to me.

I angle myself towards him, noting beads of water still on his chest where the V of his dressing gown falls open. 'You could've dried off, I would've waited outside,' I say.

Toby doesn't say anything, only waits for me to speak again. And in that moment, I recognise he's exactly the person I need to talk to. He's uninvolved, but cares for me. Maybe it's Toby's calmness, or the fact that since the moment I met him, he makes me feel simultaneously like he sees me and that I am so much more than my body, that makes me feel comfortable with him. So, I decide to tell him all about Jack. About our walks home from the bus stop with Freya and Poppy, how he'd wait until the other two had gone in before he'd pay me any more attention than a head nod. How it was Poppy he pretended to like in public, nonstop negging her and snapping her bra strap, but it was me he was video calling at midnight with his hands down his pants. How he'd laugh at me in school, then be all over me under his Man United covers hours later.

By the time I'm telling him that sometimes my *nos* got given up for *yeses* because Jack was so insistent about sex, Toby's staring at the floor, his thumb tracing the back of my hand. And when I get to the part about Jack waiting for me outside work today, gripping my arm and pulling me down a dark alley, Toby propels himself off the bed.

He roughs his knuckles against the side of his head. 'Is this guy for real? Please, I wish you had called me. If he ever pulls some shit like that again, you *have* to call me, I can't stand thinking of his hands on you like that. What did he want?'

When I talk about Poppy, my eyes fill with tears, because she doesn't believe he can be like this, or know what she's getting into. It kills me that she thinks I'm only warning her off him because I'm out to sabotage her.

'You did the right thing,' Toby says. 'You tried to tell her. Maybe if she knew you were together, that this is coming first-hand, it might really hit home for her.'

'I think you're right, but the thought of her not believing me about that either is too much right now. I can't. I will tell her soon, I just—' I take a deep breath, exhale it slow.

Toby pulls back, and I hold his gaze as his hand slips round the back of my neck, something pivotal in it. 'Seems stupid to ask, but are you OK?'

'I will be.' My work shirt rubs under my arms, the cheap

polyester stiff and uncomfortable. 'Why am I still wearing this?' I mumble, coming apart from Toby to strip down to my black vest underneath. Instead of breaking the moment though, we slot back together again, my cheek on his shoulder. 'Is it wrong if I don't tell her? I kind of want to disengage from the situation but— I don't know.'

I'm still thinking out loud, but the emotion of the situation's evaporated. I feel content being held by Toby.

'If you want to,' he says. 'But you're not a bad person if you don't. I'm sure she'll find out the truth eventually.' When he pulls back this time to look me in the eye, the V of his dressing gown loosens, exposing more of his bare chest. There's a feeling of something silken being run between my legs. Somewhere in the background of this moment, I register that there's a mutual desire and it's leading somewhere.

Before I can overthink my way out of this, I'm leaning in as Toby's thumb tugs gently on my chin. My mouth parts, his lips meeting mine. There's tongue but it's gentle, and I forget to care what I look like. His fingers slide up into my hair, and his other hand rests just inside my hip. I mirror him, my hand edging inside his dressing gown and grazing his bare thigh. But then Toby flinches, leaving me suspended in instant horror as he lurches off the bed.

'Nah, what am I doing? You're upset, this is weird. I was supposed to be comforting you.'

'Um.' It's like my whole body sighs with relief. 'I was feeling pretty comforted, believe me.'

'Yeah?'

'Yeah, this is OK.' I laugh. 'If it wasn't obvious from the moment I met you, I *want* you to be kissing me.'

'What?' Toby's smiling but shaking his head, still some distance from me. 'Seriously, what? Let me tell you, it was not obvious to me. Do you know how badly I wanted to kiss you when I first showed you the room? So bad.'

'I *knew* you were being flirty. I knew it.'

'And yet you left.' He laughs. 'Why'd you leave?'

'Because of everything I just told you about Jack.'

'Right. Shit.'

'I was too in my head, and ... I felt fat.' I look down, vulnerability making it hard to hold eye contact. 'I thought even if I wasn't imagining the flirting that you wouldn't want anything serious with me because, at the time I was like, look at me and look at you.' Toby's face falls. 'I'm in a better place now though,' I stress. 'Don't feel sorry for me or whatever. I just thought if anything were to ever happen, it'd only be a one-time thing and you might regret it, you know?'

He kneels in front of me, resting his hands on my thighs, his brows knitted together. '*No*,' he says emphatically. 'I wouldn't have done that.'

I swallow. I feel like I'm thrumming with anticipation, my heart rattling like I'm too near the speakers at Motion – and God, I so want this to happen. I start babbling. 'Also, I bolted because I was thinking if anything did happen, then it'd be this dirty secret hanging between us, when I *really* wanted to live here. I didn't want to mess that up. The rent was too cheap.' Toby laughs, but his eyes flick to my lips. 'And I'd not even known you a whole hour, my guy, how was I to know what you were thinking—' Toby cuts me off with a kiss, slow, his tongue tracing mine, before he pushes forwards, our noses bumping.

'And you and Bella?' I murmur. 'You're not?'

'Oh my God, hear me when I say no. Not at all. She's going through some shit. I'll tell you about it another time. I get it, it looks weird us spending so much time together, but nothing is going on. How could there be? It's you that I can't get out my head. And believe me, I tried. Downloading dumb dating apps to try and meet someone else, but no one compared.'

I let out all my breath, that last thing he said sinking in deep. 'I do believe you, but—'

Toby kisses me again, pressing himself further between my thighs until he's climbing up, over me, and I'm moving with him as we scramble backwards on to the bed, his hand slipping under my bra. When our lips part, he's on top of me and I can feel he's hard.

'Was that you telling me to shut up?' I say.

'Kind of.'

I laugh against his lips, initiating the kiss this time, and then switch positions so I'm kneeling over him and Toby's gazing up at me, at all the little uglies society says I should feel ashamed of. And yet he's still smiling, his hands still searching my skin. From this angle I feel mountainous, but beautiful and exact. I am powerless to change myself in this moment, so I might as well be alive in it, might as well laugh, gasp, get out of breath, stretch, feel the fullness of my belly on top of his, because life happens whether you're skinny or not. And I am worthy to be touched, to be loved.

So, I peel off my vest and accept that I'll have a double chin while I ride cowgirl. And fuck, it feels powerful not to care.

Sunday morning stretches lazily in front of me, smelling like ground expensively dark coffee, a stovetop breakfast being cooked downstairs, and boy bedsheets. I roll over on to my front to reach over and press the coffee.

About five minutes ago, he woke me as he nudged the cafetière on to his bedside table, a jangle of loose change falling to the floor.

'I wanted you to sleep, sorry. Morning,' he'd whispered. I felt the clash of his teeth as he kissed me from above, still smiling. 'Sorry, let me do that again.' And then he kissed me a second time, soft and cracked with a smile at the end, before disappearing to make us breakfast. The memory of that second kiss bleeds into the memory of last night and my insides do this liquid shiver.

As I'm pouring the coffee into two mugs, there's a knock at the door and I spill some. I scramble into a sitting position, clutching the duvet to me. 'Come in.'

Veronica cranes her head round the door, gasping when she sees me. Two strips of foil clamp the front strands of her hair like alien antennae. 'Um, so what the fuck is this?' She runs into the room and jumps on Toby's bed. 'Way to soft launch your relationship, by the way. These bedsprings?' On her knees, she throws her weight up and down to demonstrate. 'Super quiet, not squeaky at all.'

I squeal. 'Shut up, shut up, shut up. I don't know what you're talking about, didn't happen.' We giggle and it feels good to be girly. There's no hierarchy, or watering myself down to match up with her pre-approved version of me, *and* I get to live with this bitch. 'Also, girl, relationship? One shag does not a relationship make.'

'Are you joking? You're house mum and dad now.' She sucks in another gossipy breath. 'You little sneaks, was last night the first time or have you been doing it behind our backs for ages?'

'I told you I don't know what you're talking about,' I say. Veronica wags her finger, and I laugh at her as her hands thrash about under the duvet, her eyes lighting up when she's found what she's looking for. Triumphantly, she flings my bra at my head. 'OK, you got me. And, yeah, last night was the first time. But I don't know what this is. And I don't want to put too much pressure on it or make it weird in the house. I do really like him though.' Veronica lets off a noise like one of those shrieking fireworks winding its way into the sky. 'Shhh, he'll be back in a minute, let's talk about it later. I'll come find you. But quick, what are you doing to your hair?'

'Oh, I'm doing the two blonde bits at the front, you know? I know nobody really does that anymore but, bored. Me and Nairong are ordering pizza later, you wanna join? We can resume this little conversation then.'

Internally, I recoil. The ingrained Rules bark *no*, military sergeant style. But the Rules also told me nobody would ever want to be with me unless I stuck to them. And yet here I am, all sixteen and a half stone of me, in the bed of a boy who thinks I'm beautiful while he makes me breakfast.

So, fuck the Rules.

Veronica clicks her fingers in front of my face. 'Don't think too hard. You want the pizza, have the pizza.'

'I was about to say yes, I got there by myself. So yeah, I will be joining you and Nai for pizza, thanks. And hey, do you think you could help me go back to my natural colour?' I pluck at a strand of my frazzled curls. 'I think I'm over the bleach and it's taking forever to grow out.'

'Course, I still have some brown dye from a couple of months ago, no problem.'

Our heads snap to the door at the clanging crash of cookware on tiles. Shaking her head, Veronica turns to me and says, 'Saff, that boy is down there *head cheffing* to cook breakfast for you. I just saw Keith juicing a lemon. If that doesn't tell you what Toby wants, then I don't know what will.' She winks, heading for the door. 'Get it, girl.'

She's right, Toby's showing me a whole Hundred Acre Wood of green flags. I need to trust this.

From somewhere within the bedsheets, my phone goes off and in my search for it, I end up sitting cross-legged, ghost-costumed under the quilt. My screen lights up the dark.

No Caller ID

You might be able to delete Sydney but don't think you can get rid of me that easy Saffron

No Caller ID

It's Nolan, in case you had me confused with
one of the other boys you're lying to

My breath snatches back. I deleted him, deleted Sydney's
whole Reveal account. How did Nolan get *my* number? More
pressingly, how does he know my real name? Before I can spiral
too far, I hear Toby on the stairs. I thrash about in the quilt to get
my head free in time to see him backing into the room balancing
two plates on one arm, a clutch of salt, pepper, and chilli flakes
in his other hand.

'A fellow victim of the hospitality industry, I see.' Trying to
hide the shakiness from my voice, I swallow. Nolan's texts have
spiked me with cortisol. If he knows who I really am, does he
know my friends, could he find out about whatever's going on
between me and Toby and ruin it? Looking at the concentration
on his sleep-soft face as he brings me breakfast, remembering
how he made me feel last night, I can't let that happen. Even
if I deserve it. 'Most I can carry is five,' I say, gesturing to
the plates.

'I tried that once, ended up with spaghetti sauce on my box-
fresh Buffalos.'

'—I mean, why the hell were you wearing them on shift—'

'Never again.'

He laughs and I exhale, rationalising as my eyes stray to my
phone. The messages are vaguely threatening, yeah, but right
now, I decide to ignore it, because to give it any real meaning by

panicking would be exactly what Nolan wants. And what *I* want is to be able to enjoy this food, to have sex again, and maybe fall into an afternoon nap.

Toby sits cross-legged in front of me, the plates between us, and waves a hand over our food with a flourish. 'So, what we've got here is something I like to call, "back of the fridge breakfast hash" because all we had in were some potatoes, an onion, tomatoes, and garlic. Threw in some chickpeas for protein though. This OK?'

'God, yeah, thank you,' I say.

As we eat, Sydney and her entanglements fade from the present again, and I'm determined she won't make an appearance in the future either. I don't have any desire to sleuth out who Nolan really is. I don't care what his endgame might be, or whatever – probably illegal – activity was involved in getting my number. I don't want the drama, this *isn't* a TV show, it's my life. And if this was someone who knew me personally and cared about wrecking it, wouldn't they have done it already, instead of playing games behind a No Caller ID? I'll change my number, private all my social media accounts, and pretend this never happened. Then I can forget all about Nolan.

I push my mouthful of food into the side of my cheek, forcing myself to be here now. 'This is so good.'

The flavours are simple, salty, strong and pungent and I make an effort to eat consciously, gazing out the window as I chew. I try to identify the seasoning, and Toby nods when I guess correctly. Cracked black pepper, paprika, oregano, lemon (thank you,

Keith), and something potiony I've never heard of called liquid smoke.

After eating, I'm still feeling withdrawn and introspective and Toby guesses it's because of Poppy and Jack, which is there anyway, just under the surface.

'You should call her,' Toby says.

'I know, I will. Just not right now. Shall we watch a film? Or do you have things to do? I'm having a bed day.'

'A bed day?' Toby stares, considering me. I feel an *Are you OK?* coming but he leaves it. 'Alright, I'm down. You pick,' he says, reaching for his laptop and opening it in front of us.

Without thinking I go for a comfortable rewatch, *Eternal Sunshine of the Spotless Mind*. It's pure melancholy, quietly funny, and exactly what I'm in the mood for.

'Charlie Kaufman? Bro, he's like my favourite director.' Toby cocks his head, probably noting the flukiness of finding two girls in a week with whom he shares a favourite director of niche, surrealist cinema.

Fuck. What am I doing?

I swallow. 'No way. Mine too.'

'What a coincidence.'

I dissociate slightly as I act out the same discussion he had with Sydney about Kaufman. I feign surprise that we both went to the double screening at the Watershed, and purposely guess his favourite Kaufman film wrong twice, when I already know it's *I'm Thinking of Ending Things*. I roll my eyes when he tells me again that Bella said *it was a boring movie for boring people*. I

219

feel like I'm up high, watching a play from box seats behind my own eyes, everything I'm saying already rehearsed.

I press play on Toby's laptop and focus on his hand in mine as we fall into a silence I expect seems comfortable to him. His head slips into the nook of my armpit and chest as we watch and after some time, I feel the adrenalin ebb away. I allow myself to feel safe, to kiss the top of Toby's head, and to hope that everything will work out alright.

the rest of april

07/04

Mum

Mum

I need to know what size dress to order for you love??
Running out of time! Shall I just order you the 16? Do
you think you'll have slimmed down by then? Personally,
I'd buy the size down anyway for a bit of incentive but
that's just me haha. Let me know asap!!! Love you xx

Poppy

Poppy

You so are mad, stop denying it. You can't seriously be pissed at me for getting with someone you fancied ... in school??? Bffr Saff?

Nairong

Nairong

This is so so awkward, I'm sorry to be that girl but can you and Toby keep it down please? Love that you're in love ... don't love living in room next to Toby's 👀

Saffron

Mortified. Deceased. RIP.

Saffron

Seriously though, we're so sorry! Toby says he'll make pancakes in the morning x

Nairong

Apology accepted on the condition the pancakes are served with that caramel dipping sauce again, please, thank you and 😊 goodfuckingnight

09/04

girliesss

Freya

Heyyyy, anyone fancy drinks this weekend?? Or chill vibes, cinema? xx

Poppy

Can't sorry babe! I'm going on a date xx

Poppy

With someone who makes me really happy and who I genuinely see a future with tbh

Freya

Aw, OK? Felt like that was an indirect?? Happy for you though

Saffron

Sorry Frey, not a good time x

Otis

Otis

Adele vibrato Hello ... it's me

Otis

I miss you wtf!!! How are things? Come home soon pls. Mum is losing her damn mind with this whole wedding business

Saffron

I miss you too!! Things are so good, like scary good . . . I think I have a boyfriend? And tell me you're giving Mum grace, let her be excited even if this is all kinds of 90 Day Fiancé

Otis

WHAT who what where when. Why did you not tell me?

Otis

Saffron

Omg breathe please. Let me backtrack, we haven't had that conversation yet, so technically we're just seeing each other but . . . tba

Otis

Ah, Saff I'm so happy for you

Otis

WAIIIIIIT WAIT

Otis

Did you taste the forbidden fruit???? Is
it the boy next door (downstairs)

Saffron

His name is Toby!! But yes

Otis

Ahhhhh

10/04

Freya

Freya

Hey Saff, hope you're good. Bit of a weird one,
but you haven't seen Tom posting anything about
me, have you? Obviously the breakup was not an
amicable one and things have got messy. Apparently
he's been talking shit about me to all his friends

Saffron

Oh Frey, I'm so sorry. What a dick!!! But no, we don't
even follow each other. I wouldn't listen to a word he
said anyway, you know that ♥ What's he been saying?

You of course don't have to tell me! Just know I'm here if you want to talk

Mum

Mum

Hi love, had a think about the dress yet? xx

13/04

Otis

Otis

szsuishdss jwdwj its qoqqqqqqqq

Otis

Sorry, Rue stole phone!

Toby

Toby

Where are you, I'm not a 'miss the trailers' kind of guy

Saffron

Excuse me, neither am I! I'm 2 mins away. Can you get popcorn??

Saffron

Large obv

Toby

Already done. Plus pick n mix that
is 75% green jelly bean

Saffron

Oh. I know that's meant to be funny but that's
actually so sweet, thank you. I'll be there in a sec

Toby

I see you. You're looking 🔥🔥🔥 in that dress

Saffron

19/04

Mum

Mum

Seriously Saff, got to get these dresses
ordered by Friday really. 16 or 18?? xx

Poppy

Poppy

I get the sense your waiting for an apology or smthn but your going to be waiting a long time. This is stupid!!! I haven't done anything wrong?? I get it. The boy you liked in school didn't like you back and now he's with me. It's OK to be sad about that!! But it is not OK to take out your hurt feelings on me and shut me out like this without a word. We're meant to be best friends? At this point I'm waiting for an apology from you.

Saffron

Poppy. Take a second to read that back. My GOD, I love you, but would you ever climb out of your own ass??? I'm so sorry to yuck your yum but Jack is an emotionally abusive piece of shit and I'm sorry but I can't watch you get mixed up with him

Poppy

That is a BOLD statement from someone who's only ever made small talk with him on our way home from school. State your evidence, or is this just pure gossip!?

Saffron

You just need to trust me on this. I don't
want to fight with you Pop.

Poppy

How can I? Your clearly just jealous

Saffron

Maybe we should do this in person

20/04
Veronica

Veronica

Pizza?

Saffron

Pizza.

23/04
Wilder Street Massivvvve

Toby

Just got this from Elijah, what do you guys think?

Forwarded

Elijah

My guy, my guy! Congrats on your girl, bro. Myself, I've just been keeping busy, working hard. But that means I get to play hard. Speaking of. I'm planning a trip to Bristol next week which just so happens to be when Motion are hosting a payday rave 👀 Only £7 entry. Would the rest of the house be up for it u think? Miss the old days man

Veronica

Yesss! Still can't believe I didn't get to see him last time he was back. 1000% yes

Nairong

Yes, dependent on whether I've hit the halfway mark on this essay. It's worth 45% of our final grade so I cannot afford the hangover if I'm behind!

Toby

Ah mate, 45% is heavy

Veronica

You can do it I believe in you!! (And the allure of vodka cranberry)

Saffron

I'll be there!! It's about time I met Elijah, I need some answers as to who wrote the lyrics to WAP inside the wardrobe door up here

Veronica

Mystery solved. It was me

Saffron

Veronica!!! I do not need to be internalising 'certified freak, seven days a week' while I'm getting dressed

Veronica

Shut uppp, you already have. We all know what you and Toby get up to lol

Saffron

!!!!!!!!!

Toby

No comment

Keith

Suppp. Just seeing this. Tell Elijah I'll be there

Keith

And wtf is WAP

Mum

Saffron

Hey Mum. How is it all going? How did the makeup trial go? Did you end up booking them for the day? I know I've probably been adding to your already mad stress levels, so I'm sorry I've been weird about the dress. I'm a size 18

Mum

Hated the makeup. I want you to do it . . . and OK size 18 it is, if you're sure hon xx

Saffron

Yep, that's me. I want to be comfortable

april thirtieth

'OK, let me see the back?'

I spin obediently, peering over my shoulder at Veronica and Nairong taking in the scooped back of this bejewelled kiwi-coloured dress I thrifted earlier. Me and Mum were walking back to the car after a cake-tasting session for the wedding. My lips were clamped, fighting not to sound judgemental while I listened to her defend her decision to *spit out* the slivers of cake into a napkin after she'd sampled them, when this dress stopped me dead. It was exactly the same fit as the one I saw on @posibodybecky's account the other day, and I knew I had to try it on. Especially because a mannequin was wearing it in the window, a dress my size. And this mannequin was thicc, its thighs touching, bust busting, belly rounded. I realised I'd never seen a shop dummy assembled to be anything over a size eight before, never questioned it, never considered why that might be. Because thin is the blanket beauty standard we not only accept but expect.

I dragged Mum inside and there were whole rails of second-hand plus-sized clothes, curated especially for the climate-conscious big girlies. I felt the warmth of her watching me the entire time, a subtle smile on her lips. I think she was enjoying getting to watch me be teenage and girly, giddy with an armful of dresses to try on.

I told Veronica about it as soon as I got home.

'Yesss. Yes, yes. Love it. Where was this heaven-sent shop again?' she asks.

'Park Street, I wrote the name in my notes, hang on. I can't wait to take you there. How cute is this dress?' They both wordlessly agree. Veronica makes a nasally *nnn-hnng* sound through her open mouth as she slicks winged eyeliner over the eyeshadow I did for her, and Nairong nods wide-eyed, still typing close to a hundred words a minute for her essay. This dress fits right in with the rest of my revamped wardrobe. I took Bliss's *dress like you're blessed* advice and *ran* with it all through Bristol's vintage and independent shops. I'm taking denim shorts, crop tops, dungarees, and bodices into this summer, and I'm not afraid to wear them. Life is good when you allow yourself to wear the dress.

I go to my Notes app to find the name of the plus positive vintage shop, and accidentally scroll too far down. The note headed ✧New Year New Me✧ catches my eye.

1. GO ON A DIET
2. Find somewhere to live
3. Track meals in SlimIt app. Try not to go over 1,200 cals
4. NO SUGAR

5. Take self out on cinema date once a month
6. Do 30–60 minutes of cardio a day
7. Have beach body (weigh 10st) by summer
8. Find boyfriend to go to the beach with!!!

It's shocking to me, and honestly, I could cry about how little regard I had for my health as long as I was getting thinner. But credit where credit's due, I did achieve like all of these goals, if we put a different spin on them.

One: I went on two unsuccessful diets, both of which led me to the realisation that I didn't want to live like that anymore. Two: I found somewhere to live in an area scribbled with individuality on every street corner, that's diverse and inclusive and I can walk down the street and see people in all bodies, dressing and expressing however they please. Three: SlimIt's is a rulebook I no longer subscribe to, and I wouldn't know because I don't count them anymore, but I strive to eat more than 1,200 calories by mid-afternoon these days. Four: now that I don't restrict sugar, I find I don't crave it like I used to, and if I do want some chocolate, I'm not bingeing a whole box of it, then lying awake with food guilt all night. Five: the cinema is a regular date night for me and Toby, my favourite part when we come home and watch some film student's analysis of the movie's themes and metaphors on YouTube while we eat our leftover popcorn. Six: I walk a lot, to and from work and all around campus, but I don't have a regimented cardio routine, like I used to try and force myself to. Seven and eight: I don't weigh ten stone, but I do have a body that has all the business being on the beach when we're camping in Cornwall with our friends in June, me and the boy I think I'm falling for.

So no, I didn't create a new me. I found and finessed the old one instead.

'What was the name of that shop?' Veronica asks.

Smiling and feeling all types of sentimental, I scroll up. 'It's called, She Is the World.'

'Looove.'

Poppy would love this dress. I so want to take a picture and show her, but she never came through on my suggestion of meeting up and talking things over in person. We're not even liking each other's posts anymore, and this is the longest we've gone without seeing each other.

Which makes me all the more grateful for the closeness I have with these two girls.

'Nai, didn't you say you were over three quarters finished already?' I gently prod the lid of her laptop closed. 'Come on, you're done. You're done.'

If I'm being honest with myself, seeing her working so tirelessly on her essay only makes me more anxious about the fact that I haven't even got past the introduction on my own weighty assessment. I have some serious questions to ask myself about my commitment to this course that I've been head-in-the-sand avoiding for too long.

She blows a huff of air up into her face, then downs the last half of her drink. 'I am strictly on water from midnight, OK? Hold me to that.'

I salute her, Veronica following suit, when all three of our phones go off at once, meaning someone's messaged the house chat. As I glance at my screen, relief washes over me as it often does when I see my notifications clear of Nolan's exhausting message streak. Getting a new SIM worked, and I've heard nothing since. No more feebly intimidating texts. Whatever he's doing now, it's not harassing me to invest in our fake relationship anymore.

Veronica checks the group chat.

'Elijah's here! Right, let's go, everyone ready?' We file out of my room, teetering a little on the stairs. In front of me, Veronica's gripping the banister, eyes fixed on her strappy flatform shoes. 'Saff, you're gonna love him. Like, if you and Toby weren't literally perfect for each other, I'd be playing Cupid between you and Elijah.' She looks back, laughing through her teeth. 'He's such good vibes. And he's hot—' I reach out helplessly as she trips on the vacuum cord we all notice way too late, luckily only toppling off the bottom step. 'Oh my God, ow. Ow, ow, ow—' she gasps. 'My shoe!'

Veronica wiggles her foot out of the broken straps, getting to her feet.

'Shit, these shoes were *it*. The pièce de résistance. I'm gonna have to rethink the whole outfit.'

'You're bleeding,' Nairong says, pointing at where the buckle's snagged her skin.

I head down the next set of stairs as Nairong helps Veronica into her room. 'I'll find you a plaster. Corner kitchen cupboard, right?'

'Yeah. Tell Toby he's a dead man, I know this was him and his obsessive stair cleaning.'

Giggling, I make my way to the kitchen, towards bassy voices and the indefinite drone of house music.

I get closer and a familiar sting of peppery floral cologne spikes my adrenalin. As I reach the kitchen doorway, I see *him*. His twists neat, his hands that travelled my hips, my waist, gesturing animatedly as he talks to Keith in the corner.

'Oh, there you are.' My heart trebles. Toby's pouring drinks, happy he gets to introduce me. He takes my hand, taps the boy on the shoulder. A hot sickness stirs in my stomach. The boy turns, smile spreading as he remembers me, and then everything happens on fast-forward. 'This is Elijah; Elijah, this is—'

'Sydney, right?' says the boy who kissed me in the club.

'Saffron.' Toby's eyes search mine. 'This is Saffron.'

'Oh, my bad,' Elijah says, looking from me to Toby, working out what we are to each other. 'I was, uh, pretty waved that night . . . so, Saffron, is it? Ah, this is kind of awkward.'

'You two know each other?'

'Toby . . .' I don't know what to say.

He blinks with confusion, lack of recognition. 'Wait, what did he call you?'

'I said Sydney. Yo, I swear you said your name was Sydney. How embarrassing, I must've been a *mess*.' Elijah clasps the back of his neck, looking between me and Toby. 'My apologies.'

Without another word, Toby's out of the room, pulling me with him.

*

I stumble after him, our hands barely linked, numb like my body isn't my own. His fingers slip out of mine when we get to his room.

Unbearable seconds pass by where neither of us speaks. The tremble of the bass downstairs reverberates round my body, echoing the anxiety I feel. Toby stares down at his phone, scrolling for something.

'This is you, yeah?' He throws his phone on the desk behind me, and I jump, his cowboy cactus toppling out of its pot, dirt scattering over my feet. Its spines needle across my skin but it's like I don't feel it. I peer at his screen without touching it, open on his conversation with Sydney. Before I can ask how he's accessing this, because all chat history should've been wiped when I deleted her, he mumbles, 'I only took the screenshot because I wanted to search up those Korean films she recommended – *you* recommended.'

'Toby, I—'

'Nah, so let me get this straight. I meet you, I try to make it clear I like you, but you think I'm gonna turn out like your ex, OK, fine. Weeks and weeks later, I match with this girl called Sydney on Reveal. I've never met another Sydney in my life. She disappears without a word. And now one of my closest mates – he knows you somehow, and he's calling *you* Sydney. What the fuck is going on?'

'I didn't know he was your friend,' I blurt, latching on to the one shred of truth I can give him. 'I met him in town like a month ago and we kissed.' His head snaps away from me. 'I thought you were with Bella! He was just some stranger I met in a club—'

'Sydney, though. You're not even denying it. If it wasn't you, you'd be telling me to shut up. Tell me straight, was I talking to you the whole time?' The buzz of the music downstairs dies like the house is waiting with bated breath. I picture Elijah telling the others we stormed off, deliberating over whether to tell them that we kissed. 'Saffron?'

'Yes,' I say, so quiet. 'It was me.'

'Why? Why the hell would you do that?'

'It wasn't just you.' I mean it to undermine the creepy, stalkerish impression of me that must be taking form in his head. To clarify that I didn't fake Sydney up specifically to target him. I need him to know that her profile was already up and operating as my coping mechanism long before I matched with him, but of course it comes out wrong. 'It's hard to explain, I know how mental this all is. I didn't mean to match with you, I swiped on impulse, I swear that was an accident. And when I sent that first message – not only was I high as hell – but I was lonely.' I squeeze my eyes tight closed, wishing the pressure would vanish me. 'I just wanted to know how it'd feel to be liked by you—'

'I liked you anyway!'

'I didn't know that! I wasn't in a place where I could believe that. Even if you'd told me yourself, how could I believe it? I once heard the words *I love you* from a boy who'd watch and say nothing as his friends called me Queen Kong.'

He speaks to the floor. 'Well, obviously that's awful.'

'Look, I don't know how to make sense of what I did, or why I did it, so I know it's a fucking *stretch* for me to even hope that you can understand, let alone forgive me. But can I please try to explain?'

Toby sighs, collapsing on the edge of the bed, his head bowed. He says nothing but I continue anyway. I start with how hopeful Reveal made me feel with a concept so cemented in matching personalities it removed physical attraction from the equation completely. Only, Reveal's concept provided an all the more painful experience of rejection. Because when my appearance finally did get Revealed, these boys I'd already spent hours getting to know would ghost me. User not found.

'One guy told me it didn't matter what I looked like because he thought he was falling for me already. But he still disappeared once he saw I didn't look like he expected me to. I initially made a second account to find him again, to convince him we could make it work. It wasn't until he started saying the same things to me all over again that I realised everything he'd said was a lie. And then I wanted to hurt him as bad as he'd hurt me. So, I got ChatGPT to make these ultra-manipulated pictures of me. I was the source material for her, the technology just made ... a better version. A thinner one that, at the time, I thought was better.'

I sit down next to Toby, feeling the sting of tears as he moves away. 'I don't want to see the pictures.' His fingers interlock at his nape, looking straight ahead. 'So, you were basically on some vigilante catfish shit?'

'Pretty much.'

'That's ... that's weird. Really weird. Still, half of me is saying, maybe if I'd been treated so badly I'd have done the same.

Probably the fuck not, but part of me does get it. The other part that feels lied to and used is bigger though. Was that even *you* I was talking to before? Or were you pretending to be someone else too, like personality-wise?' I open my mouth to answer but he groans. 'No, you must've been you because of the Kaufman thing. I thought that was too coincidental. And then we had that conversation about it in person and you must've known some of the stuff I was about to say, right? That's the most weird.'

Toby shuffles back on the bed, to the corner where the walls meet by the window. He puts the pad of his finger to the spike of a baby succulent on the sill. I don't know how long we sit there, me watching him, waiting for a sign that this doesn't mean we're over.

In the noiselessness, I hear a scuffle in the hallway, coats and shoes being shoved on. A minute or so after the front door slams, I get a text from Veronica, sent at ten to midnight. How long have we been up here?

Veronica

> Hey. I obvsly don't have the whole picture, but Toby knows you would never do anything to hurt him. It's shit yh but you weren't to know who Elijah was! None of this is your fault OK. I'm sure you guys can work it out. Come join us. If you want company xx x

So, Elijah told them we kissed. And Veronica's showing me sympathy when she doesn't know the half of what I've done. I put my head in my hands.

Eventually, Toby says, 'It's a lot. This whole thing's a lot.'

'I know, I'm so sorry.'

'I know you are.'

I need to leave. He can't even look at me. Being in my presence only seems to be making this harder for him. I can almost feel what we have blighting, blackening the longer I stay.

'I'll give you some space then?' I say, my back to him. He says nothing but when I look over my shoulder, he's nodding. I swallow. 'Permanently?'

'I don't know.' Not meeting my eye, he takes his headphones from the windowsill and cups them over his ears. 'This all seems a bit fucked now. Me and you.'

Clamping my mouth shut, I nod once, grab my phone, and get the hell out of there. I walk briskly downstairs, shuffling my bare feet into my sliders and wrapping my coat that won't button up around me. It occurs to me what a joke that is, to have purposely kept a coat that doesn't close properly, caught in a downpour of rain. I walk with nowhere to go.

After only about ten minutes I feel stupid, my fingers too numb in this spring snap of cold, that I hold my phone up to my mouth and tell it to 'Call Otis.'

'Hello, hello.' He answers on the fourth ring. Hearing his voice releases the wracking sob I've been holding back. 'Oh my God, what, what is it?'

'Can you come pick me up, please?'

'Already leaving, send me a pin. What's happened, Saff, tell me.'

'I ruined it. I finally had it and I've ruined it.'

may

Soaked and shivering, I'm sitting on a kerb two roads away from Wilder Street when Otis pulls up, rolling his window down.

'You shit in the kitchen, didn't you?'

I blink at him. 'I— What?'

'I warned you, didn't I? Don't shit where you eat. You shit. You ate.' His mouth's cracked in a half-smile, being Otis, being us, giving me the exact kind of sibling funny I'd need if this were just about a complicated one-night stand. But it isn't. It's all convoluted and fucked up and— My throat aches and I burst into tears. 'Oh, Saff. Come on, get in.'

As Otis drives to the other side of town in after-midnight traffic, alongside taxis, night buses, and boy racers, I stitch together scraps of the truth, leaving out everything to do with Sydney. Saying it out loud once tonight was mortifying enough. I don't have the energy to explain my brainless actions all over again, and I'm not sure a lot of people would understand why I created her. I'd crumble if Otis knew the whole truth, under the weight of his disappointment too.

When I'm done talking, he only thinks I'm upset that my relationship with Toby got complicated because we live together.

'I'm sorry you're hurting, Saff,' he says, jerking up the handbrake. We idle outside the house, our features lit by the soft neon glow of the car's interior lights. 'I've only got clichés to give you, but you'll be alright. Things will work out.' I nod, blowing my nose on a drive-thru napkin. He sighs. 'Didn't know I had ads out and about saying, *call this number for therapy and taxi service* though. I should start charging.' Balling up my tissue, I side-eye him, eyebrow arched. 'Mum's home,' he explains. 'Like, *home* home. Asked me to get her from the flat this morning and she had all these bags with her. Haven't heard her on the phone to Le Dickhead once either. When I left, she was three pinots deep.'

'What?' I sniff. 'But she was so excited, everything's planned. Hasn't she told you what's happened? Did you even ask?'

'Of course I asked,' Otis snips. 'But she's not gonna say anything to me, is she? Not sure wedding bells will be ringing next month though.'

'We should get in there,' I say, sighing.

In the living room, Mum's swaying in the middle of the carpet, eyes closed singing the lyrics to 'Killing Me Softly'. Wine sloshes about in a giant novelty glass she's clutching by the stem. She looks tiny, swamped in an old Snoopy bed top of mine that comes almost down to the knee on her, her braids loose, whipping at her shoulders.

'Mum?'

She raises a finger, harmonising with the warm woodiness of Roberta Flack's voice, holding the longest note of the song. Her eyes slide open, glazed and muzzy.

'Liar,' she states bluntly, pointing at me. My chest constricts, flooded with a panic that I've missed some identifying link from Sydney's profile, or that Toby's decided to publicly out me in the time it took to get here and now my mum knows. But then her lip wobbles, and she spits, 'Liar, liar, big, fuck-off liar, that man.' With both hands she brings the balloon glass to her lips, though she's an inch or two out so it slops down her front. 'Lied about everything from day dot. The business, house in France ... the wedding.'

Mum folds herself into me, resting her head on my shoulder, and as is often the case, our roles feel reversed. I squirm, the responsibility to comfort and reassure her too soon when I'm still reeling from earlier. Still, I take a deep breath and ask her what's happened.

She takes a big swig of pinot. 'So, it started on the hen, yeah? Night one, brilliant. Tina smashed it out of the park, she'd stuck to her promise, no inflatable willy stuff, just a good time, you know.'

Out of the corner of my eye I see Otis turn quickly to face the wall and know he's sputtering over Mum's hen-do clause of no inflatable dicks. Despite having spent the last couple of hours in tears, dissecting my problematic behaviour to my could've-been-boyfriend, a smile tugs at the corner of my mouth too. There's something about being here that settles earlier's emotional storm. The worn comfort of the sofa cushions, the white noise of the always-on TV turned down low, and the musky sweetness of Mum's Black Opium perfume. It's home. No matter what I do or how big a fuck-up I make, I belong to these people, and I know there's always a room for me here.

Mum's lips are pursed as she pours herself another gallon of wine. 'Then night two comes. We're getting ready and my phone goes with a message, but I can't see it. I let it go. Since then, I've had two more I can't find either. Tina says it might be one of them message request things from someone you're not friends with. So, she has a look for me. *Natalie* comes up.'

Wordlessly, Mum taps at her phone and thrusts it under my nose. I steady her shaking hand with my own as Otis perches on the arm of the sofa to read over my shoulder.

Natalie Mullins

Hi luv . . . I know you don't know me but I was hoping to have a chat with you, probably be best to hear what I've got to say over the phone. x

Natalie Mullins

Messaging again because I've not heard from you. I'll just say everything over text and pray you read this in time. Hopefully before youv spent too much money on him. I couldn't not reach out to you . . . I'd have done anything for someone to have stopped me making the biggest mistake of my life too.

The gasp I let out sounds trashy and soap opera, but this *is* trashy and soap opera. I peer over my shoulder and glance at Otis gripping his dropped jaw.

Natalie Mullins

You did a talk at the SlimIt group my friend
goes to in Swindon and she saw you
getting into a car with my ex Andre—

'Andre!?'

—though after finding your page I see he's calling himself
'Philippe' now lol!!! Please believe me luv, the whole thing
is a SCAM. The brand he claims to run, it was called
'Pouvoir Esprit' when he was with me. He bought those
followers and the pictures are from old lululemon ads he's
photoshopped the logo out of. And let me guess ... he
asked you to help him understand some legal jargon and
in that 'jargon' it stated quite clear as day that he'd need
to pay a release fee for the so-called loan he's applying
for. And oh! All his money's tied up in the company so it's
YOU who has to pay that fee am I right?? For me it was just
shy of £8,000. But I thought it was OK because we were
getting married and once that happened I'd get my share
of the company earnings he'd promised me. God was I
wrong. And he'll have insisted the wedding is simple yeh???
It needs to be quick so he can run off with your money
before you've realised he's a lying little prick ... It's all bollox
luv!!!! I'm SO so sorry to have to tell you this. He's done it
to loads of other women, I've invited you to our group chat
if you want to talk to someone who's been through it xx

248

'Oh, Mum.'

A tear starts to roll down her cheek but she scuds it away. 'That *prick*.' She grinds the word into a growl at the end.

'How much did you give him, Mum?' Otis asks quietly.

Mum whips round, finger pointing at him. 'Don't you start—'

'How much did you give him?' I cut in. She gulps from her glass like she wants to drain it, but I put a hand on the base, slowly lowering it from her lips. 'Mum.'

Staring straight ahead, she says, 'Ten thousand.'

Otis sucks a sharp breath in through his teeth.

'*Ten thousand?* Where'd you even get that kind of money? Are you mad?' He picks up the bottle of wine and downs the rest of it, wiping his mouth on the back of his hand. 'A release fee, Mum? That's some Nigerian prince shit, like, it's *the* OG scam, how could you not know? He didn't even have to play hard, this guy was on easy mode, level one scamming. And you just threw the money at him.'

'The loan was for a hundred grand, from an offshore investor, a release fee sounded plausible. And it was from *my* savings, *my* inheritance money.'

Otis scoffs. 'Yeah, bet it was more inheritance though. From Nana Cleo, who thought you'd be using some of that money on us, on Rue. Not on a Chanel bag and a quick-time wedding to the actual Tinder Swindler. Who, might I add, you've only known for five minutes.'

'Alright, alright, you're both giving me a headache,' I say, though it's probably from the vodka I was pre-drinking with Veronica and Nairong earlier. I pull the scrunchie out of my hair, my curls pinging loose around my shoulders. 'Yeah, Otis, it's a lot of money but it's done now. Mum –' I take her hand – 'I'm so sorry this has happened, it must feel devastating to be lied to like that by someone you thought loved you.'

I let my head hang for a sec, forcing myself not to be consumed by the parallels between this and what I've done. I used to think of simulating Sydney as harmless fun, that the boys she'd ghost would slump with disappointment and move on. A tiny wickedness without lasting effect. But seeing the anguish in Mum's face slaps me with dormant accountability. This whole time I should've been trying to heal, not inflicting the pain I felt inside on somebody else. Toby should never have been the collateral damage of my processing.

'I'm so embarrassed.' Mum buries her head in her hands. 'And there's nothing I can do about it.'

I clear my throat. 'What do you mean? Surely the point of Natalie messaging you was so you could get ahead of this. Philippe doesn't have to *know* you know before it's too late, when you've got your money back and told the police—'

'I already told him.'

I sigh. 'You already told him.'

'I'd had a few drinks when I heard from Natalie. I didn't want to believe her, so I called him and confronted him. Next thing, Mrs Khatri in the flat down the hall is sending me screenshots of her Ring camera showing him carrying boxes out the flat. It's been gutted. He's gone. I'm blocked on everything.' Mum's chin juts up and she sniffs hard. 'Only thing I paid for was the venue, and my dress of course. The imaginary caterers, florists, and DJs he claimed to hire for business events were supposed to be doing the food and music and all that. *It's all bollocks, love,*' she says, quoting Natalie's message. 'Just like that, gone.'

I squeeze her hand and Otis crouches in front of her, speaking uncharacteristically tenderly. 'People don't just disappear in 2025, there'll be some trace. Tomorrow, we take everything you have on him to the police, alright?' Rolling in her bottom lip, Mum nods, as she rakes her fingers through her braids. 'But I think we should probably all get some sleep now.'

'Yeah,' she says. 'OK.' And with our arms around her waist, we help Mum up to bed.

I nudge the door open to my old room carrying a cushion and a throw from the airing cupboard under my arm. I forgot how small it was, and how big and trampling it made me feel. The newly painted walls and the bare shelves feel liminal. Since the last time I was here, Otis has bought a rug, fixed a curtain pole, and applied the finishing touches to his fairy castle mural for Rue. This space isn't my own anymore, but right now nowhere else feels like my own either.

Toby felt like mine.

I dig my phone out of my pocket, willing his name to be there, asking me to come back to the house. But there's only Rue on my home screen, her skin sun-speckled, sitting under the tree in the garden last summer. She smiles back at me, her almond-shaped eyes squinting in the light.

I come around from a deep, rolling wave of sleep, and it takes a while to surface. I sit up, disoriented, looking for the source of a persistent whining noise. When I open my door all the way up, I hear a pounding of feet and quick panting exhales. At the end of the landing, Otis is standing in Mum's doorway with his arms folded.

Taking up the exact width between the wall and the bed, Mum's running on one of those foldaway treadmills. All the blood in her body looks like it's boiling under her face, taut with rage. She's soaked in sweat and her breathing is ragged, going at a pace that suggests she's being chased.

'She's been at this speed for –' Otis reaches into the pocket of his dressing gown – 'coming up on forty-five minutes.'

'I'm.' *Huff.* 'Fine.' *Puff.*

'Did you not think to—' I climb on to Mum's bed and search for the switch behind her bedside table.

'Don't you. Dare.' I flip it and the treadmill sighs to a slow stop. Gasping for breath, Mum grabs the bottle of water I hold out to her with a shaky hand and downs it in one go, collapsing near enough on top of me.

'Refill this,' I say, holding it out to Otis. 'I bet you didn't eat anything yesterday, did you? You need to eat something, Mum.' I roll her on to her back and we lie reclined on either side of her bed.

Her chest heaves. 'I'm not ... in the mood ... to cook,' she pants as Otis reappears, throwing the bottle between us.

'Who said anything about cooking? Especially your cooking, no offence,' he says. 'I'm good for greens and evaporation, thanks.'

'Yeah, let's go out for breakfast,' I say, eager for something to do that isn't wallowing in my empty room. There's a sudden itch to check my phone, to see if Toby's text, but as I sit up, Otis feels my forehead, mock concerned.

'You OK? What happened to existing on a diet of thoughts and prayers?'

I sigh, glancing out into the hall, towards my room, my phone. 'Well, considering I almost shit myself at work and I fainted in front of all my new housemates, I decided to maybe ... not hate myself instead? Plus, I put myself through all that to only lose four and a half pounds.' I feel Mum's eyes boring into my back. 'I think this is just my body and I'm ready to accept that.'

'Four and half pounds ain't nothing,' she says breathlessly. 'It's a good start.'

I look at her, at her beetroot skin and sweat-slicked hairline, at her body's reaction to working it too hard, and instead of making me feel less than, I feel all sorts of awakened. Because I'm not blindly agreeing with that; losing four pounds that way didn't *feel* good, so why should we tell each other it is. Who said shitting your pants is something to feel good about?

'No. It isn't actually.' I look her in the eye. 'Did you not hear what I said?'

Mum shrugs but her voice is unsteady. 'No pain, no gain.'

'But why should there be any pain?' I wonder aloud, peering up at the Artex-swirled ceiling. 'And what am I gaining?' The approval of people I shouldn't want to be validated by anyway if their respect depends on my weight. How does what I look like affect anyone else in any way, shape, or form? In my head I'm passionately ranting like Bodied by Bliss in one of her video essays, but I don't say any of this out loud. Mum will go all defensive and shut down. So, I just say, 'I want to listen to my body. I've been learning a lot about this thing called intuitive eating, you should look into it.'

'I understand that it's your body, your choices, but to some people, the meal replacement side effects and feeling a bit more tired than usual is worth it.' Throwing her leaden legs off the bed, she scoffs. 'And I know what intuitive eating is, Saffron. Dieting is *what I do*, remember? SlimIt are going heavy on socials and seminars with all the body positivity stuff, trying to silence all the boohooers online.' Boohooers like me and all the other people in Bliss's comment sections, who are only now realising they've been systemically victimised by diet culture and don't want the next generation of young girls to fall into its trap of self-hatred too. 'All the talks I've got scheduled until summer are about leaning into what your body tells you is intuitively good for it, like leafy greens, citrus, and sea vegetables.'

'Well, your definition of intuitive eating is a lot different to everyone else's,' I mumble.

Otis scrolls to a stop on his phone. 'So, breakfast?' He lists off a few restaurant suggestions.

'They're all carbs, carbs, carbs,' Mum says. 'I can't eat that.'

Rolling my eyes, I bite at Mum's direct contradiction to being an intuitive eater and throw all my frustration into it.

'Who says?' I thump the bed. 'What intuitive eating means to me is hearing my body's signals for food, and respecting the fact that sometimes those signals will happen to be for a big slice of chocolate cake.' Mum shakes her head, shoving her tongue in her cheek, but I take a deep breath. I need her to know that everything she's instilled in me about diets and bodies and The Big Bad Badness of being fat isn't going to dictate my life anymore, and that it doesn't have to dictate hers. That I resent the fact she made me think a flourless, sugar-free carrot cake was all I deserved on my last five birthdays. 'I'm trying to get it in my head that no food is off limits, there aren't good foods and bad foods. I mean, obviously don't be eating pizza for breakfast, lunch, and dinner and don't eat too many ingredients that sound like industrial cleaning products, but it's all just food. And we should all be allowed to eat to feel full. I bet you can't even remember the last time you felt *satisfied* with a meal, so satisfied you're licking your fingers. Seriously, if you could eat anything in the world right now what would it be? Don't think about it, just—'

'Chips.'

Otis eyes Mum over his phone. 'Everywhere does chips, I'm gonna need you to narrow that down.'

'Just ... chips?' I ask.

'No, not just *chips*. I mean deep fried, chunky chips. Chunky, oily, golden ones. Fluffy in the middle, crispy on the outside. With bare salt and vinegar. But ...' Mum sinks back down, hugging one of her throw cushions to her stomach. 'Nah, I already had the wine last night.'

'So? The food police aren't going to arrest you. Going out for this one meal isn't going to undo all the hours of Stairmaster you've put in. You're not going to wake up tomorrow and look any different. Like you said, this is the food you want to eat the most right now, honour that.'

Otis looks between us, finger poised over his screen. 'I'm gonna have to book. Fresio's has a breakfast menu now. They do chips.'

'Yeah, Mum?' I prompt.

Mum nods once, her lips clamped tight.

'OK, so Otis you're having the open halloumi sandwich with frickles, guac, fries, and an orange juice,' I reel off from memory as I get up from the table, 'and Mum, you're having the breakfast bagel without cheese, a side of hand-cut chips – not fries, and a sparkling water.'

'Don't you need to write that down?' Otis says, pinning down our napkins so they don't blow away in the breeze. 'You should write it down.'

I scoff. 'Please. I'm a professional.'

Behind me, I hear Mum laughing as I flick some sunglasses

I dug out of Mum's dressing table down from atop my head. And I pick my way through the tables on Fresio's sundeck which overlooks the murky waters of the harbour. Luckily, with Otis's denim jacket thrown over my shoulders, my outfit from last night transitions from evening to daytime. As I head to the bar, I tug the jacket closed, suddenly going cold when I remember that Otis is driving me to Wilder Street to pick up some stuff after this.

Not wanting to get into a discussion about what happened last night, I keep things vague in my text to Veronica and Nairong.

Saffron

Hey, going to spend a few days at home. Do you know if Toby will be home in around two hours?

I don't know what answer I want to hear. If he is, I should stay away, respect his boundaries, even though everything in me is saying distance is the wrong approach here, that I need to fix this with patience and proximity. As I shuffle forward, almost at the front of the queue, their replies come through one after the other.

Veronica

Saff!! I was worried about you. Are you OK? He won't be here, no x

Nairong

There was a note on the fridge when I woke up (with a disgustingly bad hangover) saying we were welcome to eat all his food because he's going home for a few days too.

Saffron

Oh. I didn't think he would leave

My eyes fill with tears behind my sunglasses, imagining Toby packing his bags because of me, choosing not to out me to the girls despite how raging he must be. Because if they knew what I'd done, they'd be rightly judging me and protective of him, especially Veronica. But in another text Veronica says they miss me and that everything's going to be fine. I grab a napkin off a cutlery station and blot my eyes, knowing that if they do find out, our friendship will be another thing my catfishing bullshit will have cost me.

'Next, please.'

I look up, pocketing my phone as the boy who got served in front of me walks past, folding his wallet away. My memory jolts.

'Tom?' I say, without a thought for what I'm about to say next.

He hesitates, backtracking and studying my features as I step out of the queue. 'Yeah . . . It's Saffron, right? You're Freya's friend from school.'

I cross my arms, hoping my sunglasses are dark enough that he can't see me scanning over his shoulder for the girl me and

Poppy caught him cheating with at the café. 'So, you do know me?'

'From pictures. And Freya spoke about you a lot obviously.' Tom pulls a patronising smile that turns down at the corners. 'How's she doing?'

'As you can probably guess, not very fucking good, mate.' Feeling a rush of confrontational energy, I push my glasses back into my hair. 'You do know it was me who caught you, right? I served you at Jemima's when you were with that girl.'

'Caught me? What?' He looks to the side, casting back. 'I recognised you in the restaurant, yeah, but it was awkward. I'd never met you when me and Freya were together, why would I go out of my way to say hi to you?'

I open my mouth but my words stall. Something's not adding up. His face clouds as he takes a step closer to me.

'You caught me?' Tom says again. 'Caught me doing what? What's Freya said?'

A waitress tuts, holding a tray of drinks aloft as she squeezes past us.

I pull Tom to the side, the background din of conversation and easy listening piano suddenly too loud. 'Why don't you tell me?'

'Nothing. Me and Freya broke up in September,' he says. My jaw drops, the hairs on my arms prickling. 'We haven't spoken in months. She didn't tell you? She let you think we were together this whole time— Wait, she *acted* like we were together?'

My brain attempts some quick maths, but with questions firing and wires crossing in my head, I end up counting back on my fingers. 'But you got engaged in September?'

'The fuck? We weren't engaged!' All I can do is gape as Tom rakes his fingers through his hair, glaring at me like he's waiting for me to tell him I made the whole thing up. 'We were only together for *three and a half months*. She told you we were engaged?'

'I—' I don't know what to say, what to think. What the *fuck*, Freya? She did quite a bit more than simply telling us she was engaged. There was a whole announcement, a photoshoot. And everything that came after, his 'n' hers champagne flutes, selfies at the gym, posed photos by the Christmas tree in matching red pyjamas. None of that was real? Tom's staring at me, waiting for an answer. Do I lie for her, downplay it all? 'I, um. Maybe I just assumed,' I say, backing away. 'I've got to go. Sorry, Tom.'

'You assumed we were engaged?' Tom calls as I pick up the pace.

I skirt around the same waitress I almost bumped into before, carrying a tray of empties back to the bar. I whip my head back just as Tom starts after me, but wince at the tinkling waterfall sound of shattered glass crescendoing behind me. As I keep walking, getting out my buzzing phone, the waitress's tray wheels past my feet.

I'm surprised to see Poppy's name on my screen.

Poppy

Hey are you at home? Snapchat location said you were in Whitchurch with your mum earlier. Can I come over?

Poppy

I know it's been a while, but you said we should talk in person, can we still do that?

And then most recently,

Poppy

I'm on my way to yours. I'll just wait

Back at the table, Otis smirks as he sees me. 'You forgot, didn't you?'

I glance back toward the bar. Tom's shirt is soaked with beer dregs and coffee stains as he flaps about uselessly holding a wad of napkins. The waitress appears with a dustpan and brush, and shoos him away.

'Yeah,' I say, distractedly. 'Sorry.'

'I'll go.' Otis gets everyone to repeat their order, typing it into his phone while I peer past him, head ducked behind a menu. I watch Tom look for me briefly before leaving the restaurant holding his car keys.

'You OK, hon?' Mum asks, as I reply to Poppy.

'Mm-hmm.'

Saffron

OK? It's gonna be over an hour until I'm home probably

Poppy

That's fine, I'll wait

Surely, she can't still want to talk about Jack? With a jolt, I worry that maybe something happened for her to realise I was right about him.

Mum clears her throat. 'I've been thinking about something you said earlier. That you didn't want to hate yourself anymore? Tell me you were exaggerating, right? You don't actually hate yourself.'

Anxious, my hand shakes as I pour myself a glass of water from the jug on the table. 'I did, yeah. Now I don't.'

'That breaks my heart to hear you say that.'

'Well, are you surprised? How was I supposed to accept myself when . . .' I swallow. 'When you couldn't.'

'Saffron Aaliyah Saldana. What are you talking about *accept* you? I love you. And I would love you if you had two heads or a backside the size of Timbuktu, my girl.' I laugh but it snags on the lump in my throat. 'I only pushed you with your weight loss because I thought it was what you wanted,' Mum says, making a show of unfolding her napkin and laying it across her lap.

I sip my water. If I don't say this now, I never will. 'I wanted it because I've spent most of my life watching you want it *so badly* for yourself, it made me think that to be anything other than thin wasn't OK.'

Mum sits with that for a minute, clasping her hands in front of her. 'I hear you,' she says eventually, cracking a knuckle. 'I

262

know I'm a bit much with it all sometimes, but being active and watching what I'm eating kept me sane after your dad left. It gave me a focus. I didn't think about how that might affect you, and for that I really am sorry, Saff.'

She reaches for my hand, and I take it. 'It's OK. I'm OK now.'

'Good.'

Later when the food comes, we eat together, with so much to say we talk behind our hands as we chew. We share fries, order more. Otis sprays his drink, laughing, as we enjoy this rare moment of just us three. I'm not conscious of my plate emptying but of my cup filling instead. And I think Mum's starting to feel that too.

'Well, go on then.' Back home, the echo of my voice around Rue's sparsely decorated bedroom leaves a flat silence. I bite my thumbnail, my leg jiggling as I stare at the floor in front of Poppy's feet. 'What did you want to talk to me about?'

She takes a deep, juddering breath, like she's been crying. 'I'm sorry for being a brat when I was texting you,' she finally says. 'I wish I'd listened to you.'

I sigh. 'You don't have to apologise, Pop. It doesn't seem important now,' I say, remembering Tom's shock when I told him I thought he and Freya were planning a wedding. Why would she lie about something like that? With a hard tap, I wake my screen to see the time. I wonder if he's contacted Freya, if she knows I know it was all a lie yet. 'Is that all you came here to say?'

'No. Also that you were right,' she says. 'Jack is a piece of shit. And I want to know how you knew that. Because you really *knew*, didn't you?'

I nod. 'You don't have to tell me twice. Let me guess, you slept with him and he told you everything you wanted to hear. Said he wanted to make you his girlfriend—'

'*How* did you *know*?' I can tell she's already worked it out, or else combed through his texts while he was asleep or something. She's almost glaring at me, like she resents the fact I was with him first.

'I was his girlfriend, OK? He was my first kiss, the first boy I slept with. Only nobody was allowed to know, and I settled for that—'

She actually rolls her eyes. 'This isn't the fuckboy victim Olympics, babe.'

'Let me finish, seeing as you thought you could come here to tell me how toxic I already warned you he would be.' Fighting like this feels casual, inconsequential even. Like I said, we're sisters. We can be spitting teeth one second, giving forehead kisses the next. It isn't the fighting that has a finality to it, it's her showing up here after so long and apologising, like it's closure she's after. 'I couldn't even tell you about us because it felt too shameful to admit I'd accepted him not wanting anybody to know about me. That I felt I was worth so little, even that scrap of affection from him felt like some kind of win. Admitting that to you, when every boy you've ever met has tried to get with you, was too embarrassing, and by the time it was over, I wanted to repress

264

that shit, not let someone else in on it. And do you know what the most fucked up thing is? I still don't know if he actually liked me or if I was just there, easy, if the whole time he was using me. Not that you'd get what that feels like.'

'Fuck you, Saff. I do feel used. That's all I feel with boys.' Poppy swipes her sleeve across her eyes. In the seconds that pass where she fights for composure, it's the first time I wonder whether she welcomes all the attention she gets. The first time I consider that Poppy, who posts over-the-shoulder mirror selfies, post-workout in her scrunch bum shorts, might base her self-worth in how others perceive her too. And I see how they perceive her, as a sexual *thing*, her body an object. My stomach sinks, thinking of Poppy hearting the derogatory comments from the boys, and even men, who follow her. 'I know it must've all been bullshit now, but at first Jack made me think he was different. The first time it happened we were drunk—'

'I don't want to hear it, Pop.'

'I need you to hear it! I don't want you to think I'm a horrible person. It was Freya's party when her parents were on holiday, that one time I met Tom, the one you didn't come to. I got talking to this older boy who worked with Frey, and he was so drunk, like slurring with his eyes like this.' She peers dazedly through slitted eyes, and sighs. 'He grabbed my tit out of nowhere. Said I was asking for it with boobs that size. Then Jack came and decked him. I was crying my eyes out, so he took me to one of the bedrooms to calm down.' She shrugs. 'We were talking for hours, and hand on heart, I think it was the first conversation

I've ever had with a boy outside my family that wasn't about my boobs, or sex, or watching other people have sex. Now I see it was all an act. But at the time, Jack was the first boy in so long to really speak to *me* and not ...' Poppy pulls her jumper loose around her chest, like she's self-conscious even in front of me. 'And then he left for Brighton. We texted for a bit, I sent a few nudes, it was never going to be anything serious. That night at the club was the first time I'd seen him since he left. He'd been nonstop messaging me about meeting up for a week before. After we slept together, I still held out hope that it would go somewhere but he was just like the rest. And I know, right, *what did I expect*, to not get attention with these things?' She talks with her hands, mouth running her thoughts unfiltered. 'But I promise it was never about that, I got them because the thought of taking my bra off in front of a boy made me feel sick. You know how Molly Mills's are kind of like stuck here all the time?' Poppy indicates well above her already perfectly positioned boobs. 'Well, mine were down here, and all I kept thinking was there was something wrong with mine.'

What's left of her brattiness crumbles with the wobble of her bottom lip.

'Oh, for fuck's sake, Pop.' I crawl across the carpet to her. No matter how long it's been, or what she does, I'll never be able to see her like this and not go to her. My first friend. 'Don't cry,' I say, gentler, laying a hand on her arm. 'Your tits are great, always were. And I could never think you were a horrible person.'

'Oh, I am.' She wipes her eyes on her cashmere cuffs. 'I thought they would make me happy, you know? My very own thirty-two double Ds. I made an investment—'

'Technically your mum did.'

'Ew. Whatever. Where's my return?'

'You literally look like the Margot Robbie Barbie, are you for real?'

'See, you know it, I'm supposed to be happy. But I'm not. I'm really not—' Her voice strangles off.

'I'm sorry you feel that way, Pop. Genuinely didn't see that one coming.'

Looking at her with mascara streaking her face, I realise our pain and shame is nuanced, mine not to be pitted against hers. Of course, the way we're perceived is different, and Poppy's physical appearance makes it easier for her to move through the world, but on the inside, if we're all fighting the same internal battle, why are we fighting each other? Shouldn't we be raging together, at the systems that set our money alight to fuel our own self-hatred?

'I'm sorry too. If I hurt you.' Poppy rests her head on my shoulder. 'Not just by accidentally getting with your shitty ex-boyfriend, but for anything ever. I know I take you for granted and I haven't been there for you as much since uni started.'

'Yeah. But – and no shade – don't apologise for just being ... you. You're Poppy, you're an extrovert through and through, you're a little inconsiderate and messy. You're a Gemini, for God's sake.' My throat aches as I talk over the urge I have to cry. 'I want you to go off and do you, and I'll be here, doing me.'

Poppy sniffs. 'Things are different now, aren't they?' I nod, my chin against her scalp. 'Am I the problem? Are you sure I'm not a horrible person? First Lola, now you.'

'I'm sure. Lola's the Instagram girl, right?'

'My God, yes. Can you stop pretending not to know who I'm talking about, you bitch.' I shake with laughter, and feel her laughing too. 'She got weird.'

'What do you mean?'

I feel Pop wriggling to get out her phone. She scrolls to find something, then hands it to me.

Lola Hey hey where you at??

Lola Did I do something wrong?

Lola What you up too girly??

Lola Rude lol

Lola Definately didn't expect this from you

Lola Poppy wtf!!? Talk to me please

'Oh my God.'

Dread floods my chest. I reread the messages, an uncanny sense of déjà vu raising the hairs on the back of my neck.

'I wasn't trying to be mean, but I was busy with uni, and then

Jack was back in my DMs. I just didn't have time to talk all day every day like we did before,' Poppy says. 'Weird, right?'

'Not as weird as what I'm thinking.'

I get out my own phone, nerves fraying as I wait for Reveal to redownload. I open up my chat with Nolan and compare the conversations on each of our screens, my suspicions creeping into near-certainty the more I think about everything.

'Alright, I'm about to say some Scooby Doo type of shit, but does it look like they're speaking with the same texting accent to you?'

'Babe, texting accent? Aren't you the anthropologist? It's called an eye dialect, I saw a TikTok about it.' Poppy looks closer. 'Yeah, that's the same person for sure. And look, they spelled definitely wrong both times. Who's *Nolan*?'

I pinch the bridge of my nose, overwhelmed with all the soul-baring and being on the brink of even more revelations. I ignore her question because I only now feel like I might be close to finding that out for myself.

'Is there any way we could know for sure?' I ask her, more thinking out loud. 'I have a hunch about something, but I so want to be wrong.'

'I mean, there must be. But you'd have to be *smart* smart and we don't know any computer people.'

I gasp. 'I do! Come to think of it, you do too.'

I hit dial on his number, all my nervous energy propelling me up off the floor. I pace as it rings. 'Hey, Keith?'

Poppy flexes out her hand, pretends to study her nails.

'Yeah?' He sounds suspicious. 'Why are you calling me? People only call if something bad's happened.'

'I need you to do me a favour. You're at home, yeah?'

He laughs. 'Trying not to be offended you assumed that, but yes.'

'You know you said you worked in cybersecurity?' I pause at the window, staring up at the utility pole outside. 'This is probably impossible, I know, but if I gave you the details of two accounts that were sending texts via Reveal and Instagram, would you be able to, like, track if they were accessing the internet at the same IP address or something?' Poppy's nodding, connecting the same dots that I am.

'Or something, yeah.' He pulls the phone away from his ear to cough. 'If I ask, are you going to tell me what this is about?'

'Yeah, at some point, when I'm not freaking out about it. Can you do it?'

'Send me their profiles. I'll call you back in, like, ten minutes.'

I copy them into a message to Keith, my breath shuddering with adrenalin as I inhale.

'You think you know who it is, don't you?' Poppy says.

I nod. 'But I have to tell you something first, so that when all this comes out, and we have to go and deal with this, we're on the same page.' I sigh, weary with the weight of coming clean again. 'So, I used to pretend to be a girl called Sydney online. I used fake pictures and my username was Sydney-dot-Darlinghurst ...' Confessing a second time strips all the emotion away from the ugly facts; there's no desperate attempt to justify my actions, no

270

trauma-dumping. No excuses. I did a bad thing, to Toby and to all the boys before him. And I have to own that. 'And Nolan and *Sydney* were speaking for about three months, until I deleted everything a few weeks ago, which was around the same time you stopped talking to Lola, right?'

'Around then, yeah.' Poppy sucks in a breath. 'So, you're a catfish?'

'... *Was* a catfish.'

She nods slowly. 'Darlinghurst?'

'The city my dad moved to in Australia. I dunno why, I just ... it's a cool last name.'

I watch Poppy trying to keep her expression in check. She grabs her lips like she's trying to twist the smile off her face, eyes wide and incredulous, before she lets out a burst of laughter.

'I'm sorry, but that is *wild*, Saff.'

Hysterical, I laugh too, though a sudden spike of adrenalin snatches it back into my chest. My phone vibrates in my hand.

Keith

Geolocation came through. Both phones accessed the internet from the same IP address. From a router located within the postcode BS4 3PQ

'Fuck,' I groan. 'I so wanted to be wrong.'

As I climb into the passenger seat of Poppy's car, kicking through the landfill of single-use plastic in her footwell, I'm choked with nostalgia. I flip up the visor mirror and steel myself for what's to come, which feels particularly poignant sitting in this car. We've cried together here, screamed our lungs out along with Olivia Rodrigo's heartbreak, eaten drive-thru fries at 3 a.m., and got ready together sharing the rear-view mirror.

I let Poppy in on what I found out at Fresio's earlier, and when I get to the part about the engagement being fake, I screech as she nearly slams into the back of a lorry.

We drive the rest of the way in silence.

On a residential street in Brislington, the only parking space is roads away. As we walk, my own reflection floats eerily alongside me as it mirrors me in the houses' bay windows.

We trail to the front of a house like any other on this street, except parked outside of it is the same Vauxhall Corsa where Jack and I had our first kiss. Happening, and then over in seconds, his face diving into mine, tongue all too much. I flinch at the memory, and at the backscattering of bright colour as the house's front door opens and its stained-glass panels catch the sun.

Jack's saying, 'Tell your mum I said thanks for lunch. I hope you—' He sounds pained, searching for words. 'I don't know what to say. I didn't realise things were this bad, Mum never said.' He sighs. 'I hope you feel better.'

From this angle, I can only see Jack on the doorstep, the hallway in shadow.

'Come on,' Poppy whispers. She grabs my hand, but it feels numb, pins and needles pale, like all the blood in my body's beating inside my head and chest.

As we round the car, I peer over the bonnet, my eyes meeting hers, finally. I feel sick. Jack's standing between us, halfway down the garden path.

'What the hell are you doing here?' he says.

I hold her stare. 'Frey?'

As her name leaves my lips, it dissociates from the person I see in front of me. This girl's not Freya. Freya is the selfie on my feed, the carousel of holiday pics, she is #transformationtuesday, she is the goal weight, the Taylor Swift lyrics she captions her posts with. Her body belongs on the beach now, her dress size at the front of the rack in shops.

Freya's supposed to be happy. This girl looks like she's dying.

Jack steps in the way, blocking my view of her. 'I said, what are you doing here?' He's tearing down the path, on the other side of the car now, leaning over the bonnet at me. 'Haven't you both done enough, deciding you want nothing to do with her when she's like this? You and all, Pop.'

A thought finds my lips. 'What was Tom's last name again?'

'What are you on about?' Jack says.

I shake my head, drifting toward the house, registering Poppy's pleading tone.

But I don't care about that. Their voices fade and the girl in the doorway cowers. Freya cowers. Her skin's like greaseproof paper, baring her bones. Somehow, I have the awareness to suppress the gasp siphoning away all my air. She clings to the doorframe like it's hard for her to stand up, her elbow joint the thickest part of her arm. As I reach her, I realise just how ill Freya is, her face gaunt and grey without all the makeup, but her lips still drawn in a withering smile.

'It's Nolan, isn't it? Tom Nolan.'

She nods, a ghost.

In an armchair, underneath all the blankets and throws, you wouldn't know Freya's body was so emaciated. But with her hair up, the hollow vacuums of skin between her cheekbones and jaw are visible, and the skin on her face sags, her lids heavy, eyes dry. I sit uncomfortably on the cream leather sofa, feeling too hot in Otis's jacket but too pinned by Freya's stare to move.

I swallow, my throat gravelly. 'It's OK,' I whisper. 'I don't want to argue. I just came to talk.'

'Shut up,' she hisses, and I'm stunned.

I glance sideways at Poppy, who I can tell is trying hard not to stare at the starkness of Freya's appearance, her bones only a breath under her skin.

Freya's harsh expression dissolves as she glances over her shoulder towards her mum, and she looks girlish and small.

I've always loved Claire, and she's prattling about in the kitchen, through an open door behind us, her mouth running an endless stream of desperate chatter. 'No sugar, you said, Saffron? Yeah, no sugar. Milk no sugar, milk no sugar.' Mugs bang on to the counter. 'Three visitors in one day, Freya, aren't we lucky—'

'Jack didn't want to be here,' she states, bluntly.

'Do you girls see much of him anymore?' Claire natters obliviously. I cut a look at Poppy. 'I thought it was so nice when the four of you started knocking around together but then school's over and everything changes. Happened to me and my friends back in the nineties. Not like today, where you can keep in touch online, like you lot do.' Claire comes in with three teas on a tray. 'There're snacks in the kitchen if you fancy. No pressure. Just there.' I watch her eyes graze over her daughter, a smile stretched tightly across her mouth.

Freya's words come out in a sigh as she rubs her eyes. 'Thanks, Mum.'

'Yeah, thank you,' me and Poppy echo.

'Right, I'm off to do a bit of shopping, alright?' Claire bends to kiss Freya on the cheek. 'I shouldn't be too long but call if you need. See you later.' She places a hand on my shoulder on her way out and softly says, 'Thank you for coming. You look so well, love.'

Well. I've never thought of my body as a well one, and it dawns on me what a privilege it is to feel well. To feel fed, nourished, rested, and to move with ease. Freya, she doesn't look well.

The front door clicks closed and then we're alone.

Freya nods at my phone. 'So, are you you right now?'

The clock on the mantel ticks. No diverting. No skirting. Freya just straight-up calls me out.

'Yeah.' I swallow, not used to talking about this so openly. 'I don't do that anymore—'

'Sydney,' she says, gazing up at the ceiling like she's trying the name on for size. She interlocks her fingers, thin and snappable like the winter twigs of trees. 'This is all your fault really. When we matched the first time and it was *revealed* –' she air quotes – 'that the Saffron I was talking to was you, I deleted you straight away.' I flash back to nearly half a year ago, my and Nolan's Revelation Status hitting 100 per cent during the first lecture back after Christmas, the hurt and humiliation of being immediately ghosted once he'd seen my pictures, despite our connection. 'But you had other plans, didn't you, Sydney?'

I sigh, peeling off my jacket. 'Frey, can we not do this whole *Riverdale* villain thing? Why're you talking like that? Just be real. It's us. How did you work out I was Sydney? Did you pay some company for the email I signed up with?'

'There was no need, you made it *so* obvious. Sydney's job at the café, her constant *Friends* references, love of film, her sharing your refusal to ever put a kiss at the end of your messages. You forget we used to text all the time. *And* you didn't even disguise the fact you were moving into a new place. Having the exact same moving date confirmed it for me.' Because I never once considered I was being catfished by one of my closest friends. Without acknowledging it, Nolan felt like he was on the other side of the world to me, about as physically close as someone I shared a subreddit with. Emotionally, it felt like we'd never not been in each other's lives, but that's internet friendships for you. 'Oh, and you're not special, by the way. I don't fancy you. I roleplay to loads of people. As loads of people. Isn't that right, Pop?' Poppy's gripping her jaw, looking at Freya like she's a stranger. 'I also go by Lola Rae, Jackson Noel, and of course, Nolan Day. And before you ask, I'm not *confused*, I'm not having some kind of identity crisis. I don't want to be a boy, it's simpler than that.'

Freya's eyes narrow as she catches me staring at her spindly hands. 'I'm sorry,' I say, scrunching my eyes shut and trying to deep-breathe my way through the stress of this confrontation. I don't know if I can ask her about it. About how drastically thin she's got. I think of all the conversations on body image I've read over the last few months, and everything I've absorbed from the internet's collective consciousness about disordered eating and mental health, and it's all yelling, *No, absolutely not, it's personal, it could be triggering.* But the way society makes us feel about our bodies feels so uniting, it feels like something we *should* be talking about. How can I see the way diet culture has ravaged this person I love and not invite her to talk about it? If I get even the slightest sign she's uncomfortable, I'll pull back and apologise. 'You don't have to talk about it, but can I ask what happened?'

'Everyone's suddenly so interested in what I look like again, that's what. Everyone's worrying and getting involved.' I notice she's shivering as she points to the mug of tea. 'Can you pass me that, please?'

Assuming the green tea is hers, I hand her the cup printed with *This is probably wine* in a flowery scrawl. 'And you don't think they should be worried?'

'I think they should've been worried about me before, like way before.' Freya wraps both hands around it, letting the tea steam into her face. Her shoulders are humped up under her ears, and I see that same inward shrivel that I saw in Nana Cleo towards the end. Except Freya's only nineteen, her frailty shocking.

'What's way before? It was maybe early March when we saw you last, and you looked so good—'

'Pop,' I warn. I don't think that's the right thing to say. We shouldn't be commenting on her body at all. 'You were posting loads of pictures with Tom, you looked ...' Oh God, I don't know what to say either. She looked healthy, thriving, youthful and living. To say that's what she looked like *then* is to acknowledge that now, she's fading. 'You looked happy, I thought you were happy,' I settle on.

'Exactly, you *thought*. You didn't know. Didn't bother to ask.' I drop my gaze. 'I know you know about Tom, by the way. He called *my mum* and now I'm banned from the internet for a month, like I'm twelve.'

'Why'd you do it, though?' Poppy asks, still not getting that we should tread carefully. 'Get fake engaged, pretend to be all these people.'

'Because! I felt cheated. It's like after I lost all the weight, I became invisible to everyone that mattered. You think you'll be the shit when it first happens, that you won't feel unchosen anymore. Because you did it, you're *skinny*, yay. So why was it the opposite for me? Tom broke up with me after three months. My *friends* stopped replying to me. So, I kept creating scenarios that would mean you had to. You can't not congratulate your friend on their engagement, right? I just used AI and recycled old photos so my and Tom's relationship could play out like it was supposed to. I wasn't ready for him to leave me yet.'

'But wait, I FaceTimed you right after you got engaged. You were still on holiday. And the ring?' I can't help asking.

'It was my grandmother's.' Freya shrugs. 'And I was in the garden, phone angled so you could only see the sky. If you'd asked to see the hotel or the view, I was going to hang up, fake WiFi problems. But of course you didn't, that's how little attention you were paying. Anyway, enough about that – why did *you* leave?'

Even though her communication had petered out with Poppy too, Freya's glaring at me.

'I was jealous.' I say it like a shrug, the words easy to admit. 'In school, you being fat too meant I didn't feel so alone because there was someone else not getting any Valentine's cards either, someone else who didn't fit into any of the spare kit in the PE cupboard. Someone to absorb some of the blows with me. So, when you lost all the weight, I was *so* jealous. You'd become everything we wrote down in the Goals section of that fucking little red book and I couldn't stand being reminded of what I didn't have the willpower to do. There's no way I could meet up with you consumed by the horrible thoughts I was having about you. It would've been miserable. But I couldn't just come out and say that either, so I avoided you. But I am so, *so* sorry, Frey.'

For a second Freya's taken aback by my honesty, eyeing me over her mug. She nudges it on to the table, picks at the broken skin on her knuckles.

Finally, she says, 'You weren't the only one. The girls from my spin class. Nat from work, who I saw drinking FastOff one day, so we started getting steps in on our lunch breaks together. All practically disowned me.' Freya stares off to the side and her eyes get glassy. 'I don't get it. All your life everyone, everything demands you to be this thing you're not when you're a bigger girl. Thin. A size ten until society says it's too big, a size eight, a size six, and now the internet says we want a size ten again – it's so unobtainable you have to make it your entire personality to just about hang on to it. So you get up at four to make time to go for a run, to meal prep, to make the protein shake, the green juice, the lemon water. You go the gym, you do the apple cider vinegar shots, labelling, measuring, and recording everything you consume on your respective little apps. And then it finally happens, you're skinny. And everyone secretly hates you for it.' Freya huffs humourlessly. 'But by then my whole life had been adjusted to fit this lifestyle, and it's all I had left, so I threw myself into it harder. I swam, I did hot yoga, I gave myself a six-hour eating window during the day. I got on Tinder, Bumble, Reveal, looking to replace the people I'd lost, to be loved like I was promised, but all I get is ghosted, and *I'm not looking for anything serious*. I get … used.' I'm nodding, only realising I'm crying too when I taste the salt on my lips. I've felt that, the interminable treadmill run towards ever-evolving standards, like someone keeps resetting your timer, telling you to run faster, harder, uphill towards acceptance. 'All the while I'm still losing weight, because I think maybe that's it, maybe I've not lost *enough*, then maybe someone would want to stick around. Maybe I'll be happy. And if I didn't feel it at ten stone, maybe I will at eight.' She swallows. 'But I didn't, and I still don't at six.'

'Six?' Poppy gasps. 'Frey …'

'Yeah, six. Though I had to lie on the forms and tell them I was nine stone to get prescribed Ozempic.' She does stop then, the name of the drug jagged and clinical-sounding like an allergic reaction.

'*What?*'

I take in the way the blanket clings to the gaps in her body in abject terror.

'You do know what that is, don't you?' Poppy says.

I tut. 'Obviously.'

How could I not?

When news of the drug started to trickle down, my explore page got peppered with increasingly thinner celebrities paparazzied at red carpet events and award ceremonies. Their faces were suddenly sharper and more sylphlike than their buccal fat removal had already sculpted them to be. Freya would've seen this too, the miracle results of the skinny jab. At a glance, I wanted it. But I'm glad my apprehension kept me from acting on it. I don't read the news, but it filters through anyway, in shares and screenshots of articles added to social media. *My Ozempic Miracle Meds Helped Me Stuff My Face All Christmas – I Was Still Skinnier by New Year!* I imagine Freya seeing these articles on her feed, like I did. Sharing the same disillusionment I felt, double tapping on celebrities' posts, validating their blatant but silent promotion of the drug. But instead of horrifying Freya with its unknown long-term effects, it tempted her, again and again. Beguiling her with viral videos like that impossibly famous person at a gala wearing a corset so tight it was strangling her organs of oxygen so she was unable to give interviews properly. This is beauty. And you can buy it, inject it, right into the fat of your stomach.

'How – *why* would they give you Ozempic?'

She shrugs. 'Because I paid for it.'

'Where?' Poppy asks a little too eagerly. 'Online?'

Of course online. No face-to-face contact necessary, and a nameless mass-prescriber on the other side of the screen. The pharmaceutical industry made a calculated choice to put all the responsibility on the patient to self-refer, so if someone like Freya decides to lie about their weight to make them eligible, what can they do about it? How were they to know? How can they be held accountable?

'Didn't they ask for your NHS number, or referral from your doctor?' I ask, already knowing the answer.

Freya shakes her head. 'I just googled *buy Ozempic*, clicked the first link, gave them my details, some true, some false, and then this pharmacist from California pops up to tell me *Congratulations, you qualify for Ozempic as weight loss treatment*. Then I paid an obscene amount of money for a three-month supply.'

'Oh my God' is all I can say.

I don't need to ask her why she ordered the Ozempic because I can see that Freya's sick, that her eating's disordered and she's severely underweight. But I find myself thinking it over anyway and I fall silent.

Why, when she was already so beautiful, last summer and before that, as we lined up to be weighed, determined to be able to brandish bodies ready for the beach by July. To get boyfriends, to belong to somebody. I wish we both knew that we were already somebody's. We were ours.

'Aren't the Ozempic side effects pretty intense, mentally?' Poppy asks.

Freya nods, and I remember watching one of posibodybecky's awareness videos on the subject where she said Ozempic can cause anxiety, depression, even suicidal ideation.

'Frey. Do you think that had something to do with the catfishing?'

'Sure, why not. Probably.' She shuffles down further under the blankets, her eyelids drooping. 'It might've been the Ozempic, it might've been everything else, being dumped, starving, lonely,' she mumbles, her eyes sliding shut. 'But, yeah, the Ozempic kind of made me feel dead inside.' Her words bump up against each other sleepily. 'I didn't want to go *out* out anymore, alcohol tasted like poison. I didn't want to go anywhere, I started working from home. I didn't like the taste of any of my favourite foods and eating became a chore. And without my job, or the structure of mealtimes, I felt myself drifting, like away from myself. So, I decided to be someone whose body didn't matter for a while. No consequences, no people to meet, no pictures to pose for, life events to miss out on. I chose Jack because I knew anything I did wouldn't be as bad as the reality of how he treats people.' Her eyes flicker open and rest fixedly on mine for a moment before drooping again, and I wonder if she knows about us, if for some reason he decided to confide in her. 'It could've been any fuckboy, really, but because I saw how entitled he felt to everyone else's body, spinning girls whatever story fitted to get what he wanted, I thought maybe I could use his body the same way I'd seen him use theirs.'

I don't move, fingers gripping the edge of the sofa, as tears silently stream. She knows. When the sob breaks, there's an unwinding somewhere within me, as if hearing someone else was witness to Jack's cruelty means I can let it go. Demanding apologies from him wasn't something I was ever going to waste my energy on. He's shown me time and again that he'll never see what he did as wrong. So, I've been sitting with it, waiting for time to do its thing, so every day as the memories fade it hurts a little less. But in reality, this was what I needed to hear.

'Did he tell you?'

She shakes her head. 'I followed you back to his one day.'

'You little creep,' Poppy lets slip. 'Sorry. Too soon.'

Freya's eyes squint open and she sees me crying. She drags herself up and collapses on the sofa between me and Poppy, reaching for my hand.

Eventually, I say, 'But if you don't hate me, hate us, if this whole pretending to be Jack and Lola and whoever else was because you were lonely and you *wanted* to have us in your life, why did you go—' *Not crazy, can't say crazy.* 'Um—'

'Crazy?' Again, she shrugs. 'I was hungry.'

The air crackles between us and my laugh stutters, incredulous. 'No fucking shit.' Her fingers curl around my hand, and bizarrely, we laugh.

'This feels wrong.' Poppy giggles. 'You shouldn't be laughing.'

'*You* shouldn't be laughing, I'm the sick one. Cancelled,' she says, and we laugh harder, eyes glistening at each other, until our laughing falls away warmly.

'I'm sorry, Frey.' I sigh. 'I hate that I had any part in … this.' My thumb strokes the back of her hand, skimming from tendon to tendon. 'I'm not angry, I hope you're not angry at me either. Obviously, I'm not the victim here, I was lying to you too.' Without going into too much detail that feels embarrassingly insignificant sitting in front of Freya now, I give her my brief history of dating app encounters. She listens, drowsily, her head on my shoulder, to the Reveals and rejections that led to me creating Sydney, and how we got here. When I'm done, I glance at my phone and can't believe we've only been talking for forty-five minutes. 'And sorry, but I have to ask, your mum knows about the Ozempic, right? You're not still taking it? I don't want to have to grass on you.'

'Yeah. She was in the room when I got diagnosed with anorexia. The doctor told her.' Freya's eyes flutter closed, and I watch her chest rising and falling with tears in my eyes. 'Will you stay?' she breathes. And it feels like she isn't just talking about now.

I think back to how me and Poppy left things earlier, how her crying with her head on my shoulder felt like a last-time thing, a sunset scene on our years growing up together. But with me and Freya, giggling in the back of our SlimIt meetings was only the beginning. Yeah, Poppy brought us together in school, but school was about survival mode, fitting in and hoping to be left alone.

We were only just finding our feet in our own friendship when my insecurities sabotaged that, and I demoted Freya to a half-assed textationship.

There's so much we were on the cusp of.

'Yeah,' I say, stroking her hair. 'I'll stay.'

College Green is sprawled with students melting in the heatwave. Sweating after trudging uphill, I look for Veronica where she said she'd wait near the fountains, and when I see her in a metallic gold bralette and tennis skirt, lying on her back in the sun, I run to her.

It's been two weeks since I last saw her, though when you live with someone and see them every day, that feels like forever. I miss all my housemates, those late nights in the kitchen when talking about nothing feels like everything. Classes ended, and I made up the bed in my old room, still wanting to give Toby the time he needs. Temperatures soared, Freya called, and I met her wearing denim shorts for the first time. The due date for my assessment came and went without my word count surpassing 500, which at the time felt like I was going to die of anxiety, and now feels like a moment of clarity. I'm relieved, having just come from a meeting on campus with Vanessa, who's agreed to give me an extension while I figure out if Social Anthropology is still something I want to dedicate three years of my life to.

I think I already know the answer to that one, but I'm scared about the unplanned-for future stretching ahead of me. So, for now, I'm kidding myself I haven't made my mind up just yet.

When I reach her, Veronica's propped up on her elbows, headphones cupping her ears as she surveys the peopled lawn. I approach when she's looking down at her phone, surprising her as I flop down on the grass next to her.

'Oh my *God*, I've missed you.' She pins me with a hug, then veers back, up-downing my outfit. 'You're wearing shorts, exposed arms. Missy, I am so proud of you.'

'It's too hot to be self-conscious. I mean, I *am* self-conscious, but I'm getting over it.' Nodding, Veronica slides her headphones down round her neck, and my attention snaps to the tinny echo of a voice that's found a familiar place on all my social media feeds. 'Is that Bliss? Has she got a new video?'

'Yeah, just uploaded this morning.'

With a tap at her screen, Veronica disconnects her wireless headphones and refreshes the post as I lean in.

'Attention, babes. *I've got an announcement*,' Bliss sing-songs, popping her chest, and I laugh as Veronica attempts to copy her. 'I'm going to be taking a guest residency teaching a friend of mine's dancercise class towards the end of the month, right here in my hometown, Bristol. Slots are limited, and tickets go on sale tomorrow so make sure you move quick if you want to come shake with me. Comment down below what songs you want me to include in the class playlist, please. Oh, and if you want to see a realistic depiction of a body that better represents yours, check the fit.' Bliss backs up from her camera to show off her bright pink boiler suit, popping her foot, and showing how it hugs her curves from all angles. 'And remember, babes, to dress like you're blessed.'

Veronica swigs from the still-cool bottle of rosé. 'Dress like you're blessed,' she mantras. 'I'm getting us tickets, by the way, to her dancercise class. No excuses.'

'Not a one, I want to come, obviously,' I say.

'Did you see the other video she shared this week? From one of her old SlimIt Survivor features, this girl called Grace. She married herself, oh my God, you have to see.'

Veronica scrolls down to a video shared from Grace's own account. Clips roll over Natasha Bedingfield's 'Unwritten', of Grace sipping champagne with her rollers in, being embraced by her pink-robed bridesmaids and having her first dance with her sister.

My heart feels lifted as the video loops back around again and Grace gives a guttural laugh as she clocks one of her mates waiting at the end of the aisle in a three-piece suit.

'I love women,' I say, getting out my own phone to forward the video to Mum. She'd never do anything like this, but I hope seeing Grace's beautiful display of single-ladying cheers her up a bit.

The late day drips into evening, the sky's colour running cool. At some point we take a trip to the Tesco across the road for a second bottle and some salt and vinegar crisps. Time sieves quick through our conversations about Mum being jilted, Nairong asking for a deserved extension of her own to de-stress before submitting her final assessment, Keith getting a third date with that girl, Kashvi, from Toby's genetics class, and of course Toby. I ask a lot about him.

Veronica swears me to secrecy before she reveals she finally got him to be honest about why he and Bella were spending so much time together. Turns out the boy that Toby caught Bella emotionally cheating on him with over text was called *Jackson*. I sit up a little straighter. Bella and 'Jackson' carried on talking for a while after she and Toby broke up, but when her repeated attempts to meet up kept getting met with excuses, she straight-up ghosted him. Not a day later, and Bella's phone was being blasted by texts from Jackson on a withheld number.

Immediately, I make the connection between Freya and the list of alter egos she reeled off when admitting to all the aliases she was catfishing people under. Jackson Noel being one of them. And Bella not being someone Freya particularly liked.

'Out of curiosity, did Toby tell you what this Jackson's last name was?'

'No, I didn't ask. That was not a detail I cared to know, to be honest. Anyway, Toby thinks Bella played up how freaked out about it all she was. She said she didn't feel safe in her room anymore because Jackson somehow knew she lived in Manor Hall.' Because *Freya* had hung out with Poppy there of course. 'And Toby, being a good guy, wanted to be there for her. Then one night, listen to this, Bella confesses to Toby that she's still in love with him, but wait, wait, he turns her down because he thinks he loves somebody else. I wonder who that could be,' she says, elbowing me in the ribs.

My breath catches. 'He said that to you, those exact words?' Veronica *mm-hmms*. 'Not loved, but love*sss*?'

Grinning, she nods and cries, 'To love,' holding the bottle aloft to dribble the last of the wine into her mouth.

'Who do you love?' I say, sinking my weight back into my hands, spread on the grass behind me. Letting that information about Toby sink in, I feel the lingering warmth of the heatwave and the wine stirring me sleepy.

'You, of course. You're the fucking best, you know that?' The moment gets tinged with guilt, because I don't know if she'd be saying that if she knew how I played Toby. I let her finish. 'Um, I love Nairong and the boys. My girls back home. My parents and my sisters. I *love* my Nan and Pop. I love me.' She gestures around us. 'Crisps. Rosé. Your eyeliner. Being able to see the stars.' She tips the empty bottle up to the sky. 'I love a lot of things—'

'Wait a minute,' I say. 'When you spoke to Toby, he didn't tell you anything else? He didn't tell you what went down between us?'

'You know I know about the kiss with Elijah.'

'No, not that . . .'

It kills me to admit to Veronica that I catfished Toby, to see the judgement cross her face, but I couldn't let an untruth this big go unspoken between us. It felt wrong, hearing her root for me and Toby when she only had half the facts. I need to own my fuck-up and let Veronica make up her mind about whether it's something she could forgive going forward. When she asks to see what Sydney looked like, I open up the folder named 'Casper' where I keep the AI generations of her, and watch Veronica flick through the pictures. First a high-angled selfie, then a hand-on-hip

290

bikini shot taken beside the clear blue seas of some paradisiacal beach, and lastly a full-body shot, where Sydney's coincidentally wearing a dupe of the bridesmaid dress Mum's chosen for me. Her shoulders drop, and she quickly locks the screen like she's disgusted with what's on it.

'This is so sad.' She throws the phone into the grass. 'I'm not throwing shade, I don't mean it's pathetic, I mean seeing this makes me so sad for the world. That you felt you had to do this.'

'You don't hate me?'

'Never. Hear me when I say, I support women's rights and women's wrongs. You get to make a mistake, you get to apologise, Saff, I'm not going anywhere. Come here.' Veronica pulls me to her, my cheek pressed against her chest, and the reassurance melts me. 'Don't get me wrong, now I see why Toby was so mad with you. All this time, you had me thinking he was the *biggest* baby, about to throw everything he had with you away over a drunken kiss. I still don't think he should though. You guys can come back from this.' She lies back, gazing up at the emerging stars. 'Now, to combat this bout of body insanity, I'm prescribing you watch every one of Hannah Horvath's sex scene in *Girls* —' she lists on her fingers — 'thirty minutes of dancing a day in your best, saved-for-sex underwear to that Lizzo song "Fitness" . . .'

Fifteen minutes later, Veronica waves to me from the window of the bus heading back into town. I promised I'd be back at the Wilder house soon, but when it felt right.

On my own bus home, I get out my phone.

> Hey, I've had s few wines and I know I'm supposed to be giving you space but you're on my mind and you can just ignore this if you want, but I wanted to say again how fucking sorry I am that I lied to you. We were Only just starting and I felt so much already. With you. I dunno. I miss you

I rest my head against the window, contented by the evening, not feeling a need for his reply, but wishing for it anyway.

Toby

I miss you too.

Another week of indecision goes by. Another week of convincing myself this extended stay back in my childhood bedroom is just me visiting home for the holidays, like a lot of other students do. Not me avoiding confronting Toby for a yes or a no on whether he wants to be with me. Not me avoiding the overwhelming choice of quitting or committing to my degree.

No, couldn't be me.

'This time next week,' Mum says flatly, slicing off another piece of coconut bread at the breakfast table. 'The wedding.'

Shit. Otis and I catch eyes. His thumbs stop scrabbling over his screen, texting Harrison.

What with prioritising making consistent plans with Freya between doctors' appointments, finding time to see Veronica and Nairong before they leave to go back to Manchester and Kent for the summer, and all the overtime I've taken on at work as the summer season picks up, Mum's impending once-wedding date totally escaped me.

'I'm sorry, Mum,' I say, reaching for her hand.

'Heard anything from that detective yet?' Otis says, pocketing his phone.

She shakes her head. 'It's not a priority for them, I willingly gave Philippe that money—'

'Under false pretences!'

'I know, but still. If anything comes of the investigation that'll be a bonus, sure. But I'm not relying on that.' Mum drinks her tea, glancing between us. 'They've got murderers to catch. A liar getting pre-menopausal women to hand over their purses isn't exactly top of their list.' She sighs. 'I just keep thinking of the venue sitting empty next week and my dress hung up at the shop, and what a waste it all is.'

Otis bangs his mug down on the table. 'You haven't cancelled yet?'

'No, I've been burying my head in the sand. The only thing to cancel is the venue, and the deposit's lost for that anyway, so I've just kept putting it off. Such a waste,' Mum says again.

'But it doesn't have to be—'

'No, Saffron, I am not doing a solo wedding, it's just sad. Embarrassing.'

'It's only you who's calling it that. Let's just delete the word wedding. It's a ... it's a celebration of self—'

'Wank.' Otis mimes a cutting motion across his neck.

'Shut up,' I tell him. 'Call it what you want. It's a chance for you to wear your beautiful dress that you were so looking forward to seeing yourself in, surrounded by your day ones and all the people who love you. Everyone's always up for any excuse to drink and dance and have a good time. Did you look at that video I sent you?' When she stares back at me blankly, I jokingly kiss my teeth. 'Look.' I tap at my phone, finding the video of Grace's Ceremony of Self that Bliss spotlit on her page. 'Instead of letting all that money and planning go to waste, we could do something like this.'

'I ...' Mum's eyes go glassy watching the video. 'Oh, look at her, bless her. Doesn't she look gorgeous ...' I bristle waiting for the, *for a big girl*, but it doesn't come. 'I don't know, Saff.'

But I can tell she wants to be persuaded.

I nudge Rue, who tuts as I knock her colouring pencil out of the lines. 'Sorry. What do you think, Rue? Do you still want to wear your pretty dress? Do you wanna see Nanny in hers?'

'Yeah!'

Otis tucks a strand of Rue's hair behind her ear, chin in his palm as he gazes lovingly at her. 'I think you should do it, Mum. It'll be a big eff you to he who must not be named.'

Hiding her smile behind her mug, Mum rolls her eyes. 'Fine. But can you sort it? I just want to show up and for everything to go ahead.'

'Done,' I say. 'I'll do it tonight after I'm back from Freya's.'

'Back here, you mean?' Mum asks.

'Yeah ... is that OK?'

'Always,' she says matter-of-factly. 'But you're still paying rent on that place in Stokes Croft, right?'

'Mum, it's been three weeks.'

'Don't think I'm saying this because *I* want to be charging you rent, or I want you out of here. I'm just checking you do want to go back eventually?'

Otis eyes me, taking a long audible sip of tea.

I guess I never seriously considered the possibility that things might not go back to the way they were. That Toby won't forgive me, and we'll have to learn to civilly cohabit the house on Wilder Street, dividing up our time with Veronica, Nairong, and Keith like divorced parents in the midst of a custody battle. Veronica did call us house mum and dad. I'm still hoping it won't come to that though, my hope held way up high since I got that text from him saying he missed me.

'Of course I do, I love living there. I'm just ... waiting on something.'

That night, I lie back against my pillows and start drafting a mass message to the WhatsApp group Mum's friends pre-emptively set up to share wedding photos. I copy and paste it to Mum, who I know is lying in the bath right now, making the most of the annual leave she booked off for the wedding. She sends her approval, replying with a string of love hearts.

I hit send, rereading the message once it appears in the group.

Saffron

Hi people! As most of you know, we've had a bit of a change of plan for next week, and for those of you who don't, let's just say Philippe is trash and my mum needs a party, OK! Be there, same time, same place. I just have a few things to ask to pull this new kind of party together, please! Can everyone bring a dish of your favourite food, I don't care if it's shop bought, but it'd be wholesome af if we have a bunch of homemade stuff too. We want food with love in it, that's all. And we're gonna dance and eat and toast to each other. To friendship, to loving yourself, to life. And mostly to my lovely mum, who's going through it right now and deserves to feel everyone's arms around her. Things that are banned: Philippe, and any mention of him or what happened, the word 'wedding', bad vibes, self-doubt. OK!!? See you there!

People are heart-reacting already, and I get this rush of gratitude and comfort seeing people come through for Mum.

Biting my lip, I go back to my list of chats, scrolling to a stop at Toby's name. I *know* I'm supposed to be giving him time. But we were right in the middle of the bang, in the splinters of seconds before the sky's alight, our firework stubbed out against the black. I feel like if we leave things too long, things will never be the same again. I don't want to let what we had fade, and until he tells me *No, this isn't happening,* I think I have to keep trying. I think he wants me to.

Saffron

Sorry, me again. I'm shit at this. I just want to talk to you too much, and if you've blocked me, that's really good for you. Really. (Lol, can you ever say 'good for you' without it sounding like the most sarcastic thing ever!?) Anyway, if you do get this, I'm inviting you to my mum's not-wedding. I wanted to call it a Celebration of Self but my brother said it was too wellness influencer. Basically, it's a party. And I would love for you to come. Please come

I send him a screenshot of the invitation and wait for it to be marked as Seen, which it is after a few seconds.

...

The ellipsis appears as he types. Disappears. Typing. Gone. I imagine him deciding what to say, how gently to let me down.

Eventually, I stop waiting.

It's the day of Bliss Adeyemi's dancercise class and I'm standing outside some fancy-ass renovated church called Tranquillity, in leggings and an old Nike hoodie with a high-intensity sports bra underneath.

I double tap Veronica's latest message saying she's two minutes away when a bus rounds the corner and stops in front of me. I see her get up from the back row and shuffle behind the queue of people getting off.

'Are you excited?' she beams, bouncing on the balls of her feet.

'Yeah?' Veronica's smile falters and I sigh. 'I was. Really, I was. But—' I'm on day two of my period, am painfully bloated, and didn't like the way this sports bra cut in under my arms when I looked in the mirror earlier. 'I'm just having a bad day.'

'Then you are in *exactly* the right place,' she says. 'Come on. I can't believe this bus made me late to dance with Bodied by Bliss.'

Inside, we squeaky-shoe our way down a corridor lined with posters for classes like hot yoga, talking therapy, and life drawing. And before I get too far into silently rehearsing excuses to sit and watch, the bass from a song off Beyoncé's latest album rumbles down the hallway.

'I love this song.' Veronica's hand locks around mine.

I traipse slightly behind her, which is hard because she's matched her strut to the music, sashaying her hips and throwing her arms up into the air. She lets go, twirling to face me, and says, 'Quick, we're missing it.'

She swings the double doors open to a part of the old church that's been converted into a dance studio, and jumps right into line, joining the back row. Instantly, she copies what Bliss is doing at the front of the class, twerking in a squat. And, oh my God, it's actually her, it's Bliss, clad in a zebra-print gym set, her face dimpled with joy, beaming as she barks out instructions. It's like my inner Rue-sized self is watching, transfixed at a body she never thought she'd see on a stage, in Lycra, bopping her weight around and laughing while she does it. Veronica beckons me over, tripping over her feet a little as she tries to catch up with the next steps.

'Welcome, girls! Come in, join us. Come, come, don't be shy,' she says, holding my eye. 'It's your girl, Bliss.' She marches on the spot addressing the class, swagger still in her hips even in this stationary move. I slink in beside Veronica, who hip-bumps me. 'Now, as you probably all know from my content, I'm a self-confidence coach and a stubborn believer than you can wear whatever the hell you want, no matter what you look like. I also give talks on self-acceptance and body neutrality. And I hope some of that comes through today in these dances I've choreographed with freedom of expression in mind. I want to encourage you all to move your bodies for pleasure, to *feel* those endorphins, work up a sweat, and just let yourself go. Truly, dance like nobody is watching or even if they are, dance like you don't give an eff! Now for this next song, I want you to . . .'

Bliss demonstrates the next sequence of moves, incorporating chest pumps, thigh-pounding stomps, and punching the air in front of her, to 'Bootylicious' by Destiny's Child. I'm stiff at first, too worried about every wobble and fold, how quickly I get out of breath and how red I can feel my face blotching. My eyes are hyper-focused on what other people are doing and I'm stressing about how I might look to them. Subconsciously, I've ranked myself as maybe the eighth biggest person in the room, and I hate that even now, after how far I've come, I feel reassured by that. But if there's anything connecting with other girls online who are learning to accept themselves has taught me, it's that I have to remember that having days like this is normal. Especially when I'm hormonal, tired, and wearing uncomfy sportswear.

'Stop thinking,' Veronica shouts over the music at me, her body jolting in a vertical zigzag as she belly dances.

'I'm trying,' I shout back.

But it's not until Lizzo's 'Water Me' plays about twenty minutes in that I'm able to do that. Stop thinking. It happens unexpectedly when Bliss tells us to spin in circles, toes tapping as we run ourselves into a whirl in one place. In my head I picture this video that went viral a couple of years ago of Lizzo performing 'Truth Hurts' in a white bodice and bridal veil performing a flute solo while twerking, just out here *doing it* in front of the whole world. And here I am so concerned about how I look in a room full of Veronicas who are just here to dance and raise their pulses doing it. I tilt my head back and laugh, feeling this shower of happy chemicals rain down from the crown of my head. My face breaks with gladness, and the simplest of truths rings home for me: I am here, I am healthy, I can move without pain, I can feel joy, I can *dance*, I can make my muscles yawn with tiredness, I can feel sweat on my brow and the fire of my breath in my lungs. And I am *so*, so much more than the way my body looks.

'*I am free, yeah, yeah, come water me,*' Lizzo sings, and as I spin, all around me, I see women moving and breathing together, their faces aglitter, radiating with happiness.

'You're right,' I say in Veronica's ear. 'I think I did need this.'

*

At the end of the class, after Bliss delivers some parting words on the importance of surrounding ourselves with people who affirm and lift us up, my brain's still shimmering with endorphins. As I dawdle with the other women waiting for their chance to say hi to Bliss, I catch myself in one of the studio mirrors, and I look good-tired, a halo of frizz around my hairline, my face pink.

Veronica squeals, her sideburns curling with sweat. 'It's us next. What do I even say to her? I'm gonna come out with something so simpish, I just know.'

The apple-bodied lady in her sixties in front of us turns to me and asks if I can take a photo of her and her friend with Bliss. They pose, beaming, their arms around each other, her friend with a topknot of grey box braids that remind me of Mum, and as they walk off arm in arm, an idea for something I want to do for Mum sparks, and what I want to say to Bliss comes to me.

'Hey, babes!' I blink at her, momentarily gagged. It's so surreal meeting someone I've developed a big-sisterly parasocial relationship with over the last few months, and as she hugs us in turn, I feel a wriggle of nerves about the proposition I have for her. 'How did you find the class?'

Veronica jumps in. 'Amazing, I've never been so happy to be this sweaty. And you played "Girls in the Hood" – ahh, that was my suggestion. Thank you, for everything you do. You're the reason I wore my first crop top,' she gushes.

'Thank *you*. I will never, ever, ever get tired of hearing girls having the confidence to set the belly free.' Bliss laughs. 'Did you like the class?' she asks me. 'I need feedback, I want to do more of these.'

'God, yeah. I'm gonna recommend it to everybody. Especially my mum, she's so military about exercise, well, about everything she does to her body. You should see the industrial-strength shapewear she bought to wear under her wedding dress ...' And that's when I launch into my rambly elevator pitch to get Bliss to come 'officiate' Mum's self-marriage. I reference the clips I've seen of her self-love seminars that she tours around festivals in the summer, and give her an abbreviated version of Mum's situation. '... I think for so long, she's been looking for validation from whichever wasteman she's swiped right on next, that this might be my best chance to get through to her.'

Bliss nods, her curls bouncing. 'You know what, I wanna make this happen. Let me check my schedule, run this by my people, and I'll get back to you.' I give Bliss my Instagram handle and watch her follow me, Veronica gripping my arm with glee. 'Keep your phone on you!' she calls as we go through the studio's double doors.

Veronica bounds out in front of me, prancing backwards, on some kind of high from our interaction with Bliss. 'OK, tell me I'm invited to this one woman wedding too, yeah?'

'Of course. You all are, everyone in the house.' For a breath, we look at each other, knowing what that means, and Veronica clasps her hands together like she's hoping hard. 'Can you let them know?'

She says of course, hanging off my arm and rambling through all her outfit options, and before we're down the steps of the Tranquillity centre, my phone goes with a DM from Bliss.

Bliss

Wedding bells are a'ringing babe. I'll be there ♥

june

Today's the day, and I'm hiding in an alcove at the end of the room where Mum was supposed to be getting married. I'm meeting Mum at the altar, to greet her with a hug after Otis walks her down the aisle, so she's not aimlessly being marched toward Bliss. But standing at the front watching all the guests take their seats was giving me stage fright.

I peek out at Bliss now, standing with her hands on her hips, beaming, a camellia flower tucked into the top pocket of her hot coral power suit. She was *so* the right choice for this.

'That dress looks stunning on you,' she said as soon as she arrived, half an hour earlier than we'd agreed, helping me string the walls with bunting and fake flower garlands without being asked.

And you know what, it kind of does. I might even love this dress. The smooth pearliness of the pale pink contrasts with the warmth of my skin tone, bringing out the blush in my cheeks, and in the light, the silk is almost iridescent. Shimmering. And buying it in the size I am, rather than punishing myself with a size that no longer serves my body, made it fit so much better than I was imagining. OK, it's still clingy against my stomach, but to solely focus on this would be to ignore everything else the dress is doing for me.

The clopping of shoes and the scraping of chairs against the polished wood floor has gone quiet now and there's only the happy clamour of laughing and chatting, so I guess everybody's arrived. Not hopeful, I check for a reply to the message I sent Toby inviting him here today. I can't help the drop of my shoulders when I see there's nothing, cringing as I reread it, at how cloying and desperate I sound. But I'd be lying if I said I wasn't still hoping he'd show up last minute.

We're going to have to see each other next week anyway. Mum's booked a last-minute solo honeymoon to Paris, and Otis has not-so-subtly made it known that he'd like Harrison to stay while she's gone. At the threat of him bringing up guava lube again, I'd plugged my ears and promised to go back to Wilder Street to give them space.

A member of staff must've indicated that Mum and Otis are on their way because the crowd hushes and Bliss beckons me forward. I gulp back a breath and step out in front of the seated guests, resisting the urge to wrap my arms around myself. Bliss winks at me as I pull my shoulders back, letting my arms rest gently at my sides, and as I smile, I feel the glistening of tears in my eyes. Aunties and cousins I used to see at Christmases when we were small crowd the front row.

Just behind, Clara's looking shy, her phone out, ready to film Rue's flower girl moment but unsure if she should be here. I'm glad she trusted my instinct and came anyway. I convinced Mum and Otis it was important for Rue to see her parents together at events like this, believing that with the warmth of a little rum, today's festivities, and seeing their daughter so delighted to have them both in the same room, would settle their old grievances. I catch Clara's eye now and she points at me, at the dress, miming a chef's kiss as she turns her phone on me. Without hesitation, I pose, ready to capture every minute of today.

Further back, I spot Keith holding hands with Kashvi, and Veronica and Nairong mid-conversation with Freya, honouring their promise to me to make her feel extra welcome and included like I knew they would. Her small frame is shrouded in a chic, oversized, powder-blue trouser suit but already, after only a few weeks of retiring her catfishing accounts and meeting with a new therapist, she looks on her way to being healthier, stronger, the cinnamon shine back in her hair.

Then there are rows and rows of Mum's friends. Friends from the nineties when she was at school, old housemates, colleagues, clients, neighbours, all here to remind my mum of who she is, and that she is loved. And it's looking out at all these faces who have crossed paths with Mum, with me, when the realisation tingles my skin with goosebumps. Mum hasn't seen some of these people for years, and I suppose that's why she's been serial dating since Dad left, because she's scared to be alone, to be the source of her own happiness, and I know I was too. But look where that got her, throwing her trust at Philippe, pouring all her heart into someone who pulled the biggest real-life ghost on her imaginable.

It's fitting, as I'm about to watch my mum be guided towards a groomless altar, where she imagined she'd feel complete, that I'm realising I can't keep waiting on somebody else to provide my happiness. Whether that other person is another, thinner, version of me, or somebody else. I think of Freya chasing her size ten self, her size eight, size six, and it never being enough. I can't count on looking like someone else's beauty ideal, or that smaller waist, that swipe right, that text back to make me happy. So, it's time I started counting on myself for that.

The opening sax of Mum's favourite song, Odyssey's 'Native New Yorker', slinks out of the speakers as Mum's best friends, Tina and Kel, who have taken it upon themselves to act as masters of ceremonies, yank everyone's attention to them.

'Oi!' They stand either side of the arched doorway, fizzy and giggly with Prosecco, Rue hanging off Tina's hand as she grips her flower basket tight. 'Loved ones,' they call. 'May I please present to you, Dionne Saldana.' Tina gives Rue's hand a squeeze and then she's off, skipping down the aisle and scattering petals for Mum to walk through. Rue clocks me halfway and makes a beeline for me, blowing a handful of roses into my face. She giggles and I hold her to me as we watch for Mum's entrance.

The doors part and as the tinging cymbals of the disco anthem roll into a beat to strut to, arm in arm, Mum and Otis stride into the room. Mum's cowl-necked, champagne gown sweeps the floor so it looks like she's gliding, and there's a collective intake of breath. She looks gilded, elegant, and classy, with her head held high and her braids threaded with gold. But still Mum, laughing through her teeth at the performance of it all.

'*Love, love is just a passing word,*' Odyssey's lead singer croons.

When Otis lifts Mum's hand and twirls her into dancing the rest of the way, I choke out a sob that's brimming with laughter. I meet her at the end, swinging my hips to the big brassiness of the song's chorus and take Mum's hands, pulling her to me. 'Love you,' I say, nose to nose with her.

'And I love you,' she says back.

Behind us, Otis sweeps Rue off her feet, holding her and jostling her to the beat as she upends her basket, raining the rest of her petals over his head.

Bliss throws her arms wide, encircling both me and Mum. 'Oh my days, that was the most wholesome moment I've ever witnessed,' she whispers. 'OK, you ready?'

Mum nods.

Letting go of us, she positions herself side by side with Mum as I find my seat in the front row next to Otis, who slips his fingers through mine. 'Well done,' he whispers.

'Well done,' Rue echoes, sitting on his lap.

I laugh. 'You too.'

Bliss begins, and we gaze up at Mum. 'I'm here today to welcome you to this coming together, this gathering of love, friendship and support that today, we're going to use to fill the cup of our friend Dionne . . .'

*

Happiness is a bellyful of earthy spices, stirred by a loving hand. A table of world foods in warm dishes laid by family and friends. Happiness is a roomful of people raising a glass to your mum's name, sipping wishful thoughts. Happiness rolls in fat tears down your cheeks as you gasp through laughter with your brother. It is sitting comfortably in a chair and not holding your body's breath, stiff with the expectation of what others will think of you but embracing your stomach's softness.

After I finish my second plateful of pholourie, roti, black bean stew, and oven chips, I lean back in my chair and rest my hands on my belly, feeling its rise and fall. Clusters of guests sit and stand around big round tables, no centrepieces, no place names, just people finding their people, and talking and eating together. On my table, Otis looks playfully miserable as he sits in the middle of his ex, Clara, and his new boyfriend, Harrison, who have been swapping stories about him for the past ten minutes. I watch Rue darting from table to table, drawing potatoey portraits of the guests in exchange for adoring smiles. Mum floats between friends, luminous in the low lighting. I watch her now, throwing her head back in a cackle so I can see her gold fillings, somehow keeping her champagne flute gracefully aloft.

And yet, despite this fierce furnace of love surrounding me, and the sense of security I've been discovering in myself lately, despite Bliss's impassioned outpourings of the power in presence, my eyes keep straying to the door, envisioning Toby walking through it.

Mum distracts me by dragging me off to the bathroom to touch up her makeup with my essentials kit I somehow fit in my clutch bag for this very occasion. Tina and Kel are milling around waiting to perform their obligatory bridesmaid duty of helping Mum go to the toilet in her dress. They watch me powder and conceal any minor imperfections in Mum's base, before redoing her eyeliner. It got smudged when the vows Bliss made Mum recite to herself brought her to tears.

'You're telling me this was all you, Saff?' Tina asks. I nod minutely, concentrating on the slim wing of Mum's gold liner. They didn't see her final look until we got to the venue because Mum didn't want the traditional scene of matching robes and mess everywhere, as the whole bridal party got ready in the same room. It was just me, her, pastries and juice, and our favourite songs this morning, as she let me take my time with her face. 'I thought she would've paid loads for this! Can you do me for my fortieth next month? I'm serious.'

I tell her yeah, beaming as she puts her number in my phone.

'All self-taught as well, my talented girl. I thought, why pay for a professional when I've got the real thing right here. Thank you, hon,' Mum says, squinting to admire her shimmering lids in the mirror.

'Honestly, you should do this professionally,' Kel says, squeezing my shoulders as they all head back into the party.

I stuff my palette back into my clutch, pausing to look at my reflection, imagining myself with one of those black brush belts round my waist, swatches up my arm, matching colours to clients, and making them look at themselves in the mirror with the kind of awe Mum did just now. Let's face it, I was always going to drop

Social Anthropology, I just wasn't ready to admit that to myself without a plan B. But could I really get *paid* to do this? I bite my lip, smiling, as my mind flourishes with ideas on how I could turn doing something I love so much into a career. I could do bridal, like this, or editorial, or even – no, it has to be – makeup for film and TV.

I flounce back to the table, fizzing with possibility, so excited to start looking for courses. I go to check my phone again when a thick black wire snakes over my feet. I look up to see it's attached to a microphone Tina's trailing after Mum with, trying to get her to do a speech. Seeing this, a man on the table nearest her starts dinging his glass with a spoon and suddenly the whole room's tinkling.

Tugging it out of Tina's hands, Mum says, 'Sorry,' and laughs into the microphone as she strides over to me. 'Not doing it. It's my day off. Thank you all for coming and that, but nah.' She cackles, in front of me now, cupping my chin. 'I'll leave you in the capable hands of my beautiful daughter, Saffron.'

'No, Mum, I haven't written anything,' I hiss, sitting up straighter.

'So? It's better that way.'

'Oh, for God's sake,' I say, standing and unwinding the wire from around my feet. 'Hello, everyone.' My voice reverberates around the room and I recoil, laughing nervously. Mere weeks ago, the thought of having nearly a hundred pairs of eyes trained on me would've shot my adrenalin through the roof. Don't get me wrong, I'm still not totally at ease with the fact, but I'm choosing to override it, to believe these people care more about what I have to say that what I look like saying it. 'Despite public speaking being what my mum does for a living, she's refusing to get up and do a speech, so firstly, I'd like to echo her thanks and thank you all *properly* for coming, and for showing up today when it's far from the conventional. Ummm, what else?'

I hear a whoop and turn to see Veronica and Nairong picking at a shared plate of focaccia bread and olives, faces gleaming with encouraging smiles.

'My fans,' I say, scrabbling for funny stories or anecdotes to share. I catch my reflection in one of the gilded, free-standing mirrors we borrowed from the venue for decoration, and allow my thoughts to flow. 'When I convinced Mum to go ahead with today, I pitched it as a Celebration of Self and as much as she doesn't want to call it that ... it is. Mum, you could've spent the day moping in bed, and none of us would've blamed you, but what a waste that would've been, of money, yeah, but of a good time! And aren't we all having a good time?' The crowd cheers with agreement, drinks sloshing, arms in the air. 'And as much as it's a celebration of my mum as a person – enough about her for a bit – it's a celebration of all of us as individuals too.' I shut my eyes for a second, the glasses of Prosecco that've been sipped down way too casually throughout the day catching up with me. 'OK, story time. I can't believe I'm gonna say this but, a while ago, I didn't want to be myself. I thought nobody would ever want to be with someone like me.' The room *awws* like they're watching a pantomime, or sitting in the audience listening to an *X Factor* sob story. 'Awww, I know. Sad. So, I ... so I sort of pretended to be someone else for a bit, and at first it was fun.' I catch eyes with Freya, and we share a knowing look. 'And it felt like doing something naughty at school and not getting caught for it. But then I hurt someone I really cared about, like *really* cared about, someone I could've seen myself falling in love with.' From here I can see the whole room, the door I wish Toby would walk through right at this very moment, to hear what I'm about to say. But the door remains closed, and I carry on.

'Someone I do love. Anyway, I'm oversharing *hard* here – too many Proseccos – but all to say that, if I'd directed just a touch of the kind of love I have for my mum, and that I can feel you all have for her too, towards myself, maybe I wouldn't have felt the need to be something I'm not. And I hope that my mum captures some of the love in here today and keeps it close. Um, that's it, I'm embarrassed now. Love you, Mum. Can I invite everyone to stand?'

My gaze sweeps the room as it ripples with movement—

and that's when I see him, rising from a table at the back, dressed in a grey tweed suit.

'You came,' I say into the microphone, turning the attention of a hundred people in Toby's direction. 'Oops.' He's shaking his head, his cheeks reddening. But smiling. Tears gather along my lash line. God, I've missed that smile. 'Oh, yeah, the toast. Can everyone raise a glass to my mum, Dionne.'

'To Dionne,' the crowd echoes, the mic whining as I drop it, already weaving my way over to Toby.

'Hi,' I say, when I reach him. 'You're here.'

He shrugs. 'I was just on my way home from the gym, so I

thought I'd pop in.' He starts the sentence serious but he's laughing by the end of it.

I laugh too, though it knots at the base of my throat as I try to speak over the sob I'm holding back. 'How much of that did you hear?'

'Enough to know I made the right decision.'

'And what was that?'

Toby's hand brushes along my jaw and up into my hair, gently tilting my face to meet his kiss. I lean into him like my body's sighing. His other hand finds my waist and curls me closer as our lips break apart.

Behind me, Mum's guests erupt into hollers and shouts, and I feel their joy light me up in rays, like I'm standing with my back to the sunset.

I smile against his lips as Toby says, 'If it wasn't obvious, the decision is you, by the way.'

'Even though I—'

'It's a done thing, I've made my peace with it. For you to do all that stuff –' he shakes his head – 'you weren't you, even when you were *actually* you and not pretending to be someone on Reveal. For real, I feel like I'm meeting the youest you right now.'

When I turn around, everyone's still beaming, shining on us.

Toby takes my hand and soars it, like we won something. And they yell some more.

I look up at him, glimpsing my own reflection in those honey-gold eyes of his. 'You know what? Right now, I feel the most *myself* I've felt my whole life.'

Acknowledgements

Severely sleep-deprived and unsure I'd ever have another sensical idea in my head again, I wrote this book in my first year postpartum. Somehow. And like raising babies, writing a book takes a village. Thank you to my village.

Firstly, I want to thank my infinitely caring agent, Jessica Hare. You truly are the best of the best and I'm so grateful to have you in my corner. Also, Clare Mills, reading your email felt like a warm hug when I was feeling a bit lost.

My powerhouse editor, Alice Swan – thank you for your passionate and pragmatic untangling of my ramblings, and for protecting what it is I'm trying to say. You always make the right call. Ama Badu, thank you also for your affirming editorial insight. Reading your reaction notes always brings me such joy.

Thank you also to my publisher, Leah Thaxton, and to Natasha Brown, Bethany Carter, Simi Toor, Carmella Lowkis, Jack Bartram, Emma Eldridge, and to every other bright spark at

Faber. I couldn't imagine a better home for my books; every one of you is always so kind and supportive.

Mar Bertram, I'm in awe at how beautifully you've captured Saffron, exactly as I imagined her. Thank you for illustrating both of my books, you are such a talent!

Ryan, who I hope will always be credited this way in anything I write, thank you for being my first reader and for not getting mad at my sporadic replies. To my best friends, Adele, Alice, Georgia, Jenna, Ria, and Zoey – thanks Dynamos, sharing my teens and twenties with you has been a blast, here's to the rest of it.

My family, who've held me close as I learned how to mother, and cheered louder than anyone as I've continued to write; thank you for all you do. The Sunday Sitters: Mum, Auntie Zo, Rin, Ellis, and Esme – my coven, I cherish our chats and cake in the conservatory, even when we've got nothing new to say. My warm-hearted Dad. My generous step-dad, Paul. Shea, and his mini-me, Zion. Nanny Ange. Lindsey and Geoff. Nicki and Svea. To the Mannings and The Hegartys. And to my in-laws, The Sages and The Prices. I love you all.

Barney, thank you for everything, for your selflessness, patience, security, doing the lion's share, and for looking after me. With you, I know I am safe, and I am home. And Zephyr, my little love, my light, thank you for always being the youest you.